The dying woman had been knifed by one of the scalie guards as she'd tried to escape

"Should I end it for her?" Ryan asked, hand on his panga.

At the sound of his voice, the woman's eyes opened. For several long heartbeats she gazed blindly into space. Then she moved her head and her eyes locked on Ryan's face. "You," she finally whispered.

Her hand spidered up her chest to her throat and gripped a square metal pendant. "Take," she commanded, her eyes burning into Ryan's good one. "Open. Rona said to find you. Died long back. Quest. Look after." Her breathing was becoming faster and more shallow.

Slowly Ryan opened the locket and found that it contained two things—a tiny ringlet of blond hair and a picture, a faded, pale brown portrait.

"Who is it?" he asked, even though he knew what the answer was going to be.

"Your son, Ryan Cawdor. It's your son."

**Other titles in the
Deathlands saga:**

JAMES AXLER

DEATH LANDS®

Seedling

A GOLD EAGLE BOOK FROM
W🦅RLDWIDE®

TORONTO • NEW YORK • LONDON
AMSTERDAM • PARIS • SYDNEY • HAMBURG
STOCKHOLM • ATHENS • TOKYO • MILAN
MADRID • WARSAW • BUDAPEST • AUCKLAND

Second edition April 1999

ISBN 0-373-62551-0

SEEDLING

Printed in U.S.A.

This is for Geoff, Anne, Ben and Saul Kelly,
who are friends. If you don't have dreams,
then how can they come true?

Chapter One

Ryan Cawdor opened his eye, then closed it again, hoping to avoid throwing up. He'd lost count of the number of jumps he'd made over the past year or so, but there was one great truth.

They didn't get any easier.

The first moments weren't too bad—the humming and the lights glowing in floor and ceiling, the fingers of mist appearing in the chamber, hiding the colored armaglass walls.

Then the good part ended.

Ryan had thought about the sensation several times, trying to focus his mind on precisely what happened during a jump from gateway to gateway, from mat-trans chamber to mat-trans chamber.

All he could think was that it was like having a clumsy child disassemble your skull, then run a pointed file around the inside, scraping at the sensitive parts of your brain, stirring things up so that past, present and future got hopelessly scrambled.

There was pain and nausea every time, and a blinding ache in the head as though someone had been trying to remove your eyes, from the inside.

Ryan cautiously opened his good right eye, drawing a slow, whistling breath as he fought for control. He took another breath and felt relieved as he realized he definitely wasn't going to vomit this time.

"Fireblast," he muttered.

None of the others had regained consciousness yet, all lying or sitting around the chamber. It was odd not to see Jak Lauren there. The snow-headed albino boy had been with them for... For how long?

Ryan couldn't remember. It seemed like forever, and now the boy was gone.

Another surge from his stomach brought the bitter taste of bile. Ryan swallowed hard and closed his eye again.

Memories twisted in his head, one above all—the narrow face, eyes blazing with a feral hatred, staring at him. And a hand, fingers twisted in agony, vanishing into the sucking slime.

The Trader used to say he didn't have any enemies, and when someone picked up on it, as was the rule, he'd smile that wise, lopsided smile and say, "None alive."

But that wasn't true. In Deathlands there were always new enemies.

A voice jerked him from his reverie.

"Still sleeping, lover?"

"I feel like double-shit."

"We're getting too old for all these jumps."

For the third time Ryan risked opening an eye. Krysty Wroth was sitting next to him, running her fingers through her fiery hair. It tumbled over her shoulders, strangely sentient, seeming to move of its own volition.

"Some are bad," he admitted.

She smiled. "And some are worse."

"Yeah."

"Seems funny without the kid."

"Hope he and his lady make it."

Krysty reached across and touched his arm. "That cut doesn't look too good, lover."

It was a souvenir of the dizzying fight against Cort Strasser, inflicted by his bone-hilted knife. Blood had run down Ryan's arm, crusting on the fingers of his left hand, but now the long, shallow wound was dried.

"I look better than Strasser."

"Anyone looks better than Strasser." The third voice in the chamber rang off the maroon walls of armaglass.

"Thanks, J.B.," Ryan said. "Enjoy the trip?"

The slight figure of J. B. Dix, Armorer to the group of friends, straightened. He put his hands into his jacket pocket and retrieved his wire-framed spectacles. "Lost my autorifle and my Tekna knife. Go on like this, Ryan, and I'll end up naked."

"You got blood on your mouth," Krysty told him.

There was a tiny thread of crimson leaking from the corner of J.B.'s lips, and he wiped it away on his sleeve.

Krysty stood, the heels of her western-style boots clattering on the metal disks in the floor. She swayed a little and placed a hand on the wall. "Gaia! That wasn't the most fun I've had."

"How's Mildred?" Ryan asked, looking at the fourth member of their quintet.

"Old Mildred's fine, apart from some son of a bitch banging on the inside of my head with a hammer."

Mildred Wyeth was a doctor, born in December 1964, well over 130 years earlier. She'd gone into the hospital for a minor operation in the last days of December in the year 2000, just three weeks before the nuke-madness that brought utter ruin to the world. As a result of a medical accident, Mildred had been cryogenically frozen, lying in suspended animation until snatched from her endless sleep by Ryan Cawdor and his comrades.

Since then she'd been one of them, sharing their small triumphs as well as their dangers.

Now she was sitting up, rubbing at the side of her face, which was still badly swollen from the brutal beating she'd taken from Cort Strasser. "I'll never get used to these jumps," she said quietly.

"Doc doesn't look so good," J.B. observed, moving to the side of the last member of their group.

Doc had an even stranger life history than Mildred. Born Theophilus Algernon Tanner in South Strafford, Vermont, on February 14, 1868, he had a glittering career as a scientist and was married with two small children. But in November 1896 he was trawled into the future.

He was an experiment of Project Cerberus, which was a part of Overproject Whisper, itself a small cog within the vast secret machine known by the code name of the Totality Concept. The attempt to bring and send people through the barrier of time was almost totally a failure. If it had any success, then that success was Doctor Theophilus Tanner.

Doc was a prickly and difficult subject, deeply disturbed at losing his wife, family and friends. He made several illicit attempts to rejoin them, despite the risks of the unstable equipment. To get rid of him, the white-coated operators of Cerberus sent him off into the future, to the present in Deathlands.

The effects of the appalling disorientation meant that Doc would never again be totally sane. At his best he was only a couple cents short of a dollar. Sometimes he lost track of quite "when" he was living.

Now he lay on his side, knees drawn under him, a trail of spittle linking his open mouth to the polished floor of the gateway chamber.

His stubbled face was parchment-pale, and his breathing was ragged. His right hand clutched his precious swordstick, which was made of ebony, with a silver handle shaped like a lion's head.

Mildred got to her hands and knees, groaning, and crawled to the old man's side. None of them actually knew how old Doc really was. He'd only been in his late twenties when he was trawled forward, yet he looked and acted like a man in his sixties. It was a by-product of tampering with temporal paradoxes. As Doc himself once remarked, "I confess to being in fair shape for a man who is actually over two hundred years old."

"He's going to be all right?" Ryan asked.

By now all four of them were standing around Doc Tanner.

His eyes blinked open.

"By the three Kennedys!" he said feebly, looking up at them. "I feel akin to a man who has fallen down a deep well. Could you possibly stand a tad farther away while I recover myself?"

Helped by Mildred and J.B., he stood reasonably well, his knee joints cracking like snapped kindling. He wiped away the saliva and sighed. "Did anyone else find that a particularly pain-filled jump?"

"Yeah," Mildred agreed, "worst I've known."

Ryan nodded. "Could be there was a malfunction in the equipment."

Krysty was looking around the chamber. She stood still for a few moments, eyes closed, concentrating, using some of the strange mutie power of the Earth Mother to try to "see" their surroundings.

"No," she said, shaking her head. "Can't feel anything. It's always hard inside these places. They seem to sort of blanket the reception for me."

"Then we'd better go look," Ryan decided. "Everyone ready?"

"As I'll ever be, my dear fellow" was Doc's response.

The others contented themselves with nodding, and all drew their blasters—Krysty her silvered Heckler & Koch P7A-13 9 mm pistol; J.B. his trusty Steyr AUG 5.6 mm automatic; Mildred, who had represented the United States in the free-shooting pistol event in the last ever Olympic Games before sky-dark, had an exotic target blaster. It was a beautiful ZKR 551 six-shot revolver chambered to take a Smith & Wesson .38 round; Ryan had his usual SIG-Sauer P-226 blaster with the built-in baffle silencer; Doc, typically had what was probably the only Le Mat Civil War revolver in the whole of Deathlands. It exploded a single .63 round from a scattergun barrel, as well as firing nine standard .36-caliber bullets.

Ryan looked at his ragtag army, caught Krysty's emerald eyes and grinned. "Well, here we go again, lover."

She didn't return his smile.

Ryan turned away from her and reached for the lever that would open the gateway.

"Ready?" he asked quietly, and threw the lever.

Chapter Two

The opening mechanism on the gateway worked smoothly and almost silently. The thick armored glass swung back, revealing the usual small anteroom that was present in all of the redoubts the companions had visited.

This one was about twelve feet square, with benches along two walls and a fold-down table. The door set in the far wall was ajar, showing the main control room. Everything was as it had been in other gateways.

Ryan led the way out, pausing as he entered the larger room, waiting for Krysty to join him.

"Well?" he asked.

She closed her eyes and stood still, shaking her head. "Can't do it, lover."

"Why?"

"Can't override my imagination. Worst enemy of someone with the power of seeing. Doomies suffer from it even worse."

"Wouldn't of thought it."

"Wouldn't *have* thought it," she corrected automatically.

J.B. looked at the control consoles, rows of vid-screens and comp-processors, with dancing lines of details, numbers and codes. Lights flickered and shone green, amber and red.

"Looks good and clean," he observed.

In the past they'd entered control bases and found frightening evidence of malfunction. All redoubts had been built with their own nuke-gens, and most of these continued to work, long years after their human masters had vanished into ashes.

Doc glanced around, holstering the massive Le Mat pistol. "Shipshape and Bristol fashion," he commented.

"People built these complexes sure built them to last," Mildred said, running her finger along one of the desks, showing it dust free to the others. "Spotless."

"There's antistat conditioning here. Filters and cleans. Without anyone coming or going for a hundred years, there's no disturbance." Ryan looked along the consoles. "Though there's some plas-mugs along there."

It was the kind of thing that Jak Lauren would have darted toward. As it was, Krysty walked slowly and picked up one of them. She peered into it and pulled a face.

"Long, long gone," she said.

Ryan joined her and picked up another of the disposable beakers. The inside bore a faint stain of brown, but it was utterly dry.

"If they had been topped up, I would have raised

one and given you a toast." Doc picked up a single cup from another console. "To our friends—" he flourished it "—from— Oh!"

Liquid splashed all over the front of his stained frock coat, adding another layer to the patina of antique dirt.

Everyone stared at him in disbelief. Doc looked at the wetness on his clothes, dripping from his fingers. "How can this be?" he whispered. "A century come and a century gone, and this still holds—" he smelled his hands "—what is a perfectly acceptable substitute for coffee."

Ryan dipped a finger into the cup and tasted it. "Sweet, as well."

"But there isn't even any mold visible." Mildred rubbed the bruise on her cheek, lost in thought. "In a controlled temperature the cream-sub sweetener would have mold growing on it in less than seventy-two hours."

Ryan pursed his lips. "Doesn't make sense, does it? This place looks like nobody's set foot in it since 2001, but..." He looked around the big room, wondering for a moment if someone was hiding, someone who drank coffee out of plastic mugs.

"Better look out in the corridor," J.B. suggested.

Apart from the entrance to the anteroom and the gateway beyond, the control suite had only one other door. Beyond it would lie a passage, probably high, wide and curving. There would be strip lighting in the angles between walls and ceiling, and perhaps tiny vid-sec cameras watching the endless emptiness. Beyond that would lie the rest of the massive, sprawling complex of the hidden redoubt.

It was always like that.

"IT'S DIFFERENT," J.B. stated.

The usual immensely heavy sec door they'd encounter had a simple, consistent number code. To open it you keyed in 352 and to close it, 253.

This was something else.

The door was much lighter, with an armaglass panel set in its top half and a central wheel control to open and close it. There was no comp-panel at its side to work the mechanism.

Doc peered through the window, shading it with his hand against the myriad reflecting lights. "Upon my soul," he said, almost to himself.

"What is it, Doc?"

The old man answered Ryan without turning his head. "If I was fond of a wager, then I would lay a little jack that we have a sort of airlock here. But why?"

"Anything in there, Doc?" Mildred asked.

"Nothing. And there's… Ah, what have we here?" he asked, spying a series of dials and scaled displays at the right side of the door.

"Air pressure," J.B. told him, having already examined them. "Internal and external."

Mildred shook her head. "I don't get it." She

tapped them with a forefinger. "They aren't working. Show an outer pressure way too low."

"Open it up, J.B., slow and real easy," Ryan directed.

The Armorer took the central wheel and braced himself against it. Immediately it began to move, the polished chrome glittering in the bright lights of the control room.

"Easy as a war wag through a mutie's hut," he said, rubbing at the palms of his hands. "Been greased recently, Ryan."

"Keep turning."

The wheel spun until there was the faint hiss of the rubber seals releasing the door.

The intermediate room was about eight feet square, with a high ceiling. A vid-sec camera stared unblinkingly down from a corner. The walls were slightly rounded, with supporting ribs of bolted metal. Everything was painted white.

The five companions peered into it. Krysty sniffed the air. "Smells sort of stale and flat. And dusty."

Ryan sucked at his teeth. "Don't like the feel of this. What's anyone else think? How about you, Mildred?"

"I haven't done this often enough to know. But if you all think there's something wrong, then maybe we should cut our losses and get out."

"It'll mean another jump," Doc warned. "Not a prospect I think any of us welcome with particularly open arms."

J.B. was studying the far door, which also had a large polished steel ring at its center and an array of dials and readouts set into the wall. The door was sealed with a thick strip of black rubber. "Certainly looks like an airlock," he said.

"Must be a way of opening the outer door from inside here. Close this one again and then use an automatic override on the far door." Krysty looked around. "But I don't see any way of doing it."

They all looked around.

"What's that?" Mildred asked, stopping and picking something up from the floor.

Krysty frowned. "What is it?"

Mildred uncrumpled it and held it out flat on her palm. It was a torn wrapper, made from a recyc paper, silver-colored with red lettering. "N-Urgee Bar," it said.

"Energy," Doc explained.

In smaller letters it said "pecan and cinnamon."

Mildred lifted the paper and sniffed at it, shaking her head. "Yeah."

Krysty took the wrapper from her and pressed it against her nose. "Fresh as—"

"Tomorrow's sunrise," Ryan finished, breathing in the scent of pecan nuts, overlaid with the spicy tang of cinnamon. Fresh and unmistakable.

J.B. reached for it. "This can't have been here more than a few days. Couple of weeks at the most."

Doc had last go at the wrapper. Pressing his veined nose to it, he breathed in a great gush of air.

"Careful, or he'll suck it up that great hooter of his and we'll never see it again," Mildred warned.

"Either my sense of smell has deserted me or you four have breathed all the smell away. I confess I can barely catch a hint of cinnamon."

"This starts weird and gets weirder, lover," Krysty said. "Fresh coffee and now this bit of paper. Someone's been here very recently. That I can *really* feel."

"Let's go look out that door," Ryan suggested. "We can't walk away." He looked at the open chamber and the far door. "Safer I go in while you lock this inner door after me." For a moment he thought Krysty was going to raise an objection, but she said nothing.

"I'll watch through this window, and if there's any trouble—any—I'll open up here. You close the outer door, Ryan."

"Sure." There wasn't a better man in Deathlands than J. B. Dix to have at your back.

"Listen," Mildred said, "if these gauges are anywhere near right, you'll have to pull hard to open that lock. But once you do, the air could leak out faster than goose shit off a shovel."

"Hold your breath, my dear Ryan," Doc suggested.

"And keep your powder dry," Mildred added.

"Best foot forward, lover."

"Shoulder to the wheel."

"Chin up, chest out."

Ryan looked at the grinning quartet of friends. "Why don't you all place an implo-gren up your asses and pull the pin?" he suggested.

IT TOOK BOTH HANDS to work the control wheel, which meant Ryan's blaster remained tucked in his belt. Previous nightmare experiences in alien gateways had taught the one-eyed man to take extreme care or suffer the likely prospect of instant death.

Despite the dials showing lower air pressure outside, Ryan took no chances. For all they knew the redoubt might be buried five hundred feet below an ocean, and to release the locking mechanism could mean a burst of seawater surging in with lethal force.

He was aware of J.B.'s face pressed to the armaglass window. His friend was ready to react at a nanosecond's warning to any threat.

"Lock's shifting," Ryan said, his own voice heavy in his ears, the chamber muffling sound.

There was an audio link from the main room. "Slow," the Armorer said.

The wheel suddenly spun free between Ryan's fingers. He braced himself against the door, but nothing happened. Wiping a film of sweat from his forehead, he took the handle and began to pull at it. "Jammed," the one-eyed warrior growled.

He braced his boot against the frame and heaved with all his strength, losing patience with caution. Then there was a great hiss of air, and the door moved toward him.

Ryan glimpsed a bright light and a flash of limitless desert. Then his lungs emptied, and he sank helplessly into a clinging swamp of suffocating blackness.

Chapter Three

"Head feels like a bunch of stickies have been digging around inside it."

Mildred patted his head. "Man like you, Ryan, little loss of oxygen shouldn't be a problem. Thanks to J.B. getting you out in time and shutting the inner door."

Ryan had already thanked J.B. for his swift response to the danger. Now he stood and joined the others by the airlock.

"Want a look out, lover?" Krysty asked.

Ryan took a deep, slow breath. His chest and throat hurt, and his skull was throbbing with a vicious, sick ache. The dials around the doors hadn't been faulty. The air outside was much thinner than the air within the complex.

"I still don't understand it," he said finally. The far door remained ajar, giving a tantalizing glimpse at what lay outside the redoubt.

They were obviously very high up, with a landscape scrolled beneath them. It looked like late morning or early afternoon, with a bright coppery sun hanging in a sky that ranged from palest cerulean on the left side to a rich pinkish-purple on the right.

As far as Ryan could make out through the blurring armaglass, the land was untouched desert.

Rolling dunes stretched as far as Ryan's eye could see. Nothing moved. Nothing seemed to grow there. No bird flew across the flawless dome of the sky.

"Nothing," J.B. said, as taciturn as always.

"Nothing," Ryan agreed.

"Not even air we can safely breathe," Mildred added.

"So we get out of here and try another jump to some other place," Krysty offered.

Doc groaned. "Oh, my aching heart and limbs. Oh, my muddled puddled fuddled head! Can we not remain here for a day or so?"

"And do what?" Ryan asked.

"Explore the remainder of the redoubt. There may be all manner of wonders. Gold from the Incas, or fine silver from the wily Pathan of the high hills. Who knows?"

Ryan smiled and shook his head. "I know, Doc. I know."

"How do you know, old friend?"

"Because there isn't any fucking redoubt here, Doc."

"What?"

"Look around you. There's the control room. No other exits. One door into the gateway. One outside. Nothing else at all."

"There has to be a redoubt."

He looked stricken, hooded eyes darting from one

friend to another. Then the old man realized Ryan was correct. Apart from the double airlock where they stood, the only other door bore the familiar sign: Entry Absolutely Forbidden to All Except B18 and Above Personnel. All Personnel Must Have NASA-SEC Clearance Pass at All Times.

"Most said B18 Personnel, and I've never seen anything about that NASA-SEC pass before, either," he said.

"Yeah." Krysty ran her fingers through her mane of red hair. "New to me, too. You see that before, lover?"

Ryan was staring out through the small pane of armaglass, past the open door to the strange world beyond.

"Lover?"

"Best get moving," he said, turning away. "Into the gateway, *now.*" The crack of command rang on the last word.

Nobody asked him why, and nobody hesitated, questioning what he'd seen. All followed him across the control room, through the bare anteroom and into the red-walled chamber.

J.B. was last, firmly shutting the door behind them. They sat on the floor, trying to get comfortable for the jump.

Only then did Krysty pose the question they all wanted to ask. "What did you see, lover?"

"Don't know. Wish we could have shut that outer

door. Could've been that bringing it toward us. Kind of scented it.''

"What?''

Then the mists came flowing from floor and ceiling, and the lights flickered. The mat-trans jump put an end to the conversation.

STRANGELY IT WASN'T as painful a jump as the previous one. All recovered consciousness quite quickly, though Doc suffered a nose bleed that dappled his swallow's-eye kerchief with clots of crimson.

This time the walls of the chamber were a very pale golden color. As soon as Ryan was able to sit up and take notice, one of the first things he saw was a large vertical crack running from floor to ceiling on the wall directly opposite the gateway door. It was an ominous sign of deterioration.

J.B. followed his gaze, then looked around the chamber. "There's another crack in the floor in that corner over there. See it?''

Ryan nodded. It wasn't as long or deep as the fracture in the wall, but it was worrying.

Krysty ran a hand down the main flaw in the wall. "Doesn't go clean through, lover. If it had, we might all have leaked into hyperspace, or wherever it is we slurry off to during a jump.''

The sudden image of his molecules being dissipated through an infinite universe sent a chill down Ryan's spine. "Let's get out of here before the walls fall down around us. Ready?''

The room immediately adjacent to the gateway was larger than usual, about fifteen feet square, and decorated in a pale yellow that matched the color of the armaglass.

There was a steel table, one of its legs bent almost at right angles, stuck in a corner. A row of coat hooks jabbed out from the wall on the right. One of them held a torn white T-shirt. The rest were empty.

Krysty stood still and breathed in slowly while the others waited for her. "No," she said. "Nothing here. The air's very stale and flat."

Ryan could tell that for himself. So many of the hidden redoubts he'd entered had the same sour smell, a strange dullness that lingered on the tongue, flavored with a hundred years of buried nothingness. Often it bore a hint of damp.

The control room was also bigger than usual, with eight rows of consoles, screens and comp-lights. Three out of the eight rows were down, blank and dead.

This time the outer door was conventional, massive sec steel, with automatic opening and closing instructions as well as a manual override lever.

"Looks like a clean evacuation," J.B. commented, holstering his Steyr pistol.

"Shall I open it up?" Krysty asked, reaching for the opening controls.

"Slow down," Ryan said. "That last one made me more careful than before. Best use the hand lever. Easier to open an inch and shut quickly. Once those autohydraulics engage, they sometimes take time to reverse.''

"Allow me, my dear young lady." Doc offered her a courteous bow, his silver hair tumbling forward to hide his face. Unfortunately the jump had made him a little unsteady, and he nearly fell over.

"I've got it, Doc," Krysty replied. The green lever was in the closed position, and she began to push it upward. "Stiff," she grunted.

Doc had recovered his self-possession. "I trust we shall not be gazing out over the trackless wastes of Mars or Jupiter or wherever that last jump took us." He grinned mirthlessly, showing his perfect teeth.

None of them had actually verbalized where the previous jump had taken them, though Ryan had wondered if they were still on Planet Earth.

Krysty let go of the lever and looked at Ryan. "Which reminds me, lover. You never did tell us just what it was you saw through that window that made us get out triple fast."

"Don't know."

"What?"

"I didn't know then, I don't know now and I guess I'll never know."

Mildred pressed him. "Must have some idea, Ryan."

"Sure. My idea is that it was something real big, partly buried under the sand, and it was coming our way like a run-out war wag."

"Animal?" J.B. queried.

"Alive." Ryan shook his head. "No point in asking me any more, 'cause there isn't any more to say. Let's get this door open."

The door was raised about three inches. No jet of foaming water had gushed through, no sand, no wriggling creatures.

Once again Ryan missed Jak Lauren. The skinny little teenager would have been flat on the concrete, face pressed to the gap, reporting what lay beyond.

Now it was up to Ryan to get on his hands and knees and put his face against the cold floor. He squinted with his good right eye, trying to see under the huge sec door.

"Narrow passage. It's not like most redoubts. Ten feet across. Poor lighting. Can't quite… Yeah, lower ceiling, as well. Not a smell of anything moving."

Krysty and J.B. were working the control lever together. At a nod from Ryan they threw their combined strengths behind it and heaved it upward.

"Blasters ready," Ryan reminded, holding his own gun steady.

The door hissed slowly open, revealing the corridor outside. The air was still and flat, with the characteristic underground, tomblike smell.

Krysty confirmed it. "Nothing shaking down here."

"Should I close the door behind us?" Doc asked.

"Sure. No, not yet. If this is one of those buried redoubts and we're jammed down here, I'd hate to find we have a malfunctioning door, as well. Let it be.''

Mildred pointed to a single neat piece of graffito on the near wall. Hand-lettered in white, it simply said Goodbye Cruel World. We're All Going to Join the Circus.

"Cool dude," she said. "Must have done that at the last minute as they were finishing the evacuation."

"No sign of any footprints around." J.B. crouched, head cocked to one side, the dim overhead lights reflecting off the lenses of his glasses.

The passage curved away both left and right, with no sign of any other doorways.

"Which way?" Doc asked.

Ryan shrugged. "Try left first."

It was a dead end, a blank wall of raw stone, roughly smoothed down, a seam of quartz glittering like pewter in the half-light.

"Right," Ryan said with a grim smile.

"SOMETHING ODD about this place," J.B. pronounced, walking alongside Ryan at the head of the group.

"Small, you mean?"

"Yeah. It reminds me somehow of the gateway we found in Russia that time."

Ryan held up a hand and they all stopped. "We haven't passed a single doorway in nearly two hundred yards. I think you've got an ace on the line. This isn't a full-scale redoubt at all.''

"Stairs ahead, lover. I can just see them. Terrible light. If only Jak was... You know.''

"I know.''

Krysty took him by the arm, her eyes fixed to his face. "I sometimes thought... Don't laugh at me for this...''

"Won't.''

"That Jak was kind of like the son you never had. You ever think that?''

Ryan took a deep breath, nodding slowly. "Course I did. And you did the same, didn't you?'' He waited a moment, watching her face. "Sure. Krysty, there's still plenty of time.''

"Is there?'' she said bitterly. "Oh, *is* there plenty of time, Ryan?''

"Yeah. There is. And when the time's right, we'll do like we've said. Stop and rest and find that quiet place.''

"And raise us a family. Boy for you and a girl for me....'' Her emerald eyes were dull, oddly lifeless. She turned away, letting go of his arm.

"Krysty...?''

"Forget it.'' She moved toward the stairs ahead of them. Her hand came up to brush back the bright hair, which was now gathered protectively around her face. Ryan wasn't certain, but he thought she was crying.

Chapter Four

It was a wide staircase with broad treads and a sturdy handrail. Ryan joined Krysty at its bottom, followed by the other three. "See the top?" he said, aiming to restore peace.

"No." Her voice sounded a little strained and muffled. She coughed. "Dust in my throat. Sorry, lover." Krysty touched him lightly on the arm, so they both knew what she meant.

"Goes high," J.B. observed, straining his head back.

"Must've been an elevator," Mildred suggested, looking around them. "We haven't passed any other entrance or exit, and all that techno-shit must have been brought down some other way. They'd never have manhandled it down those stairs, would they?"

"Fair point and fairly put, Dr. Wyeth, if I may say so."

"You may, Dr. Tanner, you may."

"There." Ryan pointed. "The sort of design that makes an elevator look like part of the wall."

The doors were painted slate-gray, textured so that they resembled the concrete walls on either side. Ryan was surprised to see that it was only a single elevator. It contributed more fuel to his idea that this wasn't a normal redoubt at all. Apart from anything else, it felt smaller.

The neat black button was set into a mat-gray panel, with a tiny silver arrow pointing up.

"Probably sec-listed personnel only," J.B. said.

"Let's see." Mildred reached out and pushed the button.

Nothing.

Mildred pressed the button again. From somewhere above they all heard the sound of gears engaging, a grinding hiss, then a steady, whirring noise.

"By the…" Doc began, his jaw dropping in amazement.

Ryan's blaster had leaped into his hand, responding to a subconscious reflex. J.B. had also drawn his pistol.

"Taking a long time to come down to us," Krysty complained, head on one side, listening to the sound of the elevator's steady progress.

There was the distinctive pinging noise of its arrival, a sound that meant nothing to Ryan, Krysty or J.B., very little to Doc and everything to Mildred.

"Sweet Jesus on the Cross!" she exclaimed softly. "The thousand memories that thin little bell brings back to me."

The doors slid open about an inch, then stopped moving.

"Press the button again," Krysty suggested.

Ryan did, but nothing more happened. He gave the

doors an angry kick, the steel toe caps denting the gray finish. The metal quivered, then the doors jerkily began to open again.

The elevator was nearly twenty feet across, far larger than ones that Ryan had seen in ruined buildings across Deathlands. Its walls were plain gray, with a small rectangular mirror set in one. There was a simple control panel near the open doors. Inside was a rusting bicycle wheel and a battered black hat.

"Nothing else," Mildred said in a surprised voice.

Ryan stepped into the elevator, keeping a cautious eye on the heavy doors. He bent and examined the wheel and the hat. "Just garbage," he concluded.

He chucked them out. The hat flopped like a dying bat into the corner by the stairs. The wheel clattered and jangled, spokes breaking, until it rolled against the corridor wall.

"Now what, lover?"

He brushed dirt off his fingers. "I don't see much choice about the direction. Up. Only choice is how we do it. Feet up the stairs or ride the elevator. Anyone got any feelings about that?"

"I never liked elevators," Doc told him. "Always had the feeling the cables would snap."

Mildred nodded. "I agree. And after a hundred years without any oiling or servicing, I feel even worse about risking the big drop."

J.B. coughed. "Even if it falls, you don't get hurt. Wait until a fraction of a second before it hits bottom and you jump up in the air. Never fails."

Ryan looked at his colleague in amazement. "How do you know that?"

"Read it on a shithouse wall in a frontier gaudy down near Nogales. Why? You mean you think it's not true, Ryan?"

"Double-stupe bastard! Look, do you want to walk or ride?"

"Walk."

Krysty nodded. "Yeah. I'd rather walk."

THEY CLIMBED STOLIDLY up the wide stairs, the faint blur of the basement shrinking away beneath them until it vanished. They passed two intermediate levels, landings that had doors at either end. The heavy sec doors had no visible way of opening them.

"Not enough plas-ex to shift them," J.B. said sadly. "Have to keep climbing."

The air remained dull and flat, with a stale taste that lingered in the throat on every breath. The lighting was much worse, making it almost impossible to see more than twenty feet in any direction.

"How far do you think we've climbed, Doc?" Mildred asked.

"Entirely too far, ma'am. I fear we shall shortly be bumping our heads upon the lower levels of the sphere of heaven itself. Or, to put it another way, at least two hundred feet."

Ryan had been in the lead, and he heard the conversation. "Closer to three hundred. But there's good news, then Doc."

"What?"

"Won't be going any higher."

"We've reached the dark at the top of the stairs, have we?"

"Sort of."

They all stopped behind Ryan. There had been some kind of earth slide that had pushed the shaft of the stairs to one side. Rock, cut as clean as sliced butter, filled the gap above them, and the stairs disappeared into it as though they'd never been.

"That's it, folks," Mildred said.

Krysty sighed. "I suppose exercise is good for us."

"Not for my poor old knees," Doc retorted. "They've been exploding like cherry bombs for the past fifty feet or so."

Mildred patted his arm. "Us old ones'll lead the way. It just goes to prove that my father's younger brother, Josh, knew what he was talking about."

"What do you mean?" Doc asked testily.

"He used to say to me, 'Millie, what goes up must come down.' And now I see what he meant."

"WHY DON'T WE JUST go back and try another jump?" Mildred suggested.

"We haven't explored this place properly yet, and there's something odd about it. It's not like other redoubts." Ryan looked around them. "Almost like it was built *just* for the gateway."

"I say we take the elevator," Doc suddenly said

forcefully. "Having been treated like one of the men of the grand old Duke of York, I want to be up when I'm up. I've had enough of being down when I'm down. Is that clear?"

"As purest water, Doc," Krysty said. "Though you kind of lost us a bit there."

The Armorer peered into the elevator. "I still don't much like this, Ryan."

"Think it's a trap?"

J.B. shook his head slowly, a thoughtful look on his face. "Not like a deliberate trap, no. But I don't figure it can be that safe after all this time. Look how it came stumbling down and then the doors jammed. Seems real iffy to me."

"You wait here?"

"Dark night!" The slight figure turned away, biting his lip. "I don't like this a spent round, Ryan. Something's wrong. Passage is wrong. Lights, doors, stairs...this elevator."

"So you think we should get out?"

"Yeah."

Ryan knew there was another question. "Do you *want* to get out, J.B.?"

"No," he replied reluctantly. "Let's go up and see where the cross hairs meet."

"Sure."

IT TOOK ANOTHER KICK from Ryan's combat boot to get the steel doors to slide shut. Even with all five of the friends inside, there was still masses of room.

Mildred stood by the control panel, finger poised. "Not much of a decision needed," she said. "It's either up or down. I'll try up first."

The inset button, surrounded by a ring of frail golden light, clicked. The metal cage began to vibrate, slowly, then faster. They could feel, rather than hear, distant humming. Seconds ticked by, and still the elevator remained stubbornly in the basement of the building.

"How do you spell *claustrophobia,* anyone?" Mildred asked.

There was a shuddering and, at last, they began to move slowly upward.

"Haberdashery and hosiery on the second floor, with toys and facilities for the rumpus room on the third," Doc recited tonelessly.

There were beads of perspiration on Krysty's forehead, and her sharp green eyes had narrowed like a feral cat. Her hands were locked in front of her, tangling like strong, coiling snakes.

Ryan moved to stand by her, and she looked up at him, managing a shaky smile.

"Not good," he said, not bothering to make it into a question.

"Not good, lover. Too much like being buried alive. Not good."

"Least we're moving."

"For now..."

They moved steadily up in relative silence. Every now and again the side of the elevator would scrape and bump on the walls of the shaft. Ryan figured that the earth shift that had blocked off the stairway might also have damaged the running of the elevator.

Each time it happened there was a jarring rumble, and the whole thing rattled.

"How much farther?" J.B. asked, as though he were talking to himself.

The elevator hesitated at that moment, waiting poised, as though it were about to uncurl itself with a surge of energy.

"Come on," Mildred whispered.

There was an upward lurch, faster than before, taking them at least fifty feet in a couple of heartbeats.

And another stop, this time a grinding halt that had a dreadful feeling of permanence to it. Ryan pressed the "up" button several times, but nothing happened. "Looks like the end of the line."

Then, from above, they all heard the deep, sonorous twanging sound of part of a steel cable snapping.

Chapter Five

Nobody spoke for several endless seconds. Then it was Ryan who broke the silence. "Best if we move slowly and careful."

The cage still seemed jammed firmly in the damaged shaft. There was no sensation of swaying from side to side. After the thrumming sound from above them, there was only silence.

"Try the "Down" button," Krysty suggested. "Might work."

"Long as we don't go too fast." J.B. leaned a hand against the cold metal of the inner wall.

"Accelerating at a rate of thirty-two feet per second," Doc muttered, "and assuming the shaft is around two...three hundred...then...ninety-six in the...four minutes... No, that can't—"

Mildred hissed across at him. "We get the bastard picture, Doc. We'll hit the bottom kind of fast and kind of hard."

"I fear that I am unable to contradict that statement, my dear Dr. Wyeth," he said. "So sorry, ma'am."

Ryan tentatively pressed the lower control button. All that happened was that the thin ring of golden light around it went out. The interior ceiling lamps of the elevator remained on.

Above them they heard the thunderous vibration of another part of the main drive cable snapping under the strain.

J.B. pointed at the roof of the elevator. "Maintenance hatch."

There was a rectangular trapdoor, four feet long and three feet wide, set close to the far corner. A chromed handle protruded from it. Ryan didn't much fancy having to climb up through the trap, but he couldn't think of any workable alternative.

The Armorer was the lightest of the group. Doc steadied himself, hands on knees, with the two women on either side. Ryan helped J.B. to scramble onto the old man's back, holding him as he reached for the trapdoor.

"I recall playing leapfrog as a child," Doc began, but he ran out of breath and stopped talking.

"It's open. There's a folding ladder here on the roof. I'll get out and drop it down."

J.B.'s legs vanished, and they could hear his studded boots on the outside. When the others had moved out of the way, he lowered the ladder, which was thin wire with slatted rungs.

"What's it look like up there?" Ryan called. "Enough light?"

"Just. The walls come squeezing in, but... Hey! We're only a few feet from what could be the top. There's double doors there. I reckon—"

He was interrupted by another of the main support cables rupturing.

"You all right?" Mildred called.

The familiar pale face slid into view in the black rectangle. "Sure. But it looks like there's only about five more of those to go. Then..." His index finger jabbed downward, and he made a low whistling sound.

"You first, Doc," Ryan ordered. "I'll hold it steady for you."

"I'm more than capable of climbing a rope ladder, my dear fellow. I recall a square-rigger around the Horn when I—" He caught the look on Ryan's face. "Sorry. Climbing."

As soon as he was outside, Ryan gestured to Mildred. "Go."

She was halfway up, carefully planting her feet sideways on the narrow rungs, when another cable broke. This time the effect was much more spectacular, the elevator suddenly unjamming itself. It dropped four or five feet, the sides screeching against the rocky walls of the shaft. They all heard the cable take the weight, booming like a gigantic tuning fork.

"Fireblast!" Ryan growled. "Let's get the fuck out of here."

Mildred had managed to hang on to the ladder, swinging from side to side. Krysty grabbed at it, steadying it for her.

"Come on!" J.B. called. "I can see now where it's going. Frayed like an old bootlace."

"Not as 'fraid as me," Krysty said to Ryan, struggling with a fixed grin.

"Joke like that wins you next place on the elevator roof."

She knew better than to think about arguing, shinning quickly up and vanishing through the trapdoor.

Ryan glanced around. He made sure the G-12 caseless assault rifle was snug across his shoulders, then climbed effortlessly up the ladder. Just as he emerged into the black cavern above, two more strands went simultaneously, one of the broken cables lashing like a demented serpent and striking a fountain of sparks from the driving wheels.

The elevator dropped another few inches, with a jerk that sent it clanging against the walls. Ryan realized that one side now dipped markedly lower than the other. As the weight was transferred onto fewer and fewer of the support cables, so the strain would become greater and greater.

Time was running out.

Ryan swung himself onto the roof, joining the others. Doc was sitting cross-legged near the center, his shoulders hunched, head bowed. Mildred was near him, while Krysty and J.B. were standing near the farther edge, staring upward.

"You okay, Doc?"

"Never felt better, dear boy," came the muffled reply.

"There's the exit doors," the Armorer said. "Looks like ten feet."

Ryan could see them, and they were identical to the pair in the basement. He pushed away the thought of how far below the basement actually was and concentrated on how to get his friends up and out.

"Have to get up those cables," he stated.

"They're breaking," Mildred protested.

"Right. If they break and we're still here, then we're all dead. Only chance."

The cables were black and coated with old, crusted grease, each individual strand about the thickness of a child's wrist. Now that he looked carefully, Ryan could see that there were still four main sections left. He touched the nearest, feeling it thrilling and taut under his fingers. The parts of the support cables that had already snapped were hanging above them, ragged-ended and useless.

"Go for it. If one of them goes, you just gotta try and hang on tight."

"I'll take this one with you, lover," Krysty said. "Give the others one each."

"Yeah. Come on, Doc. More your ass or you're bonemeal."

Krysty, Ryan and J.B. had gloves, which made it easier to cling to the cables and climb them. It was harder for Mildred and Doc, but there wasn't time to think about offering gloves around and trying them on.

Already there was the rising scream of tortured metal. The threads of twisted wire were all trembling, the noise filling the shaft. The elevator gave another lurch, as though it had been gently rear-ended, one side dropping a further three inches.

"Going to go!" Ryan yelled. "Just hang on as tight as you can."

Krysty was immediately above him, her boots locked on the dark cable. Ryan also hung on with hands, arms, legs and feet, tangling himself into it, knowing that when the cable snapped it might go anywhere.

J.B. was crabbing his way up his chosen section, reaching level with the sealed sec doors. "Locked tight."

Krysty's voice filled the darkness. "It's coming... Now!"

The weak point was where the century-old cables were connected to the bolts on the top of the elevator. When the last four broke, almost simultaneously, the noise was appalling.

Instantly the thick wires, feeling almost like rods of iron, were transformed into whirling dervishes of malign metal. The five friends were rolled, lifted, swung and dashed against the unforgiving walls of stone.

With double weight on it, the cable that supported Krysty and Ryan steadied first, giving them a chance to look down. The elevator was falling away from them, slowly at first, then gathering momentum. The rectangle of light that was the trapdoor enabled them to follow it all the way. Its flanks scraped against the shaft, with hideous, metallic groans. The final impact, three hundred feet down, was oddly lacking in drama—a faint crunching, like a child putting his foot on a pop can.

Having followed the diminishing block of yellow light to its ending, Ryan now looked around him. It was like some macabre jolt-fantasy of a puppet show. Three marionettes dangled around him, jerking and twitching on their thick cords. Jagged, twisted ends of torn, rusted wire still thrashed at the dark air, but the violence of the movement was slowing and easing. J.B. was highest, now a little above the level of the doors. Mildred was next, clutching at the cable like a girl in the middle of a gym test.

Doc had come closest to buying the farm. His cracked knee boots were slipping down, only eighteen inches from the ragged end of the cable supporting him.

"I would be grateful for some aid," he called. "Else I fall into the abyss and perish."

"I'll get him," Krysty said, shinning up with her usual catlike ease and strength. "Come on, Doc. Grab hold of my arm and swing on over here. I've got you safe."

There was an ungainly struggle a few feet above Ryan's head, then Doc was snug, hanging on to Krysty's legs.

"How about the doors, J.B.?" Ryan called.

"Just looking."

Mildred was swinging back and forth like a pendulum. "Can you speed it up some, J.B., or I'm going to be performing the high dive and break all known records.''

''And your neck,'' Doc cackled, his good humor miraculously restored.

''Why don't you get your face out of Krysty's ass and shut your mouth?'' she yelled back, voice echoing, then dying flatly away.

''Because she's making an old man happy. You ought to try it sometime, you wizened old beldam.''

To everyone's surprise J.B. interrupted him. ''Just shut up, Doc, will you?''

''Sorry, John Barrymore, I'm sure.''

There was an awkward silence, broken by Ryan. ''If the bitching's over, can we get the sweet fuck out of this place?''

''Need some plas-ex. Got a last bit left somewhere in one of...'' The Armorer let go with one hand while he fumbled in his well-worn leather jacket. ''Yeah!'' he shouted triumphantly.

''Nowhere for us to shelter,'' Ryan observed. Above them the cables continued for another twenty feet or so, then they vanished into a self-contained power unit.

If they couldn't force the doors, then there was no doubt they would die. Maybe the strongest could contrive to hang on the dangling cables for a few hours. But at the finish they'd all go down.

''So little explosive it should dissipate out around us. Long as we close our eyes and keep our mouths open, the blast shouldn't do much damage. Could make us swing around some more."

Ryan glanced up. "You all right, Doc?"

"Passing fair, dear friend."

"Mildred?"

"Sure. How long will it be before it actually blows?"

"Got a twenty-sec detonator," the Armorer replied. "I'll have to swing myself to reach the doors."

He began to rock from side to side, pushing off with his boots from the rocky walls of the shaft, building momentum like a boy on a rope above a summer swimming hole.

"Try and turn your back, Mildred," Krysty called.

"Nearly…there…now…"

"Count us down," Ryan said.

"Haven't got…the detonator…in…yet. Setting it…now."

Ryan immediately began counting out loud. "Twenty, nineteen, eighteen…"

"Gaia, protect us all," Krysty breathed.

"Amen to that," Mildred said.

"Ten, nine, eight…"

Doc's lips moved silently.

"Two, one and—"

It was a sharp, small noise, like a gaudy whore slapping a drunken customer across the face, and the shaft filled with the characteristic bitter scent of plasex.

Ryan closed his mouth and opened his eye.

"Don't know," J.B. said, getting his answer in before anyone could ask the question.

He began to swing again, this time gathering speed so that he could kick out at the doors with his combat boots.

The others waited.

"Yeah," J.B. called.

Chapter Six

By the time they'd all struggled through the bent and damaged doors, Doc was close to total collapse.

J.B., helped eventually by Ryan, had managed to lever open the right-hand door. It had been badly dented by the plas-ex and it had been a desperate struggle, both men swinging on the pitching, greased cables.

None of them had even taken time to look around, so great was the relief at escaping from the dark shaft.

They rested in the deafening stillness. From somewhere above a faint light was filtering through. The air was cold and damp. Outside the titanium-steel elevator sec doors was a room about twenty-five feet square. It was filled with tumbled rubble and stank of urine.

J.B. broke the silence. "It's not like any redoubt I ever saw."

"More like any ruined ville anywhere," Ryan agreed. "But why build a gateway in a place like this?"

"Where is this?" Mildred asked.

"Good question." Krysty looked around. "Got a

big ville feel to it. Not like someplace out in the
deserts or mountains.''

Doc wrinkled his nose. ''I once paid a visit to old
London town. Before…before I came to when I am
now. I visited the stews of Seven Dials and the bor-
dello slums of Hoxton. I confess the scent that now
assails my nostrils is oddly reminiscent of that noisome place.''

''London in Victorian times, Doc!'' Ryan laughed.
''We've been most places and seen most things with
the jumps, but never through time.''

''Not yet,'' Doc said quietly.

''You said all the experiments failed in trawling
people through time. Except you.''

The old man stood up, kicking at a flattened piece
of metal that spun across the filthy floor. ''There
were stories, my dear old friend, stories I could tell
that would make a bold heart weep with… But what
was I saying?''

''Time travel,'' Ryan reminded him.

''You don't mean freezies, like me, do you? More
cryo-centers?'' Mildred asked eagerly.

Doc sniffed. ''I fear that I don't know. Can't recall
what I was saying. Apologies to all of this company.''

Ryan also stood up. ''Best to go take a look outside and see where we are.''

In his heart Ryan thrilled to the idea that they
might one day stumble upon a viable way of temporal travel. Like many people in Deathlands, he was

often occupied with the idea of getting back to the golden days before the long winters and sky-dark. To see the world of myth and legend when cities towered a thousand feet high, topped with onyx and chalcedony before man's madness turned inward and he rent his universe apart.

But he knew this would never happen.

The mat-trans units had been a closely guarded secret, with their ability to transport anything over thousands of miles in the blinking of an eye. But if only they could have conquered time travel...

Mildred brushed dirt off her clothes. "Kirk was wrong," she said. "It's time that's the final frontier, isn't it? Space was easy."

"HOW COME NOBODY GOT into the gateway?" Mildred asked as they picked their way slowly up the ruined stairs toward the ghostly light.

"Not many people in Deathlands have the fire-power to blow sec doors like those on the elevator," J.B. replied, pausing to offer the black woman a hand over a tangle of twisted wire.

"Thanks," she said. "What if someone comes down there now, with the doors open?"

"They'd need a lot of preparation and three hundred feet of rope," the Armorer replied.

"We'll need the same," Ryan added. "Something to bear in mind when we come to try and get back again to the gateway chamber."

Krysty had taken the lead, her heels clicking on

the moist stone. She'd drawn her silvered Heckler &
Koch 9 mm blaster, holding it cocked and ready in
her right hand.

"I can smell rain," she announced.

"Better keep talk for a red emergency," Ryan
suggested. "Could be anyone—or anything—waiting
for us out there."

They were clearly now in the basement of a devastated house. It had been totally pillaged, probably
shortly after nuke-death sprayed from the skies, and
now was no more than a hollow shell. But there was
evidence of a long-gone grandeur.

Doc paused at a turn of the stair, ignoring the
warning about keeping talk to a minimum. "If I
didn't know better, my dear Ryan, I would have said
that we were in...San Francisco or Chicago or Bos-
ton or New York or Philadelphia—a northern metropolis of some sort."

"Why?"

"The feel of the building. Angles between walls
and ceilings. Look at the shattered remnants of the
cornices and the broken plasterwork around where
the light fittings once hung."

"We visited Newyork once, didn't we? Well, sort
of sailed right on by it." Ryan remembered that trip,
on a sullen raft, floating through tendrils of miasmic
mist, along what had once been called the Hudson
River. They'd fought off grossly violent muties and
had seen what remained of the city. Darting lights

had flicked among the rubble, like corpse candles in a swampy wilderness.

"I remember that." Doc's voice boomed out, echoing through the ruins.

"Shut up, Doc."

"What was that, Ryan, my—"

"Just lip-zip, will you?"

"Roger and out."

Ryan wondered what that meant. The main thing was the old man finally kept quiet.

Krysty had paused, holding up her hand and beckoning for Ryan to join her. His own blaster ready, he climbed carefully up the stairs. Now he could feel and taste rain on his face, drifting through from the open air, close above them. It had a slightly acidic flavor to it.

"What time of day is it, lover?" she whispered.

He checked his wrist chron. "Last place we went it'd be around six in the evening. Never be sure after a jump, but it must be some time around late afternoon or near to night."

"Assuming we're still in Deathlands," she said, brushing the drizzling mist off her face. It clung in a diamond veil to the burning red hair, now curled tightly around her head and neck.

"Yeah." He glanced behind him, making sure the others were ready, knowing they would be. *Nobody ever got chilled by checking twice* was what the Trader used to say, and he'd lived long and lived hard.

The stairs ended in open air, surrounded by piles of rubble. Chunks of brick and concrete, knitted together in a mad frieze with coils of steel, were decorated with thousands of splinters of ash-smeared glass, shutting out any view of the immediate surroundings of the building.

The sky was the color of molten lead, laced through with streaks of pinkish-gold. A small rain was blowing in from Ryan's right, sending trickles of water over the top few steps. Surprisingly there were flowers growing from the fragmented stone, tiny yellow and white daisies that he'd seen in many other blasted places throughout Deathlands, and crimson-purple fireweed, waving in a light breeze.

Ryan stood still, head just below the level of the fallen ramparts, taking several slow, deep breaths, checking and analyzing what he could smell.

Behind him Krysty was doing the same thing. "Smoke. Cooking fires," she pronounced.

"Lot of them around but nothing very close," he agreed. Very cautiously the one-eyed man pushed his head above the scattered rubble, squinting around. "Fireblast." He whistled softly.

"What?" Krysty asked.

Ryan shook his head. "Real big, big ville. Could be Newyork."

"Anyone?" J.B. called from a couple of stairs lower.

"Nobody in sight. Big bastard of a gray rat just

went away over there, but there's just ruined buildings, far as I can see.''

Krysty moved carefully to join him. ''Gaia! I don't think I've ever seen... It goes for miles and miles. I never knew there was a city this big anywhere in Death—I mean in the United States. Look at it.''

''Can we come up?'' Mildred asked. ''The suspense is killing.''

''Sure,'' Krysty replied. ''But don't stick your head out too far.''

All five of them leaned on the bricks and concrete, marveling at the city of desolation before them. Over to their left Ryan noticed the distant glint of water. ''River there. Or the sea.''

''Doesn't smell strongly enough of salt to be the sea,'' Krysty said, ''but there *is* the sea somewhere not too many miles away. What big city could it be, Doc? Mildred?''

They both shook their heads. Doc scratched the silver stubble around his creviced chin. ''Not San Francisco. Not enough hills.''

''Nor Chicago,'' Mildred said.

''How about Newyork?'' J.B. offered.

''Can't we get out and have a small walk around?'' Mildred asked. ''I mean, one expanse of wrecked homes looks a lot like another.''

''Sun's setting,'' Ryan said. ''So that river over there could be the Hudson, couldn't it?''

''It's to the west of us, true enough. But it's possible that this might be the district called Queens.

Then the river to the west of us would be the East River. So confusing.''

''And it might not even be Newyork in the first place,'' Krysty said. ''That what you're both saying to us?''

Doc nodded. Mildred looked around, face puzzled. ''I don't know. There's just a sort of New York feel in the air. But...'' She shrugged.

There weren't any signs of hostile life, apart from the rat. Ryan led them out into the open.

All of them stared toward the thin ribbon of water, tinted bloodred by the sun setting over some higher ground beyond it.

Without warning a metallic click sounded behind them.

Chapter Seven

J.B.'s voice breathed in Ryan's ear. "It's an AK-47. Looks like it's got a 30-round box mag on it."

At a range of twenty yards there was a fair chance the person behind the blaster could cut all five of them into bloody tatters. If he was any good with the weapon.

"Hey! Where you outlanders coming from?"

The voice was thin and reedy, but with an infinite coldness to it that held Ryan and the others very still.

"Asked you fuckers a question."

"Passing through the ville, son," Ryan replied.

"Don't call me 'son,' you one-eyed son of a bitch. I got a name."

"What's that?"

"What's what?"

Now Ryan was becoming confused. "What's what? What's your name?"

"Name's Dred."

"Dred. How d'you spell that?"

The young man stepped out from cover, the AK-47 still threatening them. "How do I know? I never took on writing and that shit."

There was a piece of broken wood near him, and

he reached out with his left hand, scrawling painstakingly in the mud by his feet: D-R-E-D. "There. That's my tag. Dred."

Ryan nodded. "Sure. Dred."

The lad looked to be around eighteen, and he was short, barely five-six. His clothes were a ragged assortment of old and patched and makeshift. His feet were hidden inside ill-matching shoes. The left was like an ancient basketball sneaker, wound around with thin red wire. The right was a once-elegant brogue with black-and-white uppers.

Dred's hair was extremely long, twined into narrow plaits that appeared to have been coated in dark clay. He had pale skin and light blue eyes. The way he handled the heavy weapon convinced Ryan that this was a young man who'd already learned the difficult craft of chilling.

"What are your names, and why don't you have colors shown?"

"He remind you of anyone, lover?" Krysty whispered.

Ryan nodded, knowing she was thinking of Jak Lauren.

"Names." The barrel of the gun weaved a pattern in front of them.

Ryan's guesstimate was that the boy could be taken out, but it would mean at least one of them buying the farm. Maybe two or three, depending on how good Dred was.

"I'm Ryan. This is Doc, J.B., Krysty and Mildred.

We're passing through. Been looking for shelter for the night.''

"Fucking oldies. Wrinklies!" He spit in the dirt. "No gang'd take you."

"Pardon me, my young fellow," Doc said. "Could you possibly enlighten me as to the nomenclature of this fair metropolis?"

"You want your balls shot off?"

Doc sighed. "Not quite the response I'd hoped to elicit."

"He asked what's the name of this ville," Krysty explained.

"Oh." The youth nodded his understanding. "The ville... Hey, you mean this turf?"

"Turf?" Now it was Krysty's turn to look bemused.

Mildred helped her out. "I know the word. Means the territory of a street gang."

"Right, lady. That's it. This is the Hawks' turf. Me, Dred, is the pres of the Hawks. We run this section of the Southbronx."

"So it is New York!" Doc exclaimed. "Upon my soul, I thought it was."

"You going to chill us all, son?" J.B. asked casually.

"Call me 'son' again and I will."

The Armorer showed a tight, narrow grin, turning to Ryan. "He remind you of an old friend? Sure he does."

Dred looked puzzled. "How come none of you is shitting bricks at this blaster?"

Ryan took a careful half step forward. "We've been all over Deathlands, Dred, and seen plenty of killing. You've got the ace on the line here, but you can't take out more than one—mebbe two—of us. Then you're faceup with rain falling into open eyes."

"You figure?"

"I figure."

"That a threat, outie?"

"Promise."

Ryan could almost hear tiny cogs grinding in the boy's head. There was a difference from Jak. He'd been quicker, like spilled mercury. "What do you want, then?"

"The blaster down. Then tell us a place for the night and some place to get eats."

"You might be with the Peaks. Or the Chivs. Or the gang of scalies downriver."

"I'm getting tired, Dred. Put that blaster down, or pull on the trigger."

Dred grinned for the first time, revealing his truly hideous teeth. There was a variety of jagged, blackened stumps leaning into the dark gaps. "Sure."

THE BOY SHOWED THEM one of what he claimed were several gang hideouts all across that part of the ville. Mildred managed to talk quietly to Ryan as they all moved across the landscape of lunar rubble, explaining to him what and where the South Bronx had been.

"Lot of decent folks, but a lot of bandits," she said. "If that's the Hudson, then somewhere behind us must be what's left of Yankee Stadium."

"Baseball," Ryan said, dragging up an old memory. "Saw some old vids of games... Can't remember where or when that was."

Dred turned, making Ryan realize how sharp his hearing must be. "Yankee Stadium's still here. Most of the top's gone, but there's still the field. Even a bit of grass is growing."

"Is that in your part of the ville?" J.B. asked.

"Our turf? Sure is."

The sun was sinking fast across the slow-flowing streak of silvery water to the west. Ryan could just make out the vestigial remains of the piers of a massive bridge. "What's that called, over the Hudson?"

Dred laughed, a strange, almost silent convulsion. He doubled up, one hand across his ravaged mouth, shoulders shaking. "Hudson! Fucking triple-stupe outies! Not the Hudson."

"Not?" Mildred said. "But it must be. Oh, we're farther south. Then it's..." She closed her eyes with the effort of trying to remember. "I know. It's the Harlem River, isn't it?"

Dred looked disappointed, his laughter stopping as suddenly as it had started. "Right. Don't know what the bridge was called. It all fell down in the days of the smoke clouds."

"What's the rest of the ville like—" Ryan pointed southward "—that way? Manhattan. The main part of the ville. What's it like down there?"

"All fallen. Go look. Get your fucking nose scraped off and your cock nailed to your head."

Doc smiled. "Sounds to me that nothing much has changed in the past two hundred years."

Dred moved on, hopping with an ungainly ease, ducking and weaving between the devastation. It was absurdly simple to lose your way. Some of the rubble was flatter than a roach's belly. Other piles stood fifty feet high, with gaping windows and sagging doorways.

Ryan had taken a few moments to look behind as they left the building that held the hidden gateway, making sure he could memorize it, ready for when they needed to get back.

It looked as though it had once been a conventional late-nineteenth-century mansion, and he wondered how it had come to house all those expensively secret installations.

"Here, outies."

The boy had vanished, plaits flying behind him, diving into a gaping hole that looked like hundreds of other gaping holes—except for a crude drawing of a bird of prey, daubed in yellow, with crimson claws and hooked beak.

"Hawks," J.B. pronounced, "marking their turf."

Dred's voice echoed from beneath their feet. "Not

a good place to stay out after dark. Scalies creepy-crawl from rivers.''

THE FOOD WAS DIFFERENT kinds of fish and water creatures offered up in different ways. Dred got a fire going, connected to a ramshackle arrangement of old heating and drainage pipes. "Carries smoke a long way off," he boasted.

"This your own place?" Krysty asked.

"Yeah. Got three of mine. Plenty of others around the Hawks' turf for hide-ups."

It looked as if it had once been a basement apartment, built with strong supporting pillars that had held it up when the house above came crashing down. It was about fifteen feet square, with only the natural light filtering down from the open hole. Dred pointed, showing them a dented sheet of steel with a handle bolted to it.

"Any fucker tries to get in, he's got to get through that. Me and the blaster hold him out."

"You got another way out of this rat hole?" J.B. asked.

"Sure. Hey, some of you wrinklies aren't so double-stupe. Behind fire you move that door and there's a wriggle up and out behind the next house."

Ryan admired the confidence and self-sufficiency of the teenager. "How old are you, Dred?"

"Old as my teeth and younger than my cock." Again there was a paroxysm of mute laughter as he slapped his thighs at his own joke.

"Eighteen?" Ryan offered.

Like a hand turning off a spilling faucet, the laughter stopped. "Yeah. Or seventeen or nineteen. Can count to twenty and then... Then you're an oldie."

The food was in five separate containers. Most of them looked as if they'd once been old cooking pots, but none had a handle. One was split across the bottom, and liquid kept seeping out, hissing into the yellow flames.

Doc was interested in what was being offered. "Might I ask what culinary delights you intend for us, my dear young fellow?"

"You mean eats?"

"Indeed I do, Dred."

"This is shrimps," he said, stirring a mass of gelatinous pink. "This is some eels, and this is some more eels. Call this thumb chewer, 'cause it's got big teeth on it."

"And that?" Doc pointed at the largest can, which bubbled merrily and was giving off a truly original smell.

"That's some more eels."

Dred stood to slide shut the steel door, fixing a wedge of wood to prevent it from being opened from the other side, when they all heard a woman's voice calling from the darkness beyond.

"Dred! That you in there? Hey, the Hawks!"

"She's one of us. One of our sluts. Kinda special slut for me."

"Dred! Lemme in, please!"

The boy shrugged and glanced at his five guests. Ryan realized he was trying to look cool and in charge.

"Stop triggering, Retha. Got some outies here with me."

"Got some food and liquor, Dred."

He heaved at the door and managed to slide it open again. Only a foot or so, but it was enough for the girl to slip through.

"Starting to rain, Dred," she stated, eyes flicking across the faces of the strangers.

In turn they all studied her. The girl was about five feet tall with jagged yellow hair that the rain had teased into wet spikes. Ryan figured her weight around eighty pounds, including the thigh-length green rubber waders she was wearing. Her face was deathly white, her green eyes sunk into hollows of wind-washed bone. She walked forward, smiling nervously, and revealing teeth that were even worse than Dred's.

"I'm Retha," she announced. "Dred's special slut. Aren't I?"

"Sure, sure." He fixed the door back across the hole, closing out the night. "You been in the sewer tunnels again?"

She looked down at her feet. "Yeah. Borrowed these from Edie. Went under some Chivs and got half a dog and some joltsky." Retha reached under her parka and flourished a dark green bottle with a screw top.

"Shouldn't go tunneling on your own. Stupe slut!"

"Sorry, Dred."

There was an uncomfortable silence, which was broken by Doc rising from what remained of the front seat of an old Volvo. He offered his hand to the girl. "My name is Doc Tanner, my dear. I'm enchanted to make your acquaintance."

"Thanks."

"And these are my trusty companions. Searchers after the elusive truth and vagabonds upon the misty highway that winds toward the eternal mountain of spun crystal. Good people all." He introduced them one by one.

Retha shook her head. "I never seen so many oldies in one place, Dred."

"That's what outies are. Leave the turf and your hair falls out, your teeth crack and you end up shitting blood."

It occurred to Mildred, though she kept her thoughts to herself, that this was a remarkably accurate and concise description of the horrors of radiation sickness.

The girl peeled off her coat, revealing a well-darned sweater in maroon and green. The sleeves had unraveled, showing that the girl had tattoos on both arms.

The right was a reproduction of the bird of prey on the wall outside the hiding place—yellow with red claws and beak. On the other arm was a flower, yellow at the center with white petals and a wobbly green stalk. Below it was the name "Dred."

"Anyone mind if I take these big boots off?" she asked. "Only my feet stink horrible after I've been wearing them all day."

She wasn't kidding. Fortunately the smell was cloaked by the shank of a dog that Dred stuck on a spit and began to roast over the fire.

"Why you in Newyork?" she asked, addressing the question to Krysty.

"Not easy to answer that, Retha. Sort of passing through."

"To where?" Dred questioned, turning from stirring one of the glowing cans of food, a dripping spoon in his hand.

She pointed vaguely toward the west. "Out there."

"Oh, yeah. Jersey. Lot of swampies there. Watch yourself crossing the big river."

"That food ready?" J.B. asked hungrily.

"Just about."

"Did my old ears catch some passing mention of a bottle that might contain a little joltsky?" Doc asked.

"Didn't know you had a taste for joltsky," Krysty teased.

"Prefer a decent Mouton Cadet or any halfway good Spätlese, but times are passing. I developed a taste for it during my time back in the Darks with friends Teague and Strasser."

The skinny girl worked on the top, loosening it with her teeth, biting down hard on the metal and making Ryan wince. He half expected to see her damaged molars splinter around the bottle neck. But Retha succeeded, passing it first to Dred.

He gulped down a mouthful, wiping his cracked lips and smothering a cough. "Not fucking bad," he pronounced.

Doc reached out for the green bottle, holding it suspiciously to the light of the fire, then sniffing it. "Certainly raises a few gibbering spirits of evil memory. Cheers, my dears." After a quick swallow, he choked and spluttered "By the three Kennedys! That is hotter than the hobs of Hades. Excellent."

Ryan took the bottle next. Joltsky was one of the most common alcoholic drinks in Deathlands, and it varied radically from ville to ville. Battery acid had been known to find its way into some brews, but at its simplest it was just bootleg hooch, distilled over a fire of hickory wood with a sprinkling of jolt, the powerful hallucinogenic drug.

Judging by the extremely bitter flavor of this mixture, it could have contained a powerful dose of jolt. Ryan had a second, cautious sip. Then he handed it to Krysty, who shook her head and passed it to Mildred.

"What did you say it was called?" she asked Retha.

"Joltsky."

"Smells like two hundred proof distilled with a mix of animal anesthetic. No thanks."

J.B. didn't have any worries and took a long draw on the bottle, nodding. "Last time I had anything that strong must've been..." He looked at Ryan. "That gaudy house south of Reeno."

"Right. The time Hun and Finnegan took off all their clothes and painted each other with black varnish and—"

Their reminiscent laughter was interrupted by Retha, who suddenly drew a dirty Saturday night special from the back of her belt and leveled the little .32 at J.B.

Chapter Eight

Ryan's hand was already on the butt of his own blaster when he realized the skinny girl was pointing her pistol *past* the Armorer.

"Scalie," she said quietly. "Hand halfway around the door."

Then they all saw it—very long fingers webbed to the second joint, terminating in claws of hooked bone. The back of the hand was coated in thick, overlapping scales.

Dred had also drawn a small-caliber pistol of indeterminate age and pedigree. Both blasters had such short barrels that Ryan doubted their accuracy at anything over five feet.

Everyone watched the hand as it spidered slowly around the edges of the makeshift door, as though it were feeling for a lock or bolt. In the sudden silence the fingers stopped, as if the mutie outside was aware that it had been seen.

Dred took a half step toward the door, blaster leveled and steady. Ryan saw the knuckle whitening and held up a hand. "No."

"I can hit it from here," the boy protested, his face flushing with what could have been anger.

"Just a piss-ant wound. Open the door and chill the shit out of it."

"Could be several."

"We got the firepower to take out a few mutie reptiles," J.B. said.

The sound of the muttered conversation seemed to have reassured the creature outside, and its hand began its cautious exploration again.

Dred looked at the girl, who shrugged. Now everyone in the smoky room had a gun drawn.

"Come on," Ryan urged.

"I don't—"

"Do it," Retha whispered.

"I'll take the door," the Armorer said, moving lightly to the side. "Everyone ready? Keep clear of lines of fire. Right, on three. One, two and three!"

With a surge of power that belied his slender body, J.B. heaved the heavy rectangle of metal away from the opening, revealing the cold night—and also revealing three of the scalies, frozen, their olive-green flesh tinted scarlet by the glow of the cooking fire. All of them wore ragged shirts and pants.

The underground chamber reverberated with the pounding of seven blasters, all firing at once, pouring concentrated lead at the reptilian muties.

It wasn't a firefight, just a plain bloody slaughter.

The invaders, bodies slick with rain, tumbled in a tangle of flailing arms and legs and snapping jaws, all dying where they fell.

One rolled close to Doc, who hastily shifted his

feet out of the way of the raking talons, clutching at him in the spasms of death. Blood seeped down the cracked staircase, dripping and puddling on the uneven floor.

After the burst of shooting, there was a strange calm. One of the scalies was still twitching, its claws scraping on the stone. Within seconds even that stopped and there was stillness.

"Great blasters!" Dred exclaimed.

"Yeah. Where d'you outies thieve such fucking great blasters?" Retha holstered her own small handgun.

"Picked them up here and there," Ryan replied.

"Will you show them to us after?" Dred was more interested in the powerful weapons than in the corpses of the three muties that still blocked the entrance to his hiding place. And let in the rain and the dark.

"Clear the shit out of the way first," Ryan growled. "Might be more around."

Dred whooped and punched the air with his left hand. "Excellent spilling, man! You old outies are the best...and I'm talking fucking triple-best. Tore them snaky bastards from river to river!"

Retha looked at the trio of dead muties, poking at one with her bare foot, her smile showing the dental devastation that blighted her mouth. "Never seen such power from blasters," she said, shaking her head. "We had them, and the Hawks could wipe up all the shit gangs clear across Mattan."

Doc was peering at his Le Mat. "Thought I had the scattergun barrel set. Turned out to be the .36s."

"Did the job," J.B. commented.

"Something burning on the fire." Krysty moved toward the cooking food.

"Clear up and then eat. Then finish the joltsky." Dred was dancing with a manic glee, waving his .32 pistol.

"Sounds good," Mildred said. She had only fired three rounds from her ZKR 551, each of the .38 caliber bullets hitting a scalie within an inch of its mouth.

Ryan, J.B. and Doc began to drag the stinking bodies up the stairs and into the gray drizzle that was driving in from the north. Mildred moved to help them, leaving Krysty by the cooking fire. Retha and Dred watched the disposal of their enemies, hugging each other with delight.

Krysty peered into the largest of the pots, bending to stir it with an elegant metal spoon bearing a crest of a fleur-de-lis. Behind her the panel of wood that concealed the panic-run exit burst inward.

An immensely tall and fat scalie erupted into the cellar, holding a long sword in its left fist. With its right it snatched Krysty, snagging its claws in her mane of bright hair. She screamed, shrill and piercing.

By the time anyone started to react, the mutie had one arm around her throat and was holding the point of its makeshift blade at the side of her face. Ryan started to go for his blaster, seeing he was going to be a half second too late.

Only one person in the group had his gun still in his hand.

Dred.

Plaits whirling, the teenager recognized the instant of danger. He leveled his small handgun, the peeling chrome flickering with reflected firelight, and squeezed the trigger three times.

Ryan winced, knowing the effective range of the Saturday night special, one of the most common blasters in Deathlands, could spell death for his helpless lover.

The first bullet hit the wall nearly four feet to the left of the scalie; the second ricocheted off the cooking spit, sending the haunch of roasting dog into the eager flames; the third, as Dred found his balance, smashed into the long lower jaw of the reptilian mutie.

It staggered back, coughing and spitting blood and broken teeth, letting go of Krysty, who dived away to safety. Dark blood, black in the dim light, gushed across the creature's neck and chest.

Ryan aimed his SIG-Sauer P-226 and snapped off two rounds. The built-in baffle silencer did its stuff, and there was only a discreet double-cough, drowned by the agonized roaring of the scalie.

One of the 9 mm full-metal jacket rounds struck it in the center of its exposed throat, tearing through the leathery skin. The second took it high at the side of the angular skull, just below the twin-lidded eye.

The long steel blade rattled on the stone as the dying mutie fell to its knees, grasping at the gaping wound in its neck. Blood spouted, hissing in the fire, filling the cavern with the bittersweet smell of hot death.

One of the cans of eels was knocked over in the tumbling and kicking, adding an extra layer to the sickening cocktail of scents. The movements of the scalie's muscular arms and legs slowed, then finally stopped.

Dred punched the air with both hands in a gesture of triumph. "Is that more better or is that fucking more better?" he shouted.

Ryan took a halfstep toward the crowing youth, the tic of ferocious white anger working at his temple. He wanted to plant the barrel of the blaster across the kid's grinning mouth. Spraying bullets around like that—with such talentless bravado— showed a level of foolishness that made Ryan's blood race.

But Krysty had seen the look on his face, and she grabbed at his arm. "No, lover," she said, just loud enough for him to hear.

"Right through the mutie's shithead face!" Dred yelled.

"Could've chilled you," Ryan whispered through gritted teeth.

"Didn't. Everyone else was cold-cocked. The scalie could have taken me out, lover."

She was speaking the truth. Ryan, even in his killing anger, recognized that. The appearance of the huge mutie from the hidden entrance had taken all of them by surprise, including Ryan himself.

As the crimson pulse slowed, he could also accept that a part of his rage was directed at himself for allowing someone else to save Krysty's life.

"Yeah," he said. "Yeah."

IT WAS NEAR MIDNIGHT. The last body had been dragged out and thrown down the slope to join its former friends.

When Ryan went out for a piss a couple of hours after the brief battle, he saw that all of the corpses had disappeared, dragged away by God knows what hideous scavengers.

Despite one can of eels being ruined and a chunk of the dog being badly scorched, there was still enough food to go around. The bottle of joltsky was shared, mainly by Dred and Retha, though Ryan, Doc and J.B. all took small nips. Mildred tried it, shaking her head in disgust at the flavor.

"Rather drink a rabid bat's piss through a leper's shroud," she told them.

Krysty simply refused the bottle.

Doc fell asleep early, curling up in a corner, snoring steadily. Mildred and J.B. soon emulated him, though without the rhythmic snores.

Ryan and Krysty sat close together by the remnants of the dying fire, watching as Dred and his diminutive girlfriend became more and more stoned.

"Showed them scalies," the boy muttered.

"Lots more where the green-prick bastards came from," Retha responded.

Ryan was interested. "Lots more? You mean a serious gang of them?"

Dred nodded solemnly. "Sure. They push at the Hawks' turf from the river and the old sewers. Now they found this place, we'll dump it and move on."

"Where's their base?" Krysty asked.

"Who knows? Some say down the docks, southwest side. Never go that way."

"Never," Retha repeated, blinking owlishly at the boy. Her right hand had disappeared inside his pants and was busily working away there. "Never, ever, river, bother."

Eventually the teenagers fell asleep.

"Fancy a quick hug, lover?" Krysty whispered.

Ryan shook his head. "No. Not here."

"Sure." Krysty gazed at Dred and the girl. Asleep, Retha looked to be about eight years old, sucking her thumb like a cradled child. "They coming with us?"

"Maybe."

"Replace Jak, you think?"

Ryan grunted. It could have been yes. And it could have been no.

Chapter Nine

It was a relief to climb out into the cool dawn air, leaving the smoky atmosphere of the cellar with its lingering stench of blood, charred meat and roasted fish.

Ryan woke first, easing himself from Krysty's embrace, pulling on his jacket and winding the white silk scarf around his neck, tucking the weighted ends inside his shirt.

There was a mist over the limitless ruins of what many had thought had once been the greatest city in the world. Ryan shaded his eye and peered southward, trying to make out if anything remained of the golden towers that had scraped at the sky.

But that whole section was hidden in fog.

There was a breeze from the northwest, bringing the faint flavor of early-morning cooking fires. The mist slithered away, and Ryan had a clear view of the gleaming waterway. What had Mildred called it?

"Harlem River," he said to himself.

By the piles of one of the ruined bridges, he caught a glimpse of something moving. It was immensely long, with a body that was coiled like a snake or an unimaginably huge eel. It rolled lazily across his vision, and there was a snapshot of a blunt head, rising several feet from the water.

Then the fog returned, and he could no longer see the river.

There was a noise behind him on the steps, and he turned to see Dred walking toward him, holding the smooth gray shape of the G-12 caseless automatic rifle.

"The blaster's mine, Dred," Ryan said, resisting the immediate impulse to drop his hand to the butt of the SIG-Sauer.

"It's double-lethal, Ryan."

"Go put it back."

Dred's face fell. "I'm pres of the Hawks, outie. Not nobody talks like that."

"Put it back or you get hurt."

The muzzle of the Heckler & Koch G-12 swung up to center on Ryan's belt.

The one-eyed man looked into the boy's face. "You got three seconds to go and do like I told you. You made a bad mistake, and you just made it triple-worse. Put it back."

"Or?"

"Crows get to eat your eyes."

"Big talk for a one-eyed wrinklie, Ryan Cawdor."

"Oh, fuck this." Ryan drew the heavy panga from his belt and started to move toward the boy.

"Okay, okay. I'm going. Fuck a mutie duck, Ryan. No call to get so..." He turned and vanished down the staircase.

Ryan carried on admiring the morning.

Dred eventually reappeared, dragging Retha behind him. "Fucked her head, the stupe slut, with all that joltsky."

"Now what?" Krysty asked.

"Could go back to the gateway. Jump on out of here." Ryan looked at the others. "Anyone got any strong feelings?"

Mildred raised a hand. "Please, sir. I'd like to look around what's left of New York. For old times' sake."

Doc also raised a hand. "I agree with everything the last speaker said."

Krysty looked at J.B. and Ryan, knowing the final weight of the vote would be carried by them. "I'd like to look around, lover."

"Give it a day," J.B. agreed. "We can hit it as it moves."

"Yeah. Move south and keep away from the sewers and the river." Ryan looked at Dred, who was engaged in slapping the semiconscious girl to try to bring her around. "How about you?"

"Chance to stick with the best blasters in the whole ville? Got to joke me, Ryan. Course we'll go with you."

"USED TO BE WAGS RUN on steel lines, right through to Mattan," Dred told them.

"Used to run clear across Deathlands," Doc replied. "Plenty of lines. Topeka and Santa Fe. Climb aboard your coach in San Francisco, have your ham and eggs way down in Carolina. Pardon me, boy, is that the cat that shined the new shoes?'' He doubled over, cackling with laughter at what he clearly regarded as some kind of joke. The others looked on blankly.

The early mist was burning off, being replaced by a cold, bright morning. The overnight dew was disappearing, but there was still enough left to catch the dawning sun and hold it in countless diamond clusters.

"Cooking fires are dangerous," Retha said, now recovered from the alcohol and the jolt. "Brings muties like flies to shit."

"Where does the Hawks' territory—turf—stop?" J.B. asked.

"We walk where we want, and where we step, then the earth fucking dies," Dred said confidently, tossing his hair back from his face.

"Yeah, sure. But how many blocks of the ville do you control?"

"Well, around ten north and south, and four, sometimes five, from east to west."

"How many in your gang?" Mildred asked.

"Hawks got forty soldiers, the meanest fuckers who walk the valley and fear no evil."

"Dred," Retha said hesitantly.

"What?"

"Forty?"

"Shut the fuck up, slut."

KRYSTY LINKED HER ARM through Ryan's as they stood on a broad sweep of hillside, looking over ruined houses and apartments, down toward a huge bowl of tumbled concrete with a suggestion of dusty green at its center. "So that's Yankee Stadium," she said. "Like a shrine, back before the long winters."

Mildred was at their side. "My father's younger brother, Uncle Josh, he brought me here once. I'd be…about thirteen. Hot afternoon and the old guy showed us to our seats and dusted them for us. I liked that. And folks shouted, 'Beer! Yo, beer!' Cold drinks and popcorn and hot dogs. The best I ever tasted. Kids in the tiers with gloves on waited for a high fly ball. The smell and the crowd and—" She paused and swallowed hard. "If I go on like this, I'll end up in tears."

It was J.B. who put an arm around Mildred's shoulders to comfort her.

Dred was getting antsy, shuffling his feet and constantly looking over his shoulder.

Doc nudged him. "You reckon you got a frightful fiend stepping in close behind you, son?"

"Don't call me son, you—" Dred controlled himself with a visible effort. "Sorry, Doc. Listen, that blaster of yours. Big old gren-launcher. Really got two barrels on it?"

"Always keen to impart a little knowledge, Dred, though some say that can be a dangerous thing."

"What?" Total bewilderment showed on the boy's pale face.

"This single barrel fires a .63-caliber scattergun round. Close action. In fact, this gun was invented as a cavalry side arm in 1856 by Dr. Jean Alexandre François Le Mat of New Orleans, whom God preserve. They were eventually manufactured in New Orleans by the good doctor and Pierre Beauregard, later to win honors as a Confederate general at both Manassas and Shiloh."

Dred hawked and spit in the cold dirt. "Too much fucking talk, Doc. How many rounds? Gimme a short answer!"

"Well, as I was saying before that rather peremptory interruption, it has the one scattergun barrel. You then adjust the hammer here, and it will fire nine rounds of .36 caliber from this revolving chamber."

"Kind of clumsy."

"Many things are, my dear boy, until you get used to them. I have spent a large part of my adult life struggling to get used to things that were beyond my comprehension."

"You got the greatest blasters ever," Dred said, stopping to peer over his shoulder. "You all join the Hawks and—"

"We aren't big on joining, Dred. Thanks, but no thanks," Ryan replied.

"Sure, sure."

A large rat scurried in front of them, appearing to come out from a broken drain cover. It was brindled and dragged one rear leg. As it ran over the piles of bricks and shattered glass, strings of sticky intestine leaked from a savage bite on its flank.

"Supper!" Retha shrieked, pulling a small knife from her sleeve and going after the creature. But the thigh-length waders slowed her to a lumbering gallop, and the wounded rodent managed to escape among some heaped paving stones. She rejoined the companions, panting and cursing, rubbing at her ankle, which she'd turned in the rubble. "Lost food," she moaned.

Mildred glanced at J.B. "Seems I wasn't that hungry, anyway."

The Armorer smiled at her. "Yeah, but you have to admit last night's dog was good."

Dred, with his uncannily sharp hearing, caught what J.B. had said. "Yeah. With those blasters we could move in on Tuff Norris and his dogs."

Doc grinned. "Upon my soul! That sounds uncommonly like a supporting act in vaudeville. Tuff Norris and his performing dogs. A smile, a song and a bark."

"Shut it, Doc," Ryan growled. "Who's this Norris person?"

"Breeds dogs out of Saint Mary Park. East a few blocks. In Trax turf."

"Breeds dogs." Krysty shook her head. "I didn't think many people around here would be into keeping pets."

Retha looked at her as though the redhead had become demented. "What's a pet? Breeds them for food. Hundreds. Dogs for eating." She shook her head at Krysty. "What a stupe."

Chapter Ten

"What's this road called?" Ryan asked.

"Major Deeway," Dred replied. "Gotta learn the main trails so's you know how to get back to home turf."

"Is that Mattan across the river? If the bridges are all out, how d'you get over?"

"Gangs control crossings. Pay, and they ferry you over by raft."

"Pay what?" Krysty asked.

"Lotsa things. You give what you got that they want that you can give."

"If we're going down into Manhattan—Mattan—then how about all the other street gangs in the way? You got codes, laws and signals about going through each other's turf?"

Dred stopped and looked at Mildred, showing some unease. "I don't know."

The black woman sighed. "I knew about the Crips and Bloods and all the wearing of colors that street gangs used to have before the big night came."

Retha shook her head, glancing at her man for approval. "We don't have nothing like that."

"So how come we're going to walk along

these…these mean streets if they belong to other gangs?''

Dred smiled weakly at her. ''It's having you oldies along. If you weren't here with all those blasters, the other shitters'll wonder what the fuck's going down here.''

Mildred nodded. ''Terrific.''

IT WAS ABOUT NINE in the morning by the time they got to the ferry, and it had been a comparatively uneventful journey.

A stone had been thrown at them as they neared the river, skittering along the roadway, making Doc skip nimbly in the air. But there was no follow-up.

''What's the average age of the Hawks?'' Ryan had asked.

''What's average mean?''

''Like, you're around eighteen or so. How many are a lot older or a lot younger?''

''In the Hawks?''

''In any gang?''

''Mostly street kids. Sort of ten to about fourteen. You know.''

''How many older than twenty?''

Dred had looked at the one-eyed man as though he'd been asked the riddle of the universe. ''Older than twenty? Nobody. What a triple-stupe question! Hear that, Retha? Older'n twenty!''

THE FERRY OPERATED near the remains of what looked like an old railway bridge. The rusted remnants of the lines hung out over the river, reflected in the slow-moving water. There was no sign of any sort of boat.

"Now what?" J.B. asked, his eyes darting around, looking, as always, for the first sign of a potential ambush.

"Call the ferry," Dred replied.

From the behavior of the young man, Ryan was building a suspicion that he might be on jolt or some kind of speedy high. He was sweating, despite the chill of the morning, and he didn't seem able to keep still. His hands were in his pockets and out again, fingers knotting, constantly moving toward the nest of small sores around his mouth.

Behind them was a triangle of steel scaffolding, like an enormous whipping frame. Hung on a length of polished chain was a steel bar, nearly six feet long, and leaning against the apparatus was another metal bar, about two and a half feet in length.

They all watched as Dred slouched toward it, hefting the shorter bar and swinging it in a scything round-arm blow. There was a deep ringing sound, so rich and resonant that it seemed to make the marrow of the bone quiver. The noise echoed back from the wrecked buildings on the far shore.

The teenager scrambled to the top of the makeshift structure, hanging on by one arm and swinging with a studied artlessness, staring out across the water for a response to the signal.

Krysty was at Ryan's side, both of them looking at Dred. "What d'you reckon, lover?" she asked quietly so that Retha wouldn't hear.

"Got to be tough to run a street gang in New-york," he replied.

"Like him?"

"Don't feel one way or the other. How about you? What do you feel?"

Krysty brushed a strand of hair out of her eyes. "Can't tell."

"But?"

"No. Can't say I like him. But there's something about him that puts me in mind of Jak."

Ryan pursed his lips. From behind them there was another great pealing from the signaling bar. "Put Dred and Jak into a dark room together and who walks out?"

"Jak. No contest."

"Then again, Jak was...is something triple-special. Probably not anyone like that snow-headed little bastard in all Deathlands."

Krysty shaded her eyes. "Something's moving over there." She glanced behind her again at Dred, who was punching the air exultantly with his fist. "Trust him, lover?"

Ryan shook his head. "About as far as I could throw him. Then again, in all Deathlands there can't be more than about ten people I'd trust. And four of them are right here."

Krysty laughed. "King of the misanthropes, aren't you?"

"How's that?"

"Misanthropes don't care much for other folks. There must be friends left behind. Old lovers. Children. Must be."

"If there are any wives or children, I don't know nothing...anything about them."

Krysty stopped smiling, putting her hand to her eyes, as though she'd suddenly been stricken by an agonizing migraine.

"What's wrong?" Ryan asked.

"Oh, Gaia!" She swayed so much that he had to steady her with a hand on her arm. "Krysty?"

She gulped in a great shuddering breath and managed to straighten, pushing his hand away. Her face was as white as fresh-fallen snow, eyes glittering like green fire. Her brilliant hair was curled tightly around her neck.

"That was so..." she began.

"What?"

She shook her head. "Just a sort of flash of... A *seeing*. But stronger than anything I've ever known. Mother Sonja said there'd be times like this. Times like this, she said, when I'd see something so clear, so clear that—"

"But what did you see, lover?"

"I can't tell you, dearest." She held on to him now and stared intently into his face. "I can't. If what I saw is true, then it'll come. If not, then there's no point in words."

"Please."

"No. Sorry, lover. No."

"Ferry's on the way!" Retha yelled.

Ryan bent and quickly kissed Krysty on the mouth, tasting the salt chill of the water on her bloodless lips.

He turned to stare out across the river, seeing the bizarre craft that was making its way slowly toward them. It was flat-bottomed, like a raft, seeming to be based on a number of old metal and plastic drums, which were strapped to its sides. There was a rudimentary mast, but no sail. Three long oars on each side dipped and rose in a ragged rhythm. Steering was by a high rudder at the stern.

J.B. looked at Ryan, concern showing in his eyes. "Lot of men."

"I make ten," Ryan replied.

"Twelve," J.B. corrected.

"Could be fourteen," Krysty added. "Think they're down behind the planking."

Ryan beckoned to Dred, who swung down from the metal triangle.

"Yeah?"

"Need to talk fast about this ferry."

"What?"

"There's more than a dozen men on that raft, and I guess most carry blasters and blades."

"Sure. Does a rat shit in the sewers?"

"So what stops them from trying to take us out and grab our weapons, fuck the women, then cut everyone's throat? Tell me that, Dred."

"Kind of law stops them. Never heard of them doing that. They're all one family. Been here years and years. Nobody attacks them and they don't attack nobody."

Ryan looked at J.B. "Could be," he said to his oldest friend.

"Yeah. Things like it in lots of villes. It could be."

Ryan read the note of reservation and caution in the Armorer's voice. "Everyone on double-red. First sign and everyone opens up. Don't wait for any order."

Dred smiled nervously. "Hey, it'll be no-nerve. You outies don't get rules."

"And the payment?" Mildred asked.

Retha giggled. "It'll be me. Always it's me."

Chapter Eleven

The ramshackle craft coasted to a stop about twenty feet from the muddy shore of the river, the oars working slowly to keep it in position against the tug of the water. The person at the helm was so shrouded in rags and furs that it was impossible to tell whether it was a man or a woman. Most of the other crew members had long beards. All wore a similar assortment of filthy clothes.

There was no obvious threat, and Ryan began to relax a little.

"You want the ferry?" roared the person at the tiller, revealed as a tall, burly man. He threw back his hood, which looked like the pelt of a dog, and called out again. "You want to cross?"

Dred glanced at Ryan, who nodded his agreement. "Yeah."

"All of you?"

"Yeah."

"I know you. One of the Bronx gangs, near the old baseball ground. Falcons?"

"Hawks. I'm the pres. Name's Dred."

The raft was beginning to turn slowly, caught in a whirling eddy of the river.

"Back water, you brainless cockheads! Hold her steady." His attention returning to Dred. "Who's the others?"

"Outies. Most old."

"Got some pretty blasters there."

Dred grinned and half bowed. "Sure have. You carry us over to Mattan?"

"What we're here for."

"Usual charge?"

"Wait on. Hold her steady, you bastard sons of gaudy bitches!"

The man left the tiller and picked his way forward, exchanging words with some of his crew as he went. Several of them glanced toward the shore, looking along the line of would-be passengers.

Ryan half turned toward J.B., making a small movement of his right thumb, an old signal from their days with the Trader, which meant things were looking suspicious.

"Who are they?" Mildred tapped Dred on the arm, making him jump.

"Told you. Family. Name's York. That's Boss at the tiller. Rest are his sons and nephews and all. Boss York's got more kin than anyone in the whole of Newyork."

"And you reckon they can be trusted, do you, Dred?"

"Yeah, yeah. Sure."

Retha was shuffling her feet in the mud, hooking her thumbs into the waistband of the long rubber waders as though she were readying herself to slide them off.

Krysty caught Ryan's eye, biting her lip. He repeated the signal with his thumb, warning her that he shared her unease.

Boss York returned to the steering of the raft, calling out an unintelligible order to his crew. One bank of oars began to pull forward while the other rowed backward, spinning the ungainly boat neatly on its own axis, bringing it in closer to the rubble-strewn shore.

"Same as usual, Hawk!" he shouted, a red-lipped smile splitting the expanse of facial hair.

As they moved to climb aboard, Dred gripped Ryan by the elbow, pushing his face close. His rancid breath brushed against Ryan's face. "Whatever happens, don't cause trouble," he whispered.

Ryan counted fifteen on the raft, including a couple of young children who sat in the bottom between the men's feet.

The important thing was that there weren't many firearms in sight, though everyone was festooned with a variety of blades. Boss York, wearing a battered carbine with a sawed-off barrel at his hip, beckoned them to a double row of seats directly in front of the tiller.

"Keep the balance!" he bellowed. "Everyone bug-snug? Then give way both."

The Harlem River was less than a half mile across, running slow and clear. Peering over the side, Ryan could see innumerable fish moving below them, some like sinuous eels, about fifteen feet in length.

When they were a hundred yards or so out in the middle, Boss York pointed to Retha. "Time we started with the toll for the passage. Strip down, slut."

Ryan felt a faint prickling at his nape, and the pulse at his temple began to throb. Even though he knew it was ready, he looked casually down at the G-12, in his lap, checking that it was set on full-auto.

It was.

Retha kicked off the long boots and unbuttoned a pair of ragged jeans. She was wearing no underclothes.

"And your tits," Boss York ordered. "Harve, come up here and take the tiller."

Retha peeled off her sweater and the ancient T-shirt underneath. The cold wind made the nipples on her small breasts harden. Ryan looked the other way, out across the water toward the shore of Mattan.

One of the great lessons the Trader had taught him was that you didn't interfere in other people's business unless you had to. Right now there were two options. One was to ignore what was going to happen to Retha and make the ferry crossing safely. It was obvious the girl was used to this.

The second option was to take on more than a dozen men on a raft in the middle of a wide river. Ryan was fairly confident in his own ability as a swimmer, but he wasn't sure about the others. The second option became even less attractive as he glimpsed a triangular fin cut the surface only a hundred yards away from them.

Out of the corner of his eye, Ryan was aware of the pale, dirt-streaked body of the girl, kneeling submissively in front of the huge man. Her mouth opened and she lifted her hands as if in prayer. Boss York pushed his hips forward at her face.

"Use your teeth and I'll snap your fucking neck," he growled.

The oars rose and fell, moving in a ragged rhythm, carrying them south and west away from the Bronx. Nobody spoke.

The man was breathing harder and faster, finally gasping out his satisfaction. Retha coughed and choked, but he grabbed her by the neck. "Don't spit it out, bitch."

Ryan could feel his own pulse starting to beat faster, anger closing down his mind to what was sensible and what was crassly stupid.

"Who's next? Come on boys. Wet the deck and pass it around! Best go double and triple. Slut'll take what we give her."

Retha knelt in the bottom of the raft, wiping her mouth. Boss York replaced the man at the tiller, who made his way toward the girl, unzipping his pants as he went. One of the others shipped his oar and started back.

"Ryan," Krysty said, her voice shaking with emotion.

"No," he whispered in a voice strung so tight that he hardly recognized it.

The two members of the York family started in on the girl, both encouraging the other, betting jack on who came first.

Ryan suddenly realized that Boss York was deliberately steering a tacking course, running the raft in a series of lateral cuts, making their journey three times the length it needed to be.

"How come you aren't going straight?" he called.

"How come you old outies don't shut your triple-stupe mouths?" The witty riposte brought bellows of laughter from the crew.

"Gotta go with the current, outie!" one of the children shouted.

"But you're right, One-eye. It's taking a long time. Hard work with all you bastards on here. Too fucking many. Think we'll have to up the price some."

Dred's face was like wind-carved bone. "We done a deal, Boss," he protested.

"That was then and this is now."

"What's the—" Dred began.

"Triple price, friends. Redhead slut and black slut. Here and now."

"No," Ryan stated flatly.

Chapter Twelve

Dred sat on one of the oil drums, head between his legs, a trickle of vomit hanging from his open mouth. There was arterial blood splashed all over his pale face, soaked into his jacket, where one of the York boys had died on top of him. On the back of his jacket, invisible to him, was a gray splatter of brain tissue, speckled with splinters of bright white skull.

Every living person on the drifting raft was dappled with crimson. The water that sloshed around under the thwarts was clotted and murky with all the spilled blood.

Retha was being helped into her wet clothes by Mildred, who tried to wipe her clean of the worst of the shambles.

The bodies were gone, all bobbing in the Harlem River, mostly floating facedown, trailing out behind the raft like dejected flotsam. Already the scavengers were there, scenting rich pickings. Two of the dreaded triangular fins were circling the corpses, and a third was slicing through the river from the north.

"Did you have to chill the children?" Mildred asked.

Ryan glanced across at her. He was busy reloading

the G-12, fishing in the deep pockets of his jacket for more of the caseless rounds to fill the 50-shot magazine.

"Don't be a stupe."

"But they were little children," she protested. "You could have...neutralized them."

"Mildred, we did neutralize them. Permanently. They were part of the bloody gang. They lived with them and they died with them. And now they're in the river with them."

The black woman stood up, the discolored water sloshing around her ankles. "In another place, Ryan Cawdor, you might have been a real nice guy. But not in Deathlands."

He nodded. "Maybe. Nice guys, like you call them, in Deathlands don't get to be second, lady. They get to be fucking dead."

J.B. was balancing on the side of the raft, methodically cleaning and reloading his 5.6 mm pistol. He looked at Mildred, his voice quiet, barely audible above the lapping waves. "You're in shock. You just saw a mess of people get shifted from the living mode into the chilled mode. All happened so fast you could have held a single breath while it went down. We all understand that, Mildred."

Her eyes opened wide, staring fixedly at the slight figure of the Armorer. "I'm not in shock, you—" She stopped speaking and nodded slowly. "All right, you pint-size bastard. Maybe I *am* in shock. But it still doesn't make it right to butcher children."

J.B. holstered his blaster. "Tell you something, Mildred. When I rode with Trader— Around about the time we had that mess up in Towse, Ryan. Remember it?"

There was a flash in Ryan's memory of a woman with a feral scent of rutting lust, Sharona, eyes of palest lilac. Sharona Carson was a killer born who'd coupled with Ryan and then walked away, daring him to shoot her in the back. She'd kicked a big chopped Harley two-wheel wag into life and rode off into a smoke-crusted future.

"I remember it."

J.B. continued, eyes blank behind the glittering lenses of his spectacles. "About five…six months after that. Near Death Valley. We got ambushed by some desert muties. Hit a water party. Got Otis in the chest. Never the same after it. Chilled Peachy, the relief driver. Trader went after them and we hit the camp. Ragged-assed bunch of triple-poors."

Ryan checked the action on the stubby gray automatic rifle, then slung it over his shoulders. Everyone on the raft was now listening to the quiet voice of the Armorer. Ryan could recall the scene. The camp had been tattered canvas near the end of a dry draw. Lot of dogs. It hadn't been much of a firefight.

"It wasn't a clean-kill takeout. Muddle with women screaming and men running around with arms hanging off. Trader's rules meant take them all out. So we did." He coughed and wiped a smear of blood from his cheek. "After it was done, we checked out the camp. Giardino had that Enfield support weapon, Ryan. He found this toddler—could've been around three years old—wrapped in a pile of stinking blankets. Giardino picked it up and walked outside with it. Stood there and called to Trader what he'd found.''

It was one of the longest speeches Ryan had ever heard J.B. make. Behind the drifting raft most of the corpses of the York tribe had vanished. A flock of screeching, iron-billed gulls circled low over the oily water where the tangle of bodies had been.

"Go on," Mildred prompted, almost in a whisper.

"Not much more to tell. Brat had an implo-gren buckled to its belly. Pulled the pin. Giardino never knew what hit him. Him and the mutie kid kind of vanished into the sucking detonation of the gren. Found Giardino's legs and some of his left arm. Part of his skull landed in a cooking fire fifty yards away.''

Ryan could search his memory banks and almost -taste the sharp bitterness that an implo-gren left behind it. And the other scent of scorched meat. The pair of legs had bizarrely balanced for several seconds before they'd folded limply in on themselves.

"That's why—"

Mildred finished the sentence for him. "Why we chill the children, as well. Thanks, J.B. I still find it abhorrent, but at least it makes a kind of deadly sense.''

Retha seemed locked into deeper shock. Mildred

had managed to clean her up some, swilling off most of the welter of blood that had covered her when Ryan and the others had opened up the murderous tattoo. But the girl still hadn't spoken, sitting quietly on one of the thwarts, head down, staring at her feet in the long rubber boots.

Dred was perking up, punching his right fist into the palm of his left hand, cursing in a monotone. "Wiped the fuckers. All the fucking Yorks gone. We got the raft. Could take their business with your blasters. Take the ville and send every other gang out the end of the fucking pier."

Krysty moved to stand by Ryan. "What now, lover? Head for Mattan?"

"Why not? We paid some of the fare, and nobody'll ask us for any extra. Hide this boat and then use it when we want to get back into the gateway."

"Who was the woman with the lilac eyes?"

"What?" His eyes opened wider with surprise. "How d'you know?"

"Caught a strong flash of her when J.B. was opening up with his story of Towse."

"Woman I knew."

"Knew, lover?"

"We made it two or three times. I can't remember. Long time ago."

Doc was near them, struggling to complete the delicate process of reloading the old Le Mat pistol on the pitching craft. He caught the tail end of the conversation and grinned. "It was in another country. And, beside, the bitch is dead."

"That one of your quotes, Doc?" Ryan asked, eager to shift the conversation away from Sharona Carson.

"A quote?" Doc replied. "Was it, my dear boy? Perhaps, perhaps."

Once everyone had cleaned themselves up, or in the case of the teenage girl, been cleaned up, there was a general agreement that they should persist on their way. They'd cross the Harlem River and find somewhere to stash the stolen raft, then investigate what remained of old Manhattan.

Doc made another of his cackling, runic jokes. "And the Bronx and Staten Island, too," he sniggered.

Only Mildred laughed.

Chapter Thirteen

It took some time to master the clumsy raft. Ryan took the tiller, trying to keep the rounded prow headed roughly toward the distant shore without striking any of the rusting and protruding piles of tangled iron.

Doc and Krysty hefted the oars on the starboard side, while Dred and Mildred rowed on the port side. J.B. stood in the bow, like an antique figure of a harpooner, guiding Ryan away from the dangers.

Retha sat still and silent.

Before risking to take the raft close to the southern bank of the river, Ryan spent a quarter hour trying to master the eccentric steering. It had occurred to him that they might possibly need to make a swift getaway at some point, and if they floundered in helpless circles they'd be easy meat.

But he was eventually satisfied.

"Heading in over there," he shouted to J.B., pointing to a narrow inlet between two tumbled buildings.

The slow current had carried them downriver toward the piles of what had once been a massive bridge. If they'd had access to a hundred-year-old

map, they'd have known that it had been called the
Triborough Bridge, running from Randalls Island
Park on the east side to join Harlem River Drive.

As it was, the raft grounded gently on Manhattan
Island close to where the old Second Avenue intersected with 128th Street.

"All ashore that's going ashore," Doc called.
"And watch out for hostile natives!"

"Amen to that," Mildred agreed.

THE MUDDY SHORE DIDN'T show any tracks, human
or mutie. Working together, they managed to drag
the cumbersome raft up and out of sight, using some
driftwood to cover it.

Retha finally began to shake herself out of her
shocked misery and helped.

All around them stretched a limitless, devastated
wasteland—wrecked buildings and decayed road-
ways, the occasional heap of rusted metal that had
once been an automobile. There was no sign of life,
in any direction.

"Now what?" Krysty asked.

"You feel anything?"

She shook her head slowly. "Nothing, lover.
But…I'm not sure."

Ryan pressed her. "Come on, what's that mean?
Can you see danger or not?"

She rubbed her hands together. "That's a cold
wind. Bites at the skin. No. I don't feel anything
close. But there's a sort of strong, all-round feeling

of...like a blanket crawling with fleas." She sniffed. "I don't know. There aren't the right words for it, lover. Just that this feels like one of the most dangerous places we've ever been."

"Then we'll take care."

Krysty smiled at Ryan, and he felt a burst of overwhelming love for her. "We always do take care, lover."

"COULD DO WITH SOMETHING to eat," J.B. said. "Anything around here?"

Dred was staring up at the sky, head thrown back, the corded muscles of his scrawny neck standing out like spun twine. "What?"

"Food," the Armorer said, with a deceptively gentle calm.

"Where?"

"Pay attention, son. Where's a good place to get some food?"

"Food's hard," he replied.

"Food's always hard, Dred," Ryan said. "This is your ville. Tell us where to go and what to do."

The boy ran his fingers through the matted dreadlocks, looking back across the river to his own turf. It was Retha who answered the question.

"Not far from the big park. Eateries there, by where the dry lake is."

"Central Park and the Reservoir," Mildred explained. "Only a mile or so from here. Maybe two miles. Be there before noon."

It took them well over two hours to cover that mile and a half.

THE CLOUDS HAD GATHERED from over the Jersey swamps, bringing a light drizzle that smeared the gray streets. Visibility dropped, and the temperature slithered toward uncomfortable. Ryan led the way, keeping the group in a tight patrol formation.

J.B. brought up the rear, the brim of his beloved fedora keeping the light rain off his glasses. Doc was next to last, the ferrule of his swordstick rapping a smart beat on the highway. Retha and Mildred walked just in front of him. Krysty was third in line, with Dred a half-dozen paces ahead.

"Any dangers here?" Ryan asked the boy after they'd moved ten blocks south and a couple west.

"Always is danger in Mattan, Ryan. But they won't likely attack a gang like us with such extreme blasters."

As they made their way through the ville, Ryan concluded that clusters of missiles must have been responsible for such devastation. Even one of the big ones from the space programs wouldn't have taken out such a large urban area. The rad counters all showed clean and green, so it hadn't been anything dirty. And the damage told it sure as shit hadn't been caused by any neutron-based weapons.

What the explosions had done was to leave a great space ahead of them. Here and there jagged peaks of masonry stood up, rainwater trickling off in diamond rivulets. But there was nothing else.

Ryan held up his hand and the group stopped. "Dred?"

"Yeah. I been here before. Fucking dead streets. Have to go way around."

"Why not straight across?" Mildred suggested.

"Holes. All sorts of big holes. Can't see some of them. Mutie rats live in there, bigger than dogs. And there's wet places. Deep wet places you go down and you don't come up."

The woman nodded, wiping rain off her face. "Sure thing, Dred. You've convinced me."

"What a foul and noisome place is this." Doc sighed. "The Big Apple finally turned rotten."

Ryan allowed the boy to lead the way around the fringes of the totally ruined area. It involved threading back north, then east, then west, passing the 116th Lexington subway stop. The entrance gaped open, and they could smell the foul stench of rotting meat.

Finger on the trigger of his AK-47, Dred hurried them past the dark hole. No one bothered to ask what it was that dwelled down there.

As they neared the northern edge of Central Park, they began to see more signs of life.

"Newyork's about the biggest ville I've ever been in," Ryan said. "Keep seeing these shadows, dancing around right at the edge of seeing, moving from pile of stone to heap of brick. Never there when you turn and look straight at them.''

''I thought there'd be a lot of bodies still around,'' Krysty observed. ''Millions died here. Millions. Where'd all the bones go?''

Retha heard the question. ''Plenty still under the dirt.''

Krysty nodded, and droplets of water cascaded off her dazzling crimson curls. ''Think the rain's stopping. Yeah, I understand about lots of them being under the wreckage. But there must've been others.''

Retha smiled slyly, putting her fingers to her thin lips and making the unmistakable gestures of eating.

''Oh, Gaia!'' Krysty closed her eyes for a moment. ''Wish I'd never asked.''

THEY COULD ALL SMELL roasting meat and baking bread.

''What do we pay with?'' Ryan asked. ''And don't even *think* about the sort of jack that went down on the boat!''

Dred giggled. ''Not like that. Straight barter. Ammo's real good. I got me some old rounds for a nine mill. Stole them a year ago. Most don't fire, but they trade real good.''

His busy fingers rattled them in his pocket, the metal jackets tinkling.

They walked, tight-grouped, along a trodden path, trampled into the mud. Now, from all directions they could see other people, most moving south toward

the source of the scent of food. A few came back
north, eyes averted from the heavily armed strangers.
Some carried black garbage bags, hugged to their
chests. Several wore small blasters in their belts and
all hefted some kind of blade. Most were shrouded
in tattered pants and patched cloaks. Few seemed to
be more than twenty years old.

"Garden up there." Retha pointed past some
higher ground to their left. "Found a yellow flower
there once."

Just off the track in front of them lay the corpse
of a young woman, throat opened, the pool of blood
already black and scaled. Nobody took any notice of
the body, stepping around or over it.

Once they were past, Krysty inhaled the rich cooking smells. "Getting real hungered, lover."

Up ahead was the nearest thing to a crowd Ryan
had ever seen in all of his life in Deathlands. There
must have been two or three hundred men and
women. But the people seemed to sense the presence
of the outlanders the same way a witch scented evil.
They parted at the approach of Ryan and the others,
like minnows before a cruising pike.

The path had one last bend before it dropped
sharply to a great oval space, which Ryan guessed
must have once been the reservoir Mildred had mentioned.

And there was one of the more amazing sights
he'd ever seen.

Chapter Fourteen

The tall one-eyed man stood and gaped, surrounded by his friends, while the ragged crowd moved sullen and slow about them, like water roiling around a spur of granite.

"Fireblast," he said quietly. "Now that really is something."

All over Deathlands there were villes of every size and description, most ruled by a baron who held it by force of personality or arms.

Most of them had markets of varying sizes. There would be stalls cobbled together, offering all manner of local produce: food and home brew; meat, eggs and milk; clothes; and there was almost always some dealer selling ammo and blades.

But the great arena in the middle of the park was brimming with people. Some had come to sell, but most had come to buy or trade.

"Any local jack?" J.B. asked. "Any baron around Newyork big enough to issue his own scrip?"

Dred laughed. "No fucking way. There's some big dealers around Mattan, but no barons. No."

"Harry," Retha said.

"Who?"

She grinned crookedly at Ryan. "Harry Stanton. Calls himself the King of the... What is it, Dred?"

"Underworld. Yeah. There's him. But he's not a baron. No, jack isn't worth a candlelit fart in a fucking hurricane."

"How come nobody comes thieving?" Krysty asked. "Take over this place?"

Dred shook his head slowly and thoughtfully. "No. There's a sort of a rule. Anyone tried it, then they'd be marked down and hunted by everyone in the whole of the ville."

"Nobody ever try it?" Ryan was trying to guesstimate how many people were down there, but he ran out after he hit three hundred.

"Sure. Triple stupes. Sort of thickshits that'd catch a horse turd in midflight. They got chilled. Nobody for weeks tried that on."

"Let's go look around," Ryan said. "Stick together. Anyone drifts could get lost. And on-line red."

Everywhere they encountered the same sort of dull resentment. One young girl, reeling on jolt, spit at Ryan, but an older man grabbed at her and pulled her away to safety. Nobody else looked directly at them.

Even the dealers checked their hoarse chants and pitches as the small group of strangers stepped by their stalls, waiting until they'd walked on before resuming their efforts to sell.

"Never seen anything like this." J.B. was at

Ryan's elbow, looking at the goods on offer on both sides of them.

There was the rotting detritus of an entire civilization. So vast had been the metropolis of New York that the scattered survivors, a century later, were still scavenging a living from the remains.

Some stalls held pots and pans, plates and glasses. Many were filthy, dented or chipped. Some showed the clearest signs of severe scorching during the skyborn holocaust. One stall had a number of books and comics, which attracted both Ryan and Krysty. But nearly all were badly damaged with pages missing and spines broken. Mildred joined them, picking up a copy of a magazine called *Love and Rocke*— She handled it with a reverential awe.

"This was the best around. The Hernandez brothers." Mildred looked at the young woman behind the stall. "How much is this?"

"What kinda question's that, lady? You a coupla fingers short a hand?"

"I just wondered what you wanted for this old comic."

"Jeez! You outies? Yeah, I see you are. We don't take outie jack here. You tell me what you want to give me for it!"

Mildred looked at the others. "What can I…?"

"Clothes or some sort of weapons'd do fine, lady."

"No. Thanks, but no thanks." She put the tattered,

dry-leaved magazine back down, and they moved on through the market.

They pushed along crowded aisles. Dred had told them the food was served on the south side of the old reservoir. They could see the smoke of cooking fires and ovens ahead of them.

There were so many people there that they could only glimpse odd items on some of the trestles and boxes. People in Deathlands weren't that concerned with personal hygiene. You washed when you could, but if it was only every couple of weeks, then that was the way it was. But even Ryan was aware of the appalling stench that washed around them. Not just sweat, but sweat layered upon old sweat. And everyone seemed to have an aura of damp glowing around them, from wet clothes that never dried properly.

One stall had a pile of tiles that Doc claimed must have dated from the middle of the nineteenth century, entwining floral patterns in faded crimsons and yellows.

There was one young boy selling only lengths of string, rope and wire, of all sorts of dimensions and strengths.

A long table, with three armed men behind it, was covered with handfuls of ammo of all calibers. J.B. paused and browsed awhile, coming up with a dozen antique rounds to fit Doc's .36. One of the men seemed delighted to take two of the Armorer's own 5.6 mm rounds in exchange.

One of the busiest sections of the market was the

one selling clothes and footwear. A foxy-faced teenager with dreadful smallpox scars disfiguring his cheeks grabbed at Krysty's arm, nearly earning himself a slashed groin from Ryan's panga.

"Love the boots, Red."

Krysty was wearing the same boots she'd had on when she and Ryan had first met—dark blue leather, now badly scuffed and stained, with chiseled silver points on both toes. There were also silver leather falcons with their wings spread across the fronts of the boots. The heels were worn down, and she'd had them repaired once. The soles were also becoming perilously thin.

"So do I," she replied.

"Give you any five pairs from the stall in trade. Good deal, Red."

"No."

"Come on. Eight pairs."

Krysty smiled at him and started to move on.

He clung to her arm. "Ten. Ten pairs of any kind!"

She tried to shrug him off, but he persisted. Still smiling, the tall woman reached down and closed her fingers over his hand, squeezing hard enough to make him yelp in shock and pain. "No. I mean it." Her face was like Sierra ice. Krysty let go of him and walked on, leaving him to nurse bruised fingers.

"Could do with a decent coat," Mildred said, sidling close to Ryan. "Freezing wind."

"See anything you want? We can barter some bullets for it."

She sighed, glancing at a stall they were passing. Even from where they stood they could see the myriad fleas and mites skipping all over the rags.

"Maybe I'll stick with being cold for a while."

"Let me do the talking," Dred said as they reached the first line of food and drink stalls. Smoke billowed around them, stinging their eyes and snatching at the backs of their throats.

But it was a smell they'd all encountered in many frontier villes.

"Sure," Ryan agreed. "Get something we can eat now and something to take with us."

A hand suddenly snatched at his sleeve, and he spun around to find himself looking down into the ravaged face of a middle-aged woman. Her hair was graying and tied back in a long ponytail. At one time she must have been very attractive, but someone had once taken a thin, sharp knife to her and marred her beauty. A network of long, narrow scars seamed her from forehead to chin, tugging down her eyes and making her look vaguely Oriental. Her nose had been deliberately split up both nostrils and had healed crookedly. The corners of her mouth had been extended with a knife, making it seem as if she were always smiling.

There was a small metal locket around her neck on a length of plaited steel wire. She let go of his arm, and now both hands were reaching for the locket. Ryan noticed that both of her thumbs had been hacked off, showing only cauterized stumps.

Dred had also turned, and he pushed the woman a few steps away from Ryan. "Fuck off, beggar! Go slut some other place!"

"Want to ask him a question." The voice was plaintive, hoarse, used to rejection.

"Let her ask," Ryan said.

"She's a beggar," the teenager spit.

"One-eyed man. What's his name?"

Ryan opened his mouth to ask why she wanted to know, but Dred was quicker. He slapped at the woman, catching her a glancing blow across the cheek, making her stagger away. "His name's Chiller, so now you know. And that's what'll happen to you if you don't wheel that cut-up face of yours out of the fucking way."

The crowd whirled around them, put on edge by the shouted anger in the youth's voice. When they stilled again, the woman was gone.

Dred, cocky, strutted on.

Ryan was close to Krysty. "Didn't have to do that," he said.

"Young and wants to show off. Jak was a bit like that, some of the time."

"Some of the time," he agreed.

AMMO WAS AT SUCH a premium in the ville of New-york that they were able to eat and drink well, and

take some dried meat and bread with them—all for
only five perfect 9 mm full-metal jacket rounds.

They ate a rich stew from homemade bowls. The
meat was almost certainly dog, though the seller
claimed there was also some rabbit and even some
tinned beef in there someplace. Chunks of some un-
identified root vegetable floated stringily in the dark
brown gravy, as well as a handful of pallid beans. It
was spiced with too little salt and too much pepper,
as well as the ragged remains of some red chilis.
With it there were some fresh sourdough biscuits,
still warm from a portable clay oven that stood at the
side of the caldron of stew.

The man offered them watery milk or some home
brew. All of them chose the latter.

Mildred stifled a belch and popped the last of her
bread, soaked in the last of the gravy, into her mouth.
She swigged at the container of colorless hooch,
coughing, eyes protruding. "Judas and his silver!
That's strong stuff. Must be two hundred proof."

"I have dined at some of the finest restaurants Eu-
rope or the United States can offer, and I doubt I
have ever dined better than that." Doc wiped at his
lips and smiled. "Hits the spot and layers the stomach most perfectly. I declare that this establishment
is worthy of three stars from Mongsoor Michelin."

"Not bad," J.B. agreed.

The stall holder had slipped the bullets into a
leather pouch at his waist. "Anyone want some good

jolt? All the way from the Amazon. Best you can find. Dreamland for hours."

"Yeah, please," Retha said.

Dred looked eagerly at Ryan, who shook his head at him. "No."

"Why not?"

"Why put a thief into your skull that'll steal your brains?"

"Some sluts at the gaudy tent up that far hill, by that stump of the obelisk. I'll give you scrip to go." The man was eager for more trade.

Mildred spit in the dirt. "Nothing changes, does it?"

Retha looked puzzled. "You can make good jack there. Few hours fucking means a few hours eating."

Mildred patted her gently on the shoulder. "Sure. Sorry, child. Shouldn't have spoken the way I did."

Their stomachs pleasantly filled, the five old friends and their two young companions moved southward across Manhattan.

Chapter Fifteen

Once they were past the straggly line of gaudy tents, with their ragged crimson banners and ragged whores parading in their tawdry finery, the crowds thinned fast.

There was an occasional stall or small tent, holding a tattoo artist or a mutie seer or teller. A lean, hungry-looking man offered a strange selection of rings, bracelets and necklaces. Krysty picked one up to look at it and dropped it with an expression of disgust. "They're all human bones."

"Yeah." The man grinned wolfishly, showing a mouth filled with jumbled yellow teeth. "And I knowed 'em all."

"THIS WOULD HAVE BEEN Fifth Avenue, would it not, my dear Mildred?"

"Guess so, Doc."

"Look upon my works, ye mighty… This part has been devilishly hard hit. I can recall…but what is the point of all that? What *is* the point of all that? Yesterday is gone. One day we will all die. In life, my friends, there is but that one great certainty. Dust, brothers and sisters. Dust."

His shoulders started to shake, and tears ran through the grizzled furrows of his cheeks. Mildred went toward him, but Retha was quicker.

"Hey, don't cry, old Doc. You said, least I think that's what you was saying, about us all dying, and yeah, we will. But you do the best while you can. That's all."

"Out of the mouths of babes, Doc," Mildred said.

"What's that weird place?" J.B. asked.

"Where?" Mildred and the others looked a couple of blocks north, following the Armorer's pointing finger.

"Like a kind of broken seashell."

The haze from the cooking fires was drifting eastward across the ruined buildings, making it hard to see more than a hundred yards in that direction. But they could all see what he meant.

"Like a sort of small redoubt," Ryan said. "But I guess it can't be that, right smack in the center of the ville."

The smoke thickened and the building vanished. J.B. asked Dred and Retha if they knew what it had been, but they both shook their heads.

"Let's go see," Krysty suggested.

Ryan wasn't happy at that. "Day's wearing on, lover. If we want to get south and find some place for the night, we need to move on."

The wind gusted and the smoke cleared, showing the peculiar building more clearly. Doc and Mildred spoke in unison. "The Guggenheim," they chorused.

"How's that?" Ryan asked.

Mildred got in first. "Classic art gallery. One of the best in the world. Architect called Frank Lloyd Wright designed it. It's like being inside the shell of a great snail. I saw a wonderful exhibition of Georgia O'Keeffe. Let's go and look at it."

Ryan glanced at the sky. It was darkening from the northwest, with the promise of more rain, though the falling temperatures threatened snow. "Could we hole up there for the night, Dred?"

"Don't know. Yeah. Sure. Why not? Yeah."

THE BUILDINGS around the Guggenheim were totally wrecked. Nothing stood more than a single story. But the stained white concrete museum was remarkably untouched. Ryan guessed that its peculiar shape and structure must have protected it from the blast that had demolished everything around it.

"Anything worthwhile inside?" he asked Mildred.

"Used to be some of the finest pictures the world ever saw. Renoir, Picasso, Mondrian, Klee, Van Gogh...names go on forever, Ryan."

"I fear that little will remain of that collection now," Doc said.

Sadly he was right.

The outer doors and windows were smashed, and the lobby was filled with piles of rotting leaves. The air smelled cold and damp, unused. It was, oddly, very much like the smell they'd encountered in many of the hidden redoubts they'd entered.

Ryan glanced across at Krysty. "Anything?"

"No. Feels like nobody's been in here for a hundred years."

Doc had wandered across the floor and was looking up at the enormous winding ramp that went clear to the roof. "Suppose there's nothing here for anyone. It's so damnably cold in here, and there's nothing to burn for a fire."

Typically J.B. saw the situation from his own, personal direction. "More than that, Doc. Way it's built, there's no way of defending it. You get trapped up that ramp and you're dead meat. No way of establishing cross fire or any defensive positions."

Doc smiled, his perfect white teeth showing up with an almost fluorescent whiteness in the dimness. "I'm sure you're correct, my dear fellow. If I had access to a temporal transporter, I would hasten back and ask Mr. Lloyd Wright to redesign it so that it could be defended in the event of a firefight. I'm sure he'd be most happy to oblige."

The Armorer didn't smile, throwing a finger at the old man.

"Enough," Ryan snapped. "We going to stay here for the night?"

"Not much heat here." Mildred looked around. "Some of those leaves might burn." But she sounded as doubtful as she felt.

Behind what had once been some sort of sales section, J.B. had rummaged out a pile of white plastic strips. "These'll go. Keep away from the fumes, and

they'll do. Them and some of the leaves. Once they
dry out.''

Dred nodded. ''Why don't me and Retha go hunt
the park for branches and stuff? This far south there
aren't many gangs, so's there could be some. What
d'you say, Ryan?''

''Sure. Good as anywhere. We've got enough to
keep a watch. Solid roof. Worth something. But
don't take long.''

''Can we borrow your blasters?'' The question
was asked very casually.

''Nobody ever borrows anyone's blaster,'' J.B. replied curtly. ''Never.''

AN HOUR AFTER DARK they had a good fire going.
Ryan had decided to light it to one side of the bottom
floor, where the smoke would be sucked away out of
some of the broken windows. The plastic sent out a
thick cloud of noxious black fumes, but it served to
ignite the pile of twigs and branches that the teenagers had dragged in, as well as drying out the big
piles of leaves collected around the building.

Before full dark came Doc and Mildred climbed
up the winding, circular ramp, clear to the top of the
building. The woman laughed quietly as they reached
the haunted, shadowed level, with the floor sweeping
gently away from them, around and around and down
toward the lobby.

''What is so risible, my dear doctor?''

''Take me an hour or more to answer that one,

Doc. But if you mean right now... Well, I just had a thought."

"I'm all attention and quivering eagerness, madam. Tell me."

"Just looking around here. Masses of rubbish and dead leaves and rags and all kinds of windblown and human shit. If this was a book or a movie...well, we'd burrow around and find a buried masterpiece by Van Gogh or someone."

Doc nodded, his silvery mane luminous in the evening gloom. "Yes, yes. And we would look at it, and then one of us would say that we wondered what the old picture was. But it would..."

"Sure burn well," Mildred completed, and they both laughed loud and long.

They made so much noise that they didn't hear the light-footed approach of the Armorer. His quiet voice made them both jump. "Private joke?"

Doc shook his head. "No, but it would take a frightfully long time to try to explain it."

J.B. shrugged. The last feeble glow from beyond some broken windows bounced off the metal-rimmed glasses. "Fire's going well down there, and there's some food readied."

"I think my belly and backbone are getting used to being stuck together," Doc said. "I shall go and force down a little something. What do you say to a little something, Mildred?"

"I probably say, 'Hello, little something.' Sorry.

Wasn't that good a joke a hundred years ago, and it hasn't improved with age.''

"You going down?" J.B. asked.

"Not yet. But you go ahead, Doc, and if you find any Renoirs, put them on the fire."

They watched the old man pick his careful way down and out of sight. J.B. moved a few steps to stand by the window, looking down across Fifth Avenue. "Cold night."

"It is."

She joined him, standing so close that their bodies brushed together. They stared as a figure moved past, heading north. It was difficult to make out, but it looked like the stunted little creature they'd passed earlier as they'd made their way to the Guggenheim.

"J.B." She grabbed his arm.

"I seen them."

There were two more shadows skulking against the tumbled wall of the park. They were closing in on the solitary figure that marched stolidly up the center of the road.

Mildred started to draw her ZKR 551, but J.B. laid a hand on her wrist. "No. Not our fight, Mildred. And it'll attract attention to us."

They watched the tiny drama of life and death. The victim only became aware of the threat at the very last moment, whirling around and drawing some sort of blade. But it was way too late, and the two attackers closed in.

A soundless scuffle, then the street was suddenly

empty again. Except for the small, huddled corpse at its center.

"I could've chilled them both," Mildred said softly.

"Not the way."

She sighed. "Guess not." She looked over her shoulder across the landing at what had been some kind of administrative suite. There were a couple of seat cushions in the dark room. "John Barrymore?"

"Yeah."

"If we went in there, we could lie down for a few minutes."

"We could." He was as laconic as ever, no surprise or question hiding in his voice.

"And you could make love to me."

"I could."

"Would you like that?"

She saw the specter of his narrow smile in the darkness and felt his lips brush against hers.

"I would."

Chapter Sixteen

"Think they're okay up there?" Ryan picked his teeth, locating bits of grainy bread and sucking at his long fingers.

Krysty laughed very softly. She was stretched out on the floor, the firelight playing off the planes of her face and the tumbled curtain of her dazzling hair. "I think they're very probably okay up there, lover."

"What's that supposed to mean?" The penny dropped. "You don't think they're...? Not Mildred and... Not J. B. Dix!"

At that moment they all heard the sound of feet coming down the long ramp, out of the cold darkness above. Two pairs of feet.

Dred had been dozing and he started awake, hand going for his Saturday night special.

"Relax," Krysty said.

J.B. and Mildred walked into the pool of warm light cast by the dancing flames of the fire. They were standing close together, then glanced at each other and took an uncomfortable step away.

"Better in here," the Armorer said. "Saw someone go down to a street attack. It's a jungle out there. The beasts come out at night."

"Yeah," Mildred added, her words tumbling over the end of J.B.'s sentence. "Safer in here."

"I'm sure it is," Ryan said. "As far as you and—" He stopped as Krysty lifted her head and gave him a withering glare. "I mean... Sure. Here, Mildred, have some food."

OUTSIDE, THE VAST sprawling ville was surprisingly quiet. The dominant sound was the howling of dogs. Sometimes the noise was more like a hunting pack of wolves. Once there was a terrible scream, long and bubbling, rising and falling and finally falling away into stillness again.

Once there was a bark of a single blaster, which J.B. guessed as being a Smith & Wesson .38. And once came the brief stutter of automatic gunfire that both Ryan and the Armorer agreed unhesitatingly was an Uzi.

"Time for some sleep," Krysty suggested. "Retha's crashed already."

The girl was curled up in a fetal position, sucking at her thumb.

Ryan nodded. "Right. Have to take a watch. Only one entrance, isn't there?"

"No." J.B. had been sitting on the far side of the fire, close to Mildred. "Sort of rear exit through that door. Leads into a kind of alley, mostly blocked. But someone could get in if they tried hard."

"Right." Ryan stood and looked around. "Still cover that from the bottom of the ramp. Best bet is we all sleep one level up. Guard stays here." He pointed at the main lobby area, where the floor began to circle upward.

"Better do it in pairs," J.B. suggested, "in case anyone drops off."

"You're on watch and you don't fall asleep," Ryan snapped.

"You wouldn't and I wouldn't, but…" He looked around at the others.

Mildred's head was nodding, and Doc's eyes were already closed and he was snoring gently. Krysty was still wide awake, and Dred was watching from the corner where Retha was fast asleep.

"All right. But you and me do it on our own. Spread the load."

"Sure."

PART OF THE PASSAGE that spiraled around the shell-like interior of the Guggenheim still retained patches of carpet, making it possible to move around in almost total silence.

Doc had been roused enough to take the first watch, and Ryan took over from him. Dred and Retha were to go next, followed by Krysty and Mildred, with J.B. taking the last round until dawn.

Now everyone was sleeping as Ryan picked his way cautiously around the abandoned museum. The G-12 was down by his sleeping place, and he had the SIG-Sauer P-226 in its holster. There were times when you felt the spice of danger and times you didn't. The Guggenheim had such an atmosphere of long-abandonment that there didn't seem any serious risk.

He walked clear to the top. There were high clouds racing across the face of a bright moon. Its light came through the broken windows and splashed over the walls, showing the faint, rectangular marks where paintings had been hung a hundred years ago.

Ryan leaned his elbows on the sill, staring out across the sleeping ruins. This was *the* place. Damn near the biggest city in the world. The true capital of the United States of America. He'd seen it several times on old, flickering vids and in pix in torn books and faded magazines. Now he was in its center, looking over the finest street in the whole ville.

On Fifth Avenue it was beginning to snow.

The first frail flakes whirled down on the teeth of the blue norther, settling immediately on the cold, cold ground. It covered the sharp edges of the tumbled masonry and metal, veiling the old horror of the biggest slaughterhouse in history. There had never been such a killing as when the missiles dropped over Manhattan Island.

And there never would be again.

Dred was already awake when Ryan returned to the lobby. "Time for us?"

"Yeah. It's snowing outside."

The boy uncoiled with a coltish grace, rubbing at his eyes. "Had some bad winters in this ville. Cold-er'n a well-digger's cock."

Ryan tossed a few more broken branches onto the smoldering embers of the fire, generating flaring orange flames. "Wake Krysty and Mildred on time."

"Sure, Chief. Can I borrow that… No. Nobody borrows blasters."

Ryan sat down and tucked his coat around his feet, glancing around. "Where's Doc gone?"

The old man's voice answered from the valley of black shadows at the very rear of the building. "Been out to point my peter at the porcelain. When you reach my age, my dear friends, you will find that you want to do less more often, if you take my meaning. I'm all right now. Until next time."

The pressure of the double-jump, combined with the firefight and the tension of being in this alien ville all worked to make Ryan feel utterly bone-tired. By the warm fire, with a double watch out, he felt reasonably secure, so he fell asleep quickly.

As THEY BURNED THROUGH, the branches crumbled away into frail columns of ash. They tumbled one upon the other with a soft, whispering sound, but it was loud enough to wake Ryan.

He started to sit up and felt the jar of something poked into his chest. There was just enough light left from the dying fire to make out the silhouette of Dred, holding the G-12 caseless, the muzzle touching Ryan's breastbone. Retha was on the other side of him, the homebuilt blaster in her small fist.

"So fucking long, outie," the teenage boy said.

Chapter Seventeen

The trigger pressure on the Heckler & Koch G-12 caseless had been adjusted by J.B. at Ryan's own request, pulling it down a few notches. It was only in misinformed vids that the hero had a weapon with a hair trigger. Have that and you'd be shooting anything and everything, including your friends and your own feet.

What you wanted was a light trigger tuned to your own reflexes.

Ryan knew he was only a couple of ounces of finger-tightness away from death. The blaster was on full-auto and would pour out twenty rounds in a fraction of a minute, pulping his heart and lungs.

"Lie down, outie," Dred whispered.

Under his coat Ryan's fingers were also reaching for the hilt of the long panga, the only weapon he could get at without making a fatal move. "Sure."

The boy giggled, a bizarre, feathering sound that rasped at the nerves. "Got your fucking gun you wouldn't borrow me, outie."

"Yeah."

The muzzle had moved away from his chest, but still pointed at him.

"You, then that smart-bastard Dix. Old man with triple-stupe talk. Black bitch and redhead last. Save them for fucking last—" again the obscene snigger "—or for last fucking."

"Yeah," Ryan repeated, racking his brain for something to say.

"Now, outie," Dred whispered.

"No," Doc said, his voice as calm and reasoned as if he were refusing a nephew a third trip to the cookie jar.

It was as though Dred were an android who'd malfunctioned. A metal spring had broken and uncoiled from within his throat, bursting from the front, standing out by at least eight inches.

A tiny fragment of time passed, and Ryan realized what he'd seen.

The tip of Doc's swordstick, thrust with a savage force into the back of the teenager's neck, had penetrated and emerged from the front.

As quickly as he'd struck, so Doc withdrew his blade, lunging again, this time into the boy's back, two fingers to the left of the spine and four fingers below the scapula.

Dred started dying.

He gave a strangled, bubbling gasp, blood beginning to froth from his gaping mouth. He was already falling, the Heckler & Koch sliding from nerveless fingers. Retha half turned, looking around at Doc's monosyllable, seeing Dred run through by the slim blade. She began to scream, uncertain whether to shoot at the old man or at Ryan, still flat on his back in front of her.

"You…" she said.

With his left hand Ryan threw off the encumbrance of the long coat. He'd drawn the panga with its eighteen-inch blade. He gripped it in his right hand, swinging it sideways in a short, hacking arc, aiming at Retha's skinny legs.

The heavy rubber boots did little to deflect the ferocious power of the blow. Ryan used his wrist to give extra bite, pulling the panga back and across after the clunk of the impact. Behind Retha's scream was the frail sound of snapping bone.

Her pistol fired once, a thin crack in the echoing stone vault of the museum. The bullet whined off the roof, then disappeared into the upper blackness.

Ryan rolled sideways, avoiding the toppling body of Dred. Retha hopped backward, dropping her gun, starting to fall. She clutched at Doc, who was about to deliver the coup de grace to the moaning figure of the boy.

In the dim half-light the others were waking. J.B. was instantly on his feet, blaster probing the darkness, trying to work out what was going down.

Krysty was also up, hair seeming to crackle with a fiery electricity, her own Heckler & Koch P7A-13 pistol in her fist.

Close to J.B., Mildred was just coming to life, sitting up, fumbling for her own gun, her softer reflexes leaving her several vital seconds behind the others.

Ryan was now standing, falling naturally into a classic knife fighter's half crouch, ready to take out Dred if the boy showed any sign of recovery.

But the teenager was flailing around on the cold floor, both hands at his throat, as if he might be able to check the blood that was pouring through the narrow lips of the wound. His movements were slowing, and Ryan knew the boy was already inexorably set on the last train to the coast.

The girl was a different matter.

Screeching like a gut-shot horse, she was clinging to Doc, arms locked around his neck, making it impossible for him to shorten his grip on the lion's-head hilt of the swordstick to stab her. Blood was filling the long boots, sloshing out through the cut across the shin.

"Push her away, Doc!" Ryan shouted, shifting closer, waiting for a clear chance to kill the girl with his panga.

"Can't. I fear…"

It was like watching a hideous dance of death. The old man, frock coat whirling, spun around, almost whisking Retha clear off the floor. She was crying out in a reedy, babbling voice, begging for her life, tightening her grip around Doc's neck, almost strangling him.

By now Krysty, J.B. and Mildred all had their blasters drawn, but it was impossibly risky, in the poor light of the dying fire, to try to shoot the girl.

Dred gave them the chance.

He rolled over and over, his struggle weakening, until his feet and legs rested in the glowing embers. Smoke began to rise, and there was the smell of scorching cloth and flesh.

Retha noticed it and broke away from Doc, her pale face frantic. "He's burning, you bastards!"

It was Ryan's opportunity, and he took it.

As she moved toward Dred, he swung the panga in a singing blow. The edge was razor-honed, and he put enough power behind it to sever the skull from the neck.

It wasn't the perfect, clean kill he'd hoped for. At the last moment the girl's street awareness made her glance toward him. Her arm came up to try to fend off the weapon.

She might as well have tried to fend off a great white shark with a breadstick.

The severed hand went spinning up into the air, the fingers opening wide as the tendons relaxed. Blood fountained, hissing into the ruby embers of the fire, splashing all over the corpse of Dred.

Retha tottered, her broken leg failing to support her. As she dropped to her knees, J.B. put a single bullet through the side of her head. It smashed her down and she twitched a few times, the boots sliding and squeaking on the wet concrete.

Then there was the final and unmistakable stillness that marked the ending of life.

"Thanks, Doc," Ryan said, stooping and wiping the dulled steel on the girl's coat.

"You're more than welcome, my dear chap. Nasty business." He was also cleaning his slim swordstick, wiping it on one of the few dry patches on the lad's clothes.

"How come you were up and awake, Doc?" J.B. asked.

"My little problem, for once, came in frightfully useful."

"What problem's that?" Mildred asked. Then she smiled. "Ah, you mean the little problem that makes bad-tempered old farts like you have to get up in the middle of the night?"

"Indeed, yes."

Krysty grinned. "More power to your pisser, Doc."

"I was returning to my sleeping place when I saw our two deceased companions whispering together. I closed in as quietly as my creaking knee joints would permit. The lad plucked up your rifle, Ryan, and that was when I decided I would need to draw my steel."

Ryan pulled the charring corpse of Dred out of the fire, waving his hands to dispel the smoke. "Again, Doc, thanks. Owe you one."

Doc sniffed. "Nonsense. Stuff and bloody nonsense! By the three Kennedys, Ryan, if you owe me one, then I must owe you at least fifty."

J.B. shared the remainder of the night guard's duties with Krysty and Mildred. The bodies were heaved out of the way, through the shattered doors and onto what had once been the bustling sidewalk of Fifth Avenue.

In the morning it was no great surprise to find that both were gone.

As the dawn's early light came creeping up from behind the Guggenheim, Ryan and Krysty stood together and looked out at the ruins that stretched as far as the eye could see.

And so much farther than that.

The woman put her arm around the man's waist, drawing him closer to her, savoring his strength and power. "Lover?"

"Yeah?"

"Now what? Do we go on back to the redoubt and jump out of Newyork?"

He rubbed the stubble that was sprouting from his chin, darkening the angle beneath the jaw. "We can spare enough ammo to trade food for a few days yet. Or we can just take it when we want."

"So we're staying." It was a statement, not a question, and he didn't bother to speak. Krysty went on. "What about this big gang of scalies the kid talked about? Down at the docks."

"We can keep clear and walk careful."

"You sorry about them? Retha and the boy?"

"Dred? Not specially. Tried their luck and lost. I know you thought he might have been a sort of... replacement. Tell you this, lover. He was no Jak Lauren." He paused. "Never would have been."

Chapter Eighteen

Now it was back to the five of them, and they were able to revert to the familiar loose skirmishing pattern that they all knew so well. Ryan was out on point, the G-12 held ready in his hands, eye raking the heaps of stone and metal that lined every street in Manhattan. Krysty was immediately behind him, then Doc, still stepping out with a dandyish elegance, rapping his cane on the frosted cobbles. J.B. and Mildred shared the rearguard position, walking close together and occasionally talking quietly and earnestly.

"You sure they actually screwed last night, lover?" Ryan asked, speaking quietly over his shoulder to Krysty.

"I think they'd prefer to call it making love," she said chillingly. "I know that's what I prefer to call it, *lover*. But, yeah, I'm damn sure they did. That bother you, Ryan?"

He didn't reply, shaking his head, walking briskly on along the wide street.

Krysty closed up on him, whispering, "You must see how they are, lover. It's like looking at the desert just after the spring rains."

THE SNOW HAD STOPPED at some point during the night. The temperature was very close to freezing, and the ville seemed to be completely deserted. Not even a rat moved against the cold, glittering wasteland.

"Wish we'd kept some of our warm clothes," Ryan said. "Lost so much along the way."

"Reason to keep moving," J.B. replied.

"Is there anything in particular we're searching for in these forsaken ruins?" Doc asked. "I'm more than happy to stride along with any man—or woman—but to wander aimlessly has never been one of my favored hobbies."

They'd reached the southern end of Central Park. The farther they walked, the worse the devastation seemed to get.

Mildred stopped, blowing at her hands, rubbing them together, her breath gathering in front of her like plumes of steam. "Sure is chilly."

"Borrow my coat?" J.B. offered. "I don't feel the cold too much."

Ryan avoided the temptation to glance sideways at Krysty.

"Thanks, John. I'll struggle on a while longer."

The wind was still biting in from the north, bringing occasional flakes of snow or a brief rattle of venomous hail.

Mildred shaded her eyes with her hand, bracing herself against the breeze. "Stand hereabouts back in the days before...well, before. You could see all the great skyscrapers. Empire State and down to the Twin Towers of the World Trade Center.''

"I scaled them both," Doc said. "The Empire State Building was somehow more amusing. On that floor below the top of the Trade Center I confess to a slight loosening of the bowels at the drop through the glass. Now they're large piles of urban rubble."

"In the end I guess this'll finish up like it used to be before we bought it from the Indians." Mildred shook her head. "I'm not truly sure I like this too much, Ryan."

At a cross-street a block ahead of them they watched a five-legged dog—a brindled pit bull— dash over, carrying something dead in its jaws. At that distance it was impossible to make out what it might be.

It was about then that they heard the distant rumble of a heavy-duty wag. They waited, but the noise faded away into stillness.

"One of Trader's war wags?" Ryan asked, looking at J.B.

Over the past year or so they'd occasionally discussed the possibility that the original War Wag One might still be lumbering around Deathlands. Trader had gone some time earlier, but the survivors might still be moving on.

"Doubt that. Never get it into the middle of a honey-ambush like this ville."

"It's not good as I'd hoped," Ryan said. "Damage is triple-total. I somehow hoped...I don't know what I hoped.''

But he knew in his heart.

It was all a part of the grail he'd been seeking for years. Perhaps for most of his life. What fascinated Ryan Cawdor wasn't the present. That was for surviving in, a place for dodging the skull-faced figure with the whispering scythe.

The past was interesting because it linked directly to the future. The more you knew about the one, the better you could anticipate the other. Since he'd met Krysty Wroth and their destinies had become inextricably linked, Ryan had been looking for a special kind of tomorrow. Amazingly Jak Lauren was the only person who might have found that tomorrow.

When he eventually found it for himself, Ryan felt he'd know. Perhaps in some sun-bleached Arizona arroyo. A house surrounded with dogwoods, dripping with Spanish moss, deep in the bayous. Or something, preserved like a fly in amber, in the untouched kernel of a great ville. A place like Newyork.

Now Ryan appreciated the total desolation and realized his dream wasn't going to be found in the city.

"We might as well turn around," he finally said. "Trouble is, the weather's getting worse. Wouldn't fancy trying to get the raft across the river against it."

J.B. nodded. "Can't argue with that. Like Trader used to say, 'Living's mistakes you don't make.' Could head west and find somewhere to shelter."

"Night before last the boy was saying that some of the old subway stations had been excavated and people used the tunnels." Krysty hesitated. "I just have this feeling about the kind of people who'd live down in there."

Mildred had a vague feeling they might not be too far away from one of the stations for the E train. But she wasn't at all certain.

Doc's memory was a great deal more vague. "I could do adequately if I had to show you around the streets of Omaha, Nebraska, two hundred years ago. But I have scant experience of the subways and bus routes of this city, a mere century back. My apologies, friends."

J.B. carried a selection of miniature maps, along with a micro-magnifier, but none of them showed the rectangular web of streets that covered Manhattan Island.

Though the sky had been dull, like cut slate, there was a momentary clearance of cloud. A watery sun peeked through, veiled by the light snow, producing a blurred rainbow that arched high over the island, to the north of them. It was a beautiful sight and they all gazed at it until the curtain in the clouds slid shut again and the sun vanished, dragging the rainbow behind it.

"Is that a good omen?" Mildred asked.

J.B. answered her. "If we all live through the next twenty-four hours, then it's a good omen. If not... then it wasn't."

IN LESS THAN FIFTEEN minutes the temperature had dropped like a pebble down a well. The wind freshened and strengthened, turning into a full-size gale. And it began to snow.

First came a few ragged flakes, large and cottony, like the drifting feathers from a plucked goose. But the flakes grew smaller and more frequent. The day darkened, and visibility fell from four or five hundred yards to less than a hundred feet.

Then to less than fifty feet as the blizzard sharpened its icy teeth.

Ryan was aware that death wasn't all that far away if they didn't find themselves some cover. Fast.

Mildred was already shivering like an aspen, even though J.B. had insisted on her borrowing his coat. Her teeth were chattering and her skin was turning gray. "Sorry, us black folks needs the sun," she joked weakly.

"Lover," Krysty said urgently.

"I know. Before it closed in there seemed to be some slightly bigger ruins toward the west. Let's go. And keep close together."

IT WAS THE WORST OF TIMES. The streets were uneven, snow covering the frozen puddles and making every step perilous. If it hadn't been for J.B.'s steadying hand, Mildred would have fallen again and again. Doc was the worst affected, slipping and going down several times, ending up with a wrenched ankle and a limp.

The layer of whiteness blurred everything. Ryan squinted against the wind, now beating in on the right side of his face. His eye was watering, and every time he opened his mouth to draw breath, the tiny flakes drove in between his cold lips. Everywhere he looked there seemed nothing but piles of stone and metal, sometimes fifty or sixty feet high.

Nothing but rubble, with no sign of any sort of entrance or shelter anywhere.

They blindly staggered on, leaning against the wind like a quintet of ragged mimes.

Ryan had a fine sense of spatial awareness, but even he began to lose touch with the realities of distance, time and direction.

In fact they were blundering roughly toward the west. Some roads were totally blocked off by the ruined buildings, making it necessary to detour for three or four blocks to north or south. Because of the relentless wind, Ryan was tending to take the path of least resistance and move toward the south.

"Can't," Mildred protested, her voice so faint that nobody except the Armorer heard her.

"Ryan!"

"Yo? What is it?" Both men had to shout at the tops of their voices to be heard over the crazed screaming of the wind.

"Got to stop."

"Dead if we do. There's nothing."

J.B. was almost carrying Mildred. "Find lee of ruins. Get close and hope."

Ryan looked at him, reading the desperation in his old friend's eyes.

"Yeah," he yelled. "Right."

Krysty was tugging at his sleeve, trying to attract his attention. She pointed with gloved fingers ahead of them into a wall of unrelieved whiteout.

"Something!"

"What?"

"Big block. Just for a second."

Ryan relayed the message to J.B. and to Doc. The old man was also close to the end of his tether, staggering with exhaustion, ice crusting around his eyes and nose.

Ryan led them in the direction Krysty had shown him.

And there it was, a massive, looming block, hewn from concrete, towering several stories into the snow-filled sky.

There were several entrances at street level, as well as numerous window holes blasted into its long flanks.

"Thank you, Gaia," Krysty breathed, now bringing up the rear with Doc hanging on to her, slowing her progress.

They were all so near the limit that none of them bothered to think about danger. The only menace to them was the weather, and that was relenting.

Ryan was first, leading them into a maze of narrow passages, blacker than midnight. The wind still howled like a demented banshee, but they were out of the snow. He emerged into a wider space, with a faint light filtering from somewhere above him. J.B. was at his shoulder, one arm supporting the semi-conscious figure of Mildred.

Krysty and Doc hadn't appeared yet.

Ryan and the others waited for several minutes, but there was no sign of them. And even though he retraced his steps into the whirling storm, Ryan could find no trace of them.

They'd vanished as completely as though they'd been sucked off the face of the earth.

Chapter Nineteen

The blow across the back of the neck that felled Krysty also dragged Doc down with her. The thick cushion of red hair protected the woman from the worst of the impact, but it still knocked her to the cold stone floor, head spinning, barely conscious.

She was just aware that she was being dragged away, gripped by the wrists, her heels dragging behind her.

The vicious swing of the club that had been aimed at Doc missed him completely, as he was already falling on top of Krysty.

His senses had been numbed by the ferocious power of the storm, and he hardly even noticed he was suddenly lying on his side. There was scuffling going on all around him, and someone kicked him hard under the ribs. It jerked him back toward a sort of awareness, and he realized they had been attacked. Doc tried to yell out, but all of his breath had been snatched from him.

He had just enough awareness to wriggle around and stuff his precious swordstick down his left leg, inside his breeches.

Then he was being dragged, like Krysty, from

darkness into a deeper blackness. His nostrils could catch the stink of sweat, and he heard muttered, guttural voices all around him.

Krysty, with her greater sensitivity, knew what had taken them. Her skin crawled at the feeling of the clawed hands holding her. Her sharp ears could catch the rustling of scaled flesh.

They'd been captured by a large force of scalies, maybe the gang Dred had mentioned with an almost superstitious awe.

Help me, Earth Mother, she prayed silently.

ONCE THE DEADLY combination of driving snow and a horrific windchill factor had been thwarted, Mildred began to recover. She sat pressed between Ryan and J.B., all of them sharing the two men's coats. The storm seemed to be passing outside the cavernous building, and there were frail shafts of light appearing from high above them.

"Some kind of warehouse or garage," J.B. guessed.

"Garage," Ryan offered.

"No."

It was the first word Mildred had spoken since they'd all sat together. Her body still trembled, but her lips were recovering normal color. She'd folded her hands inside her clothes, squeezing them to try to bring back circulation.

"No?" Ryan said.

"Bus terminal."

"Buses? Big wags that carried a lot of people all at once."

There was the ghost of a smile. "Good definition, John. Wins the doll. Yeah. The Port Authority Bus Terminal and Air Transcenter. That was what it was called. Means we're way over west, between Eighth and Ninth, fronting on Forty-second."

"How far from the river does that put us?" Ryan asked.

"Close."

"How far?"

"It's about three blocks."

"Mile?"

She shook her head. "Not even that far."

Ryan closed his eye, fighting against anger, a rage at his own stupidity. They'd been warned that the territory close to the river was rampant with gangs of scalies, and he'd pulled them on through the snowstorm right smack into the middle of the reptilian muties' turf. "Fireblast!"

Mildred felt the depths of his anger. "Where d'you think they've gone?"

Ryan took three slow, deep breaths, fighting for self-control. "If I had any idea, then we'd be moving after them. We don't know. Storm's passing. You're getting better. Then we go take a look."

KRYSTY WAS NO LIGHTWEIGHT, and it wasn't long before she was unceremoniously dumped, the fall jarring the base of her spine. She rolled around, moaning, clutching at herself, exaggerating how hurt she was so that she could slide the silvered Heckler & Koch P7A-13 from its holster and stuff it into the small of her back, under the jacket.

"Get up or I'll chill ya." The harsh, grating voice lacked any emotion. There was no anger or hatred, yet the flat, unemotional tone made the threat seem that much more savage.

Krysty stood. Doc had also been dropped and was now dusting himself, standing in a curiously stiff-legged way that Krysty guessed immediately was due to his concealed swordstick. There was also enough light for her to see that the old man had also managed to hide his cannon of a Le Mat away from their mutie captors.

As her eyes grew accustomed to the dimness, her heart sank. In her years in Deathlands she'd seen plenty of muties. But she'd never seen what looked peculiarly like an army of them.

There were about fifteen scalies surrounding their two captives. All of them were male, mostly standing between five foot six and five foot nine. You didn't very often see a tall mutie. Or an old one, come to that.

They all wore heavy combat boots studded with iron, dark pants with a variety of thick woolens and furs over the top, and all wore identical black berets, with a crude silver lightning flash sewn to the front. The "uniforms" gave them a bizarre, almost militaristic appearance, quite out of keeping with their faces.

Apart from the webbed fingers, which ended in hooked, hornlike nails, the skins of the creatures were a dark greenish-gray and covered in thick, overlapping scales. They mostly had very prominent jaws and small noses, more like porcine snouts, a double row of snaggle teeth, with serrated, rear-facing points, tiny eyes with vertically split pupils and ridges of protective bone over them, and their ears were set flat against the sides of their narrow skulls.

"Stop looking and walk," the nearest of the scalies said, nudging Krysty with a long-shafted spear. Most of them were armed with cudgels, nail-tipped, or with metal bars. Nearly all had daggers stuck into broad belts of rope or leather. Krysty could only see a couple of blasters—one unbelievably battered M-16 carbine and a Saturday night special almost identical to the ones worn by Dred and Retha.

Krysty began to move forward, alongside Doc, and noticed for the first time that they weren't the only prisoners of the scalies' raiding party. Walking in single file ahead of them, linked by chains attached to neck collars, were a dozen or more men and women. Most carried various pieces of scrap metal and wood.

"Slavers," Doc whispered.

"Right."

The passage in front of them opened up into what

had probably once been a part of a shopping mall, now completely stripped.

They walked quickly through it, across a place where several different corridors intersected. Krysty looked up and saw that there had once been a great dome over it, but that was melted a century ago and now stood open to the sky. The clouds had peeled away, showing a patch of bright blue. But around their feet lay several inches of fresh-fallen snow, trampled by boots. She carefully picked her way over to an untouched patch a little to one side so that her distinctive boot heels would leave a trail for Ryan and the others to follow.

Come on, lover, she thought to herself.

"SUNSHINE," Mildred said, hissing through her teeth at the cold air that still lay over them.

Bright golden spears, darting in high above them, lanced into corners of the huge concourse. Now they could see faded signs pointing the way to different bus routes, and empty boxes that had once been smart little stores. Rubble filled the corners and was piled against the stout walls.

"You feel ready?" J.B. asked, uncoiling himself and cracking his finger joints.

"Yes, John, I'm ready. I won't slow you down, Ryan. No, don't say you didn't think that. I can recognize the look in your eye. Krysty's been taken, and you want to be off after her on burning feet of fire.

I'm ready for that.'' She reached out and squeezed his hand in hers.

Ryan nodded. "Go back to the street where we came in. Then try and pick up their trail. Shouldn't be that difficult to track them.''

"You think she and Doc are…'' Mildred hesitated, allowing the words to fall into the cold, dusty stillness.

"Alive?''

"Alive.''

Ryan looked at her. "I don't have a single moment of choice, Mildred. I *have* to believe Krysty—and Doc—are still living. Now let's go and find them.''

THE SCALIES DROVE THEM faster, briefly out into the open and then into another deep passage that Krysty suspected might have once been linked to some kind of subway system. One of the slaves ahead tripped and fell, bringing down four others. Several of the guards also carried short, club-handled whips with vicious wire flails. They moved in quickly, using them unsparingly until everyone was back on their feet again.

"That woman,'' Krysty whispered to Doc. "Third in the line.''

"I see her. Was she not the one who tried to speak to Ryan back in the market? I do believe it was she.''

Even in that shifting half-light there was no mistaking the dreadful facial scarring, or the missing thumbs. And she still wore the small metal locket around her neck.

"Wonder where we're going?" Krysty mused.

A whip cracked across her shoulders in a shocking explosion of sound. "You be going to have tongue cut off at back if you talk again," the scalie at her elbow said.

Krysty nodded.

THERE WAS A PLACE where several of the linked passages all joined up, under what had once been a large dome. Now it was flooded with bright sunlight, showing the tracks of a large number of people who'd passed there recently. Ryan and J.B. crouched in the snow, studying the marks intently.

"That's Krysty, all right," the Armorer agreed. "Think these here are Doc, but he's walking funny. Like he's limping some."

"And there's a load of folks in ragged shoes. But what about...?" Ryan pointed to the number of cleated boot marks, all more or less identical, crisp and clear in the fresh-fallen snow.

"Some kind of baron's sec men?" J.B. suggested, his voice revealing his doubts. "Not around here. Not this kind of a ruined ville."

"That scalie gang Dred said were near the west river. Got to be them." Ryan straightened. "Must be a dozen or more of them."

"Could be they saw us, and they might leave a couple of snipers behind."

Mildred shivered. "Day'll be done soon. Shouldn't we be thinking about somewhere for the night?"

Ryan turned toward her, and she winced at the totally empty expression on his face. Then it was as if someone had wiped a cloth over it, restoring the polish of humanity again. "Tonight? Soon. But not yet."

THE SCALIES HAD REACHED their destination. Krysty could taste the salt of the river, close by, and there was a bone-damp feel to the air. They had stopped at what looked like a linked complex of warehouses and industrial installations. The jagged skeletons of old cranes were etched against the bright sky.

They were herded, with the neck-chained group, into one of the massive buildings. All around the outer walls were huge metal tanks that had once held hundreds of thousands of gallons of various chemicals. Some still had painted symbols on their sides, faded and barely legible.

But there was no time to look at them, not with so much bustle going on around them. One of the scalies pushed them down onto the floor, waving the metal butt of his whip to reinforce the order.

"Be glad when Ryan and the others arrive with much blowing of bugles and waving of banners," Doc whispered.

"They can forget the bugles and banners. Just as long as they get here."

Chapter Twenty

Ryan learned the hard way that pursuing Krysty and Doc was going to be a whole lot more dangerous than he'd hoped. It was one of the moments when the trail took them out into the open air. They'd been moving as fast as they dared, with Ryan leading, Mildred second and J.B. in his habitual position at rear guard.

An archway was supported by heavy iron girders, opening into a street, and Ryan led the way under it, stopping so abruptly that Mildred bumped into him. He backed away, dragging her with him.

She had the sense to keep her mouth shut, flattening herself against the rough bricks of the wall behind her. There was the sound of boots clattering over stone, and voices singing a flat, atonal chant. The ugly, harsh words made the hairs prickle at the base of her skull.

Ryan leveled the G-12 at his hip, finger tight on the trigger, while J.B. had drawn his blaster, head turning around to make sure they weren't going to get cold-cocked from the rear. Mildred pulled out her own target pistol, swallowing hard and struggling to calm her breathing.

The feet and the song disappeared together, fading into the distance.

"Scalies," Ryan said, "like we thought. This part must be filled with their bastard runs."

J.B. sighed, taking his glasses off to give them an extra polish. "Know what worries me about them, Ryan?"

"What?"

"The noise."

"Sure. They must feel safe here, singing and stamping. Like they're snug as bugs in their own part of the ville. Could be we'll run into a lot more of them."

Mildred began the motion of reholstering her blaster, then changed her mind, keeping it fisted in her hand, ready.

THE LEADER OF THE SCALIES, its beret sporting a crimson flash alongside the lightning symbol, stalked over to stand in front of Krysty and Doc. "Up."

Both of them knew from bitter experience that there was a time to resist and a time to obey. This was one of those latter times. They both stood, Doc moving clumsily because of the long swordstick down his pants.

"Outies?"

"Indeed that is correct," Doc replied. "Strangers passing through your beautiful town."

"Words needed are yes and no. Nothing more. Understand?"

"Yes," they said in unison.

There was no response from the mutie, no flicker of life or emotion in the green soulless eyes. A sinuous tongue darted out across the protuberant lips.

"Can I ask a question?" Krysty said, pitching her voice low, making sure she avoided any sort of eye contact.

"What?"

"Will we work here for you? Or are you going to take us somewhere else?"

"It's all same, outie. We got roads all through the ville. Under-roads."

"Sewers," Doc offered.

The long head moved slowly toward him and the jaws opened an inch or so, revealing its edged teeth. The hand holding the whip began to lift, then stopped. "You didn't ask to speak, old man."

"I'm sorry. Yes. I'm sorry."

A considered nodding came from the scalie. "Not tell again, old man."

"Can we eat, please?" Krysty asked.

"Work ends, then eat. Then go to sleep place. Have neck chains fitted. Now, end questions." The scalie left them alone.

Doc glanced at Krysty, then looked around to make sure none of the scalies were nearby. "If they move us..."

"He'll be here," she replied confidently.

"THINK THEY'LL KEEP moving them?" J.B. asked.

Ryan hesitated, finally stopping and turning.

"Could be. Number we've seen means it's going to be triple-tough to spring them free, and they seem well organized. More like mutie sec men. Got loads of prisoners, so they must have a system for feeding and working them. And places for them to sleep."

Mildred looked around. "Didn't Dred say something about them using a lot of the tunnels? The old sewers and subways of New York? There must be hundreds and hundreds of miles of tunnels. A maze of them."

Ryan glanced at the sky. "Going to be night, and I'm not sure we're close yet. Probably they'll cut right back on their patrols after dark. What we need is to try and find them before then. Make a try in the blackness."

ONE OF THE SCALIES, a rippling belly hanging out of its pants, waddled to a great triangle of iron, like the one that had been used to summon the ferry raft. The creature hammered at it, filling the cavern with ringing echoes.

"Food!" the scalie shouted in a thick, barely comprehensible voice.

Doc clambered to his feet, knees cracking, helping Krysty to stand. But one of the nearby muties lashed at him with its whip, hitting him a stinging blow across the upper arm. "Not you!" it croaked.

"I'm really most frightfully sorry, my dear freak of genetic accident."

"Don't push it, Doc," Krysty warned.

Around them the hustle of meaningless work was ceasing and the nonscalies were filing in groups, chains rattling, toward the central area. There was a large fire there, with a long metal trough suspended over it. From the steam and the smell it appeared to be supper.

The guards had also gone to eat, leaving Doc and Krysty unattended. They were between two of the monstrous tanks and Krysty rapped thoughtfully, first on one and then on the other. The first one rang empty, but the second sounded dull and solid.

"Full," Doc said. "Wonder what it's got in it? This place looks as if it was some kind of chemical store back in those good, good old days."

"Lettering on it. Can't... The light's so bad. Unless I can move to...yeah, I can read it now."

"What's it say? The Colonel's Lip-smacking Special Sauce?"

"Letters. An *H*, then an *M*. No, it's an *N* with a streak of paint on it. And then a zero or an *O*. And at the end, kind of tucked underneath, there's a little number. Three. And a bit more in brackets. This bit's in red. The rest was white. It's a word. *Conk*. What's that?"

"Is that spelled *Conc* or *Conk?*" he asked with a strange note of tension in his voice.

"With a *C*. Why?"

He sniffed. "Because I know what's in this tank.

Must have a special lining to have lasted all these years. By the three Kennedys! Suppose it is!''

''What, Doc?''

''HNO$_3$. Conc. It means concentrated nitric acid, Krysty.''

''Scalies have taken the collars off some of them,'' Krysty observed a moment later.

''Women, so they can serve the food. I suspect it's probably the most appalling gruel, but the smell is beginning to tantalize the taste buds.''

''Looks like they won't be tantalized any longer. Young girl's been told to... Hey, see that?''

''Yeah. Woman from the park took the bowls off her. Wonder why.''

Her gray ponytail swinging slowly behind her, the elderly captive was picking her way over the uneven floor toward them. In each thumbless hand she held a steaming can.

''See the way the floor slopes down from us?'' Doc asked quietly. ''Interesting.''

''Why?''

''Later.''

Now the woman was very close to them, her head darting over her shoulder to keep looking behind, making sure none of the scalies was anywhere near her.

''That punk kid made up that stupid name, didn't he?''

Now she was so near that the zigzag pattern of scars on her face was even more striking. Krysty found herself wondering, with a shudder of revulsion, what the wounds must have looked like when they were fresh-made.

"Didn't he?" she repeated.

"What?"

"You were with him. Both of you. In the park there by the food market. They caught me that same afternoon. Came out of the pipes in the road. Took me and some friends."

"We thought we saw you there," Doc said cautiously reaching up for the cans. "Allow me to relieve you of the burden of those containers of nourishing—" he looked into it "—gunk."

"Knew you. Not many's old as you in this ville. Been here with...here for months. On me quest. What I call it. Your hair. Red like fire. Remembered that was what she said."

"Who?"

"Rona. Dead now. Best out of it. But handed me her quest. Trusted me. Said to find him."

"Find who?" Krysty asked, taking one of the hot tins from Doc, finding it contained what looked like mushy fungus in a watery stew.

"The one-eyed man. Knowed that wasn't his real name. Shit-stupid punk. Chiller. Not his real name. Rona knew him."

Krysty nearly dropped the container as she "felt" an almost overpowering wave of shock, sensing something apocalyptic was in the air.

"Who?"

The woman smiled, distorting the scarred mouth further. "Ryan, lady. Ryan Cawdor."

Chapter Twenty-One

The scalie had appeared out of a well of shadows beneath one of the great tanks and struck the gray-haired woman a single, clubbing blow across the side of her head, felling her to the dirt. He stooped and locked his claws in her ponytail and hauled her, with effortless strength, back toward the cooking fires, where they saw him dump her among some other women. Not a single word had been said during the attack.

Doc and Krysty silently began to slurp up their food. It was bland, unsalted, but it was hot and seemed to contain plenty of mushrooms. Only when they were sure the guard wasn't returning their way, did Krysty speak in a low whisper.

"What did she mean, Doc? Ryan's name. A quest. Rona. You ever hear Ryan speak of someone called Rona? No, me, neither. And she was covering up something else, or someone else."

"I fear we should deposit this mystery at the rear of our minds. There are more pressing worries, my dear lady."

"What?"

"I believe they will be driving us elsewhere after

the meal is done. Then come the chains and the collar. If we are to effect any chance of escape..."

"But Ryan's name? Something that..." She bit her lip. "But you're right, Doc. Time we thought about getting away from here. I know Ryan sometimes quotes Trader. 'Best chance you get if you're caught is right at the beginning. After that it gets harder.' What's your plan?"

Doc looked behind and above them. "See this tank? If we are correct and it's still filled with acid, then it would be interesting to open that red handle and see what transpires."

Krysty peered at the large metal faucet, seeing a crust of yellowish rust around it. "Looks like it hasn't been moved in a hundred years, Doc."

"If you used the power, Krysty?"

She looked at him. "Oh."

RYAN, J.B. AND MILDRED were crouched in a narrow alcove, a side passage that ended in a blank wall of fallen rubble after about twenty feet. It was pitch-dark. Every now and again a patrol of the scalies would stomp by, boots crashing in the confines of the corridors.

"Now what?" the woman whispered.

Ryan sat in silence for a few moments, trying to think what was the best plan. They could go out and get back into the open by way of the ghostly relic of the bus terminal, even if they had to shoot their way past any muties they encountered. But that would draw attention to them and might seriously harm any chances of rescuing Krysty and Doc.

The patrols were so frequent and numerous that it didn't seem worth the risk of going deeper into the complex. From an occasional burst of distant noise and the strong smell of food, they knew they were very close. Probably less than two hundred paces.

"We stay here and wait," he finally decided. "Maybe they wind down their guards after midnight. We could go then."

"If they haven't moved," J.B. said.

"Right."

THE MEAL SEEMED to be nearing its end. Doc and Krysty were in one of the darkest parts of the old warehouse, but there were dozens of scalies between them and the main exit. None of the reptilian muties took much notice of them, and Krysty was able to stand and surreptitiously check out the massive handle without drawing attention to herself. She threw all her considerable strength against it, but it was totally unmovable.

"Well?" Doc said, as she sat down by him, breathing hard.

"No hope. Take plas-ex and plenty of it."

"But if you used the power, Krysty?"

She was using her healing techniques to bring her respiration quickly back to normal. "Might not even be acid in there. You know I can hardly walk after

I use it. Suppose I manage and out comes fifty thousand gallons of rusty water?"

"Then they'll probably kill us, my dear," Doc replied.

Krysty managed a quiet laugh. "Sure, Doc. But if I don't try, then they'll probably kill us."

"If you don't have dreams, then how can your dreams ever come true?"

"THEY'RE GETTING READY to move," Doc said sometime later. "That woman is on her feet, but they haven't chained her to the others yet. If it's to be done, my dear young friend, then it is as well that we do it quickly!"

"But what about the prisoners if…?"

"Might it not allow them the opportunity to seek their own freedom?"

"Right."

She stood up, feeling her knees trembling. Her nails clenched so hard into the palms of her hands that they nearly drew blood. The power of the Earth Mother had been slowly and painstakingly taught to her by Mother Sonja during her adolescence in Harmony ville. The key phrase was to "strive for life," and it had been drilled into her that the power was something special and secret. And should only be used in the direst need.

The dark warehouse began to fade from her as she gripped the cold, damp metal. Krysty closed her eyes and began to send herself into a trance.

Help me, Mother Sonja, she prayed, her pale lips moving soundlessly. May the force of Gaia flow through my body and give me power.

She could sense the hot sun of summer on her shoulders and taste the freshness of new-mown hay in her nostrils.

Cool fresh water was flowing over her naked breasts as she stood beneath the weir that surged past the old mill. Now the power was coming, rising within her like a fierce, uncontrollable fire, racing through her nerves and muscles, making her skin tingle. Krysty's mouth opened, and her tongue danced out across her dry lips. A quivering moan forced its way out between the clenched teeth.

Doc was standing by her, anxiously watching, part of his attention directed back toward the fires, hoping that none of the scalies decided to come and investigate what was going on in the shadows.

Now the sun was in her eyes, dazzling her, a hand on her shoulder that was her mother's, gripping her. The sun, bright and golden. Burning.

The sun.

"Gaia!" she whispered.

Doc watched, mesmerized, his mouth sagging open. He could actually hear her muscles cracking with the strain. There were a few strands of rotted hose beneath the foot-wide faucet, and they trembled and dropped to the floor. The rust crumbled into powder.

He reached out a hand to try to lend his own puny

help, but jumped back as though his fingers had entered a high-voltage energy field. Somewhere behind him he heard a voice shouting, but nothing else mattered.

Krysty was exalted.

Her mind and body combined into an almost supernatural demonstration of mutie power. She had never tested herself to the limit, but this was close. The valve resisted, locked tight by the passing ages.

Metal squealed and the wheel started to move, a millimeter, then another.

"Help us, Lord," Doc prayed.

Behind him the shouting was swelling, and there came the sudden, sharp crack of a blaster. A gleaming dimple of raw metal appeared in the tank, a couple of inches to the left of Krysty's head.

Doc spun around, seeing that the scalies had spotted what was happening and were moving toward them in force. Ten or fifteen, shouting and waving their weapons.

"Krysty," he said, blinking as he realized he wasn't even sure whether he'd spoken out loud or not. In case he hadn't, Doc decided to try again. "Krysty!"

But she wasn't there.

Her body stood at his side, its hands gripping the metal, twisting. Her knuckles were white, and the skin had peeled off the ends of two of the fingers under the unthinkable pressure. Her flaming hair was packed so tightly against her skull that it looked like a cap of crimson plastic. Her emerald eyes were open a narrow slit, looking blankly ahead of her.

"Krysty!"

MILDRED STARTED AWAKE, conscious that the two men with her were both on their feet. "What's happening?"

"Something," Ryan said, from the pitch-dark.

LESS THAN THIRTY SECONDS away from them, in the shadowy warehouse, everything was happening. The scalies were closer, barely fifty yards from the redhead and the decrepit old man. They'd only fired one more shot, then a guttural order had been coughed out. They were sufficiently well armed not to have to use their blasters.

Doc was fumbling to pull out his swordstick, cursing under his breath as it snagged on his belt. Gripping it in his left hand, he drew the Le Mat from its hiding place with his right, thumbing back the hammer and readying himself. "Take some with us, eh?" he croaked.

Krysty was still heaving on the wheel valve, finding it moving more and more easily. She didn't see the scalies or the rough brick wall or the massive metal tank. Her eyes were focused inward, and she saw only the smiling, gentle face of her mother.

A few drops of clear liquid leaked from the faucet, then a trickle. And then a great gushing torrent.

The screams began almost immediately afterward.

Chapter Twenty-Two

Doc tried to move Krysty out of the way, scared that she might slip into the flood of concentrated nitric acid. But she was still deep in thrall to Gaia's power and ignored him, continuing to pull with both hands at the red metal wheel, turning it until it moved no farther, jammed full open.

"Krysty!" The old man finally charged at her, dropping his shoulder, hitting her under the ribs and knocking her loose.

Krysty cried out in protest, but her legs shook and she suddenly sat down, head slumped on her chest, eyes shut.

At least she was safe, for a time, out of the way of the river of acid. Doc turned back to see what was happening.

"Oh, God..." he said to himself, holstering the Le Mat.

Blasters weren't necessary now.

The clear liquid, fuming as soon as it began to spread out, was running down the slight slope, filling the dips and hollows, toward the fire and the line of chained prisoners. It foamed and frothed around the feet, ankles and knees of the group of scalies that had been charging forward.

And they began to melt.

There was a period of several long seconds when the muties froze, puzzled at what appeared to be water surging toward them, lapping at their boots. Then gray-brown tendrils, like smoke, came bubbling up from the surface of the liquid.

There was a tiny splinter of a second when Doc almost started to smile. There was something about the behavior of the scalies that reminded him of giving a hotfoot to a fellow student back at Harvard— the same startled expression and the hopping up and down and yelling out.

Then, one by one, they began to fall. Doc watched them, the flickering light from the fires giving a demonic hue to the deaths, making them even more macabre.

The acid began by eating through their boots into their feet. As it gushed from the tank it grew deeper, corroding their pants, starting to blister the skin on their legs, through the skin to the flesh and through the flesh to the network of muscle, ligament and tendons.

To the clean white bones.

The first shouts were bewilderment, turning to pain, sliding up the scale to a hysterical, agonized scream of panic.

The helpless, doomed scalies fell, kicking, splashing and flailing. But each part of them that came into contact with the concentrated acid began immediately to disintegrate, vanishing, stripped away into a slurry of bloody gruel.

"Oh, my dear God," the old man breathed. The fumes were choking, but it wasn't that bringing tears to his eyes. "Oh, the horror, the horror."

THE NOISE WAS AMPLIFIED by the narrow passages. Where Ryan waited with J.B. and Mildred, the screams were deafening, rising louder and louder.

"Something real bad!" the Armorer shouted. "Shall we go take a look?"

Ryan nodded.

He put his head around the end of the corridor, looking toward the source of the noise. As well as the noise, there was a strange smell drifting toward them.

"What's...?"

"My Lord," Mildred said. "That's acid. Maybe nitric acid."

Within twenty yards the fumes were so thick and choking that they had to stop. "No good," Ryan panted. "Have to get back toward the bus terminal. Fresh air. Come on."

"Doc?"

Krysty's voice was weak, barely audible, but he heard it. He turned from his contemplation of the vast stillness of the warehouse.

"I'm here, child."

"We do it?"

"Oh, yes." He sighed. "Indeed, we did it. How are you?"

"Feel like an hour-old chick. Give me a hand up, will you?"

He reached down to help, finding that he needed all of his strength to get her to her feet. She slumped and would have fallen again if he hadn't put an arm around her waist.

"There."

"Thanks. Gaia! The smell's dreadful. Where's all the scalies?"

At the far, higher end the cooking fires still burned, their dying flames reflected in the sullen surface of the acid lake. The tank was drained, and only an occasional drop now spluttered from the nozzle of the faucet.

"Most under that. Some escaped out the far side. I believe the majority of their prisoners got away, but they were chained, so I have some serious doubts as to their potential for ultimate survival. If there are more in this mutie army, then this will cause them considerable anger. We should get away and try to find Ryan and the others."

"Can't walk too fast. What happened to the woman with the scars?"

"Saw her grapple with a scalie, then the aqua fortis threw its veil of night across the place. Can't see her now."

Krysty's boots dragged on the stone floor as Doc

began to pull her toward the nearest exit, the one they'd been brought through. The light was now almost gone, but he hoped his sense of direction might eventually get them reunited with Ryan, Mildred and J.B.

But two factors combined to dash Doc's hopes. One was that his sense of direction in pitch-black, interwoven tunnels and corridors wasn't as good as he'd reckoned. The second was that Krysty's use of the power, as always, had weakened her to such an extent that she had to rest. They had only been stumbling along for about ten blind minutes when her legs completely gave way. Doc was able to lower her to the floor, kneeling by her.

"Sorry. Can't go on any farther. Must sleep awhile, Doc."

"That's fine my child. Let me sit down here, and you shall lay your sleepy head in my lap. Nowhere to go tonight, is there?"

The old man realized he was talking to himself. The young woman was already fast asleep.

In his rich, rounded voice Doc crooned a lullaby. Buried beneath the ruins of New York, Doc Tanner ran his fingers through the mane of hair, feeling it almost respond to his touch. And his mind wandered away, back through time, to the little daughter he'd hardly known. And who was now dead for well over a hundred years.

"Sleep well, my dearest," he whispered. "Sleep well, my dear, dear Rachel. Sleep well."

Chapter Twenty-Three

The city was silent. The air tasted fresh and clean, with just a faint flavor of woodsmoke. They still had a little food left from two days earlier, but that would soon be running out.

Ryan stretched, bracing his shoulders. After a cold night, he invariably felt stiff, his old wounds and injuries coming back to haunt him, each one with its whispered memories of pain.

He brushed them to the back of his mind. "Time to be up and doing."

J.B.'s eyes opened immediately. From hundreds of similar moments Ryan knew precisely what his old friend would do and in what order.

The glasses first, unfolded from a pocket of his coat, followed by a swift check of all his weapons. Then he sat up. "Nothing?"

"Not a sight and not a sound."

Mildred awakened and stretched, her mouth gaping open in a huge yawn. "God, it's freezing. Any sign of Krysty or Doc? Stupid question. Sorry, not properly awake yet."

"We'll have a bite of dried meat, then go look," Ryan said.

DOC HAD BEEN DREAMING. The visions of the night were rarely about the present or the immediate past. Occasionally he had black nightmares about the period in the Darks when he had been a plaything for Jordan Teague, baron of Mocsin, and his skull-faced sec boss, Cort Strasser.

Mostly his dreams were of the late 1890s, summery dreams of picnics with Emily and the two children, Rachel, toddling in her frills and petticoats, and little Jolyon, lying on a blanket, kicking his chubby legs.

But the idyllic dreams were almost always shadowed by clouds across the sun, or the faint, menacing rumble of distant thunder.

Last night they'd been on a sloping, shingled beach. Jolyon had been close to the edge of the rippling waves, with Rachel tending him. Doc himself had been sitting up, smoking a pipe, Emily's head in his lap, her long hair streaming over his thighs. Suddenly he'd seen triangular fins cutting the water, heading toward the beach. The notches in the dorsals revealed that they were a pod of killer whales, driving toward the two little figures on the beach. He'd wanted to run to pull them to safety, but his wife's head was heavy and he didn't like to disturb her sleep.

He'd awakened, sweating and gasping, just as one of the creatures had lunged from the waves, surrounded by a surging swell of foaming green and silver.

Krysty's eyes were open, looking up at him from his lap. "Bad dream, Doc?"

"Not one of the very best. But how are you this fine morning?"

"Better. My head feels as though it's been rolled between a couple of millstones. That'll pass."

The place where they'd spent the night was now illuminated by the first, gentle light of dawn. Doc had dozed, waking frequently, straining his hearing for any warning of the scalies' return. But all he'd heard had been the rustling of rats, one of the most common nighttime noises in Deathlands.

"I think we should move if you feel strong enough. We don't want our reptilian friends of yesternight to find us here."

"Sure." With a visible effort Krysty stood, helped by Doc's hand. She leaned for a few moments against the chipped brick wall, taking slow breaths. "Every time I use the power I tell myself I'll never, ever do it again. Makes you feel like triple-shit."

"STILL SMELL THE FUMES from the acid or whatever the chemical was," Mildred said.

Ryan was leading the way through the maze. "I got a feeling it has to be linked with Krysty and Doc. Some way."

"No movement of those scalie patrols this morning." J.B. looked behind them. "I reckon that could be Doc and Krysty, as well."

Neither of them actually put into words the fear that their friends could very possibly be dead.

THOUGH STILL WEAKENED, Krysty was recovering fast.

As they made their way along dappled corridors, trying to track the route toward the old bus terminal, she had to stop every few minutes, squatting, hands on knees. But each time she was able to go that much farther between rests.

It was during the fourth or fifth such break that she suddenly looked up, head to one side as though she were listening to the tiny sound of a far-off bell.

Doc recognized the pose. "What can you hear, my young friend?"

There was a point close ahead of them where the passage forked into a T-junction.

"Something both ways. Not scalics. Much too quiet. To the right there's…I can feel pain in that direction. The other way, left, it could be Ryan and the others."

It was.

THE EMOTION AT THEIR reunion was intense, but quickly over. Ryan, still holding Krysty's hand, summed it up. "Tell us about it later. And we'll have later for some close times. But for now we can get the ace on the line out of here. Back north. Cross the river and down into the gateway. And gone."

"I'll drink to that." Doc beamed. "I fear New

York is no longer the toddling town it once was. Best I leave it to my memories.''

"You're right, Doc.'' Mildred gave Krysty another hug. "So great to see you again. We thought we wouldn't.''

"Me, too. Tell you all about it on the way back to the redoubt.''

"No scalies around, lover?'' Ryan asked.

"Not one. Though there was something a little ways back.''

"What?''

Krysty took her hand from Ryan's. "Let me just listen a moment. Quiet, everyone. Real quiet.''

There was an infinite stillness in the concrete tomb. Ryan strained his hearing, but all he could catch was the blood pounding through the narrow thoroughfares of his skull.

Krysty's startlingly green eyes snapped open. "Yes. Something.''

"Danger?'' Ryan asked.

She shook her head. "No. Pain. Someone suffering and ill. Very sick. Close to passing over to the other side. That way.'' She pointed in the direction they'd come from.

"Near?'' Ryan trusted Krysty's mutie skills implicitly. She'd never guess at anything unless she felt sure.

"Underground you can't be certain. But, yeah, she's not far from here.''

"She?" J.B. said. "You sure it's a woman out there?"

"Course. Come on."

THEY FOUND HER just where Krysty had predicted, up the other corridor off the T-junction.

She sat with her back against the stone wall, knees drawn toward her chest. Her face was dust-white, the pattern of scars standing out even more clearly, a random design of raised weals. The metal locket around her neck glistened faintly in the dim light.

The five friends stood in a loose half circle around her.

"She gone?" Krysty asked.

"Breathing." J.B. stooped closer. "But only just."

"Let me." Mildred knelt and peered at the woman. She took her wrist between finger and thumb, looking into the distance as she counted to herself. "Very low."

"The cold?" Ryan offered.

"Maybe."

Doc coughed. "Forgive an elderly man's interruption, but it appears from where I'm standing that the poor woman is sitting in the middle of a pool of drying blood."

Mildred gently unfolded the arms from across the chest and stomach. "Oh, shit," she said quietly.

"What?" Krysty took a half step to the side so that she could see over Mildred's shoulders. "Oh."

Mildred straightened, and they were all able to see what had happened.

The dying woman had been knifed, presumably by one of the scalie guards, perhaps as she tried to escape. Somehow she'd managed to get away from the acid-flooded warehouse. The bloody sores on her knees told their own story of how she'd gotten as far as she had.

The knife had been thrust in with a ferocious anger, a little to the left, then drawn across and twisted. In among the sodden clothes, crusted with congealing, clotted blood, they could all see the thin loops and twists of intestines tumbled into her lap.

"Least the rats didn't find her during the night," J.B. commented.

"I don't think she'd have known much about it if they had," Mildred replied. "Whatever bad times she's had in her life are nearly finished."

"Should I end it for her?" Ryan asked, his hand slipping to the hilt of his panga.

At the sound of his voice the woman's eyes opened. For several long heartbeats she gazed blindly into space, not focusing on anything. Then she moved her head and her eyes locked on Ryan's face.

Her lips moved, but no sound came out. Her tongue tried desperately to moisten her cracked lips. Krysty had a small container of water, and she knelt quickly and splashed a little into the palm of her hand, offering it to the woman. She lapped at it, then coughed, the breath wheezing in her chest.

But her eyes never left Ryan.

"You," she finally whispered.

"What is it you want?" he asked, feeling an almost supernatural wonder at what was possibly keeping her alive with her guts spilled out.

"Rona."

"What?"

Doc looked at Mildred. "That was the name she said before." He explained to the others. "She gave us food when the scalies had us. She didn't make sense. About wanting to find you, Ryan, my dear fellow. But wouldn't say why."

"Look," Krysty breathed. "Her hand."

It was spidering up her chest, with a life of its own, to her throat. It stopped and gripped the square metal pendant. "Take," she said, her eyes burning into Ryan's good one.

"This?" He touched it with his fingers. A nod of the head, slow and painful, answered him. He carefully pulled it up, wincing as he realized it was stuck to her with dried blood. He peeled it loose and over the tangled gray hair.

"Open."

He turned it in his hand. The workmanship reminded him vaguely of silver he'd seen down in the Southwest. Indian crafts. For a moment he couldn't see how to get inside it.

"Open."

"I'm trying. But it's…" He spit in his hand and wiped off some of the blood, seeing, then, that it had a catch on one side. Ryan levered a nail into it and pried. "Stiff," he said. "Don't want to break it when... Ah, here."

"Rona said to find you. Died long back. Find you. Quest. Look after." Her breathing was becoming faster and more shallow.

Slowly Ryan opened the locket and found that it contained two things—a tiny ringlet of blond hair and a picture. A faded, pale brown portrait.

"Who is it?" he asked, even though he knew what the answer was going to be.

"Your son, Ryan Cawdor. It's your son."

Chapter Twenty-Four

The woman coughed again, spitting a tiny thread of fresh blood from the corner of her mouth. Krysty, still kneeling at her side, wiped it away.

"My son."

"Rona."

Ryan nodded, her face flooding his memory. "Sharona," he said almost to himself. "Sharona Carson from Towse ville."

"Yes. Dead. Boy lives."

The only sound was that of labored breathing. Everybody was looking down at the dying woman, each locked in his or her own thoughts.

Ryan stared again at the tiny picture, at a solemn-faced boy with short, dark curling hair, dark eyes, stubborn jaw and pronounced cheekbones.

Krysty reached and took the locket from him, glanced down at it and nodded. "Certainly looks a lot like you, lover."

"How old is he? How old is the boy?"

His mind was frantically calculating backward. When had the Trader been in Towse? When had he slept with that feral bitch, Sharona Carson? Rutted with her, until they were both spent with the venom of their coupling. Whatever else it might have been, it certainly hadn't come within a country mile of being lovemaking.

"He's ten years old, Ryan Cawdor."

That sounded about right. He glanced at J.B. and saw that the Armorer had been occupied with the same arithmetic. There was the slightest nod of the head.

Ryan couldn't think of what to do or say, his mind completely blanked by this astounding revelation. Part of him wanted to question it, to shake the woman until her remaining teeth rattled in her skull, to make her admit it was a pointless lie. A macabre joke. Simply a mistake.

But he knew it wasn't, not with those solemn eyes staring back at him from the little square of paper.

He knew.

"Name's... Name's..." But it wouldn't come. The woman's eyes closed as though she were gathering her strength for a final assault on an unclimbable peak. "His name is Dean."

"Dean." Ryan tried the sound in his mouth, letting it slide into his mind. "Dean." Ten years old. What in fireblast was a ten-year-old boy like? He couldn't properly remember himself at ten, and if the boy had been out on the road in Deathlands for those ten years, then what might he be?

The breathing was suddenly slowing, becoming more erratic.

"She's going," Mildred said, taking her pulse again.

J.B. took off his fedora, turning it in his hands. "Woman spends a chunk of her life trying to find you, Ryan. Finds you, then she hasn't got any life left anymore."

"Least she handed the quest on," Krysty whispered.

"Yeah." Ryan nodded, his mind still in a blurred turmoil.

Doc coughed. "I have no wish to intrude a note of reality into this solemn and sad moment, but I have a question. One which I feel might be somewhat relevant here."

"What's that, Doc?" Mildred looked up at the old man with a slightly irritated expression on her face. "Can't it just wait a few moments? It's very near, now, for her."

"That's the point. It will shortly be too late. Forever."

Ryan looked at Doc. "Then spit it out."

"Where is the boy?"

It was like slicing into a beautiful cake and finding a ticking implo-gren inside.

"Fireblast!"

Mildred half raised her left hand, as though to protect the dying woman. "I think it's too late, Ryan. Sorry, but—"

"Get out of the fucking way," he grated, kneeling at her side. "Move, Mildred!"

Reluctantly she did as he ordered, shuffling to her left.

He took the woman's hand in both his, squeezing, his face inches from hers. "Where is he? Where is Dean? Tell me."

Her eyelids fluttered and her lips moved, but there wasn't a sound.

Ryan lifted his right and brought it down in a vicious round-arm swing, catching the woman across the left cheek, and bringing a flush of pink to her skin.

"Ryan!" Krysty shouted.

He ignored her. "Where is the boy now? Quick, or your quest's fucked forever. Where is Dean?"

This time there were words, just audible. "Not here..."

"Where?" No answer. No response. He shook her, a small part of his mind aware of the slippery sound of her intestines sliding in her lap. Ryan shouted again, spittle spraying in her face. "Where is he?"

"Ninth Avenue."

"More."

"Twenty-eighth, old park. One block."

"Go on!" he shouted, shaking her again.

"Cellar. Friends there. I'm real cold. Where's Rona gone?"

"A park near Twenty-eighth and Ninth. What else? Come on," he demanded, his voice cracking.

"Ryan, she doesn't..." J.B., urged by Mildred, a hand on his shoulder.

The one-eyed man didn't turn, but his body stiffened. "Leave me be," he warned.

"Old cellar under the ground. Get in back of tumbled... Dean! Here, son. Going to get cold."

Now the voice was fading. The woman's breathing was slowing and becoming painfully irregular. Seconds would pass between each shuddering intake. All of them knew time was being measured in those breaths.

"You left him there?"

"I really don't think she can hear you now, Ryan," Mildred said gently.

Ryan wasn't done yet. He lifted his hand again, this time clenching it into a fist. But he hesitated, sighing, feeling the crimson mist of anger beginning to drift away from him. "No point."

The breathing stopped.

Long seconds passed and he began to stand up, his mind racing with myriad thoughts.

But there was a hoarse, grating moan, and the woman half sat up, eyes staring, pupils dilated. One hand grabbed at Ryan, catching his sleeve, holding him frozen. "You're like him. Like Rona said you was. He's going to...to be special, Ryan Cawdor. Now I done what I said, and there isn't..."

Mildred stooped, putting a finger to the artery beneath the woman's left ear. "Gone this time."

Ryan gently disengaged the clawed fingers from his arm and folded it across the woman's chest. "You did it right. Now I'll carry it on."

Chapter Twenty-Five

"I had to do that."

"I know that."

"If I hadn't—"

"Then she'd probably have died, and you wouldn't have known where the boy was. Just that he was somewhere in the Newyork ville."

"But I... Slapping a dying woman who's maybe saved the life of..."

"Your son," Krysty said. "Come on, lover. It's not that difficult to say, is it?"

"Yeah." He stopped and glared at her. "Yeah, Krysty, it's actually very fucking difficult to say. My *son*. Up to fifteen minutes ago I didn't even know I had a son. Or a daughter. Or any children. It's going to take me a while to get used to that. My son, my son, my son. Right?"

She smiled at his anger and his uncertainty, then stepped in close and kissed him on the cheek. "Course. Glad you've gotten that off your chest, lover. Easier all around. Be easier for Dean, as well."

"Krysty..." He hesitated. "Look, I think we should talk some about this. It doesn't make any difference to you and me, you know. It was ten years ago.''

Doc, with J.B. and Mildred, had been waiting, listening. The old man repeated a runic remark he'd made once before. ''And it was in another country, and besides, the bitch is dead.''

THE SKIES OVER NEW YORK had cleared and it was a bright, fresh morning. The shadows were sharp-edged as they walked south.

Once again they slipped naturally into a skirmish line, keeping to the center of what remained of the streets, Ryan leading, holding his G-12 caseless. Then came Krysty, Doc, Mildred and J.B.

As he walked on, Ryan's mind kept sliding back ten years to the blazing heat and murderous winds of the baked Southwest. And Sharona Carson. ''Rona.'' He'd never heard anyone call her that. As the wife of Baron Alias Carson, she'd been entitled to respect. Sharona—dazzling blond hair, beautifully styled; expensive jewels; fabulous clothes that fitted her like a second skin; skin, with its sharp, exciting taste; teeth that had nipped at him, leaving him marked and bleeding; and deep violet eyes that had suckered him.

''Something ahead left,'' Krysty called from just behind him, jerking Ryan out of the reverie about the past and back into the dangers of the present.

He realized he'd lost concentration by brooding on Towse and the woman. And his son.

He stopped and raised his G-12, looking where
Krysty had pointed. Something was watching them
from around the corner of a pile of rubbish, but it
was in shadow and he couldn't make it out. As soon
as they paused and looked, the creature darted away
out of sight again.

"Scalie?" J.B. called.

"Don't think so. The head looked normal shape.
Just a scavenger, one of the triple-dirties who lives
here."

THE FARTHER THEY TRAVELED, the worse the desolation grew. Hardly a building stood above ground-
floor level, and virtually all had been stripped of
wood. To their left, where there had once been great
buildings that scraped at the lower edges of the sky,
there was a permanent haze.

Ryan noticed that the tiny lapel rad counters he,
J.B. and Krysty wore were showing a potential haz-
ard. The color had shifted from the faded green of
safety through the middle band of orange toward the
crimson of danger.

J.B. was also aware of it. "Some serious hot spots
over east."

Ryan looked around. "Can't be that far. How
many blocks should it be?" he asked, addressing the
question to either Doc or Mildred.

It was the old man who answered. "The bus terminal was around Fortieth Street. It backed on to

Ninth Avenue. Woman said down to Twenty-eighth. Twelve or thirteen blocks.''

Mildred looked around. "Not all that far from Greenwich Village, but it's impossible to work out. Some roads have totally vanished. No landmarks. Just head south and look for that park she mentioned.''

"Chelsea Park," Ryan said.

They did what they could to quarter the area, looking for anything that might resemble a park. As far as they could tell, they were in roughly the right part of the ville, but they drew a blank.

"Noon," J.B. announced, glancing up at the bright sun from under the brim of his fedora.

"Not that much food left." Krysty turned to face Ryan. "What do you reckon, lover?"

"Keep moving. Woman was dying. She wouldn't tell us lies. Got to be around here.''

In some of the shadowed parts in the lee of the piles of debris, there were small patches of unmelted snow. J.B. stepped aside to take a leak behind a heap of dark red bricks near one of the white drifts. "Hey! Look here. Some scalies been here.''

They made out the marks of studded boots and a few scuffed smears of heelless footwear as well as the clear imprint of a set of small bare toes.

"Still sending out their hunting parties," Ryan commented. "Never known muties so well organized. Really are like fireblasted sec men.''

Doc gazed vaguely at the fallen walls and ice-coated rubble. "That's most interesting," he observed.

"How's that, Doc?"

"Well, my dear Ryan, unless I am much mistaken, someone has painted the number over there as an indication of the street. Twenty-seven. Of course, it may be the merest coincidence."

The numbers were in faded white paint, poorly executed, the dribbles running from both the two and the eight.

Ryan looked toward the west and took a deep breath. "River's close. Can taste it. Let's go two or three blocks to the east and then cut south. If we move west along what's left of that highway, we should hit this Chelsea Park."

"MUST BE."

"Some park."

The only thing that made them think this had once been a park was the fact that there were no piles of rubble on the ground, merely a narrow rectangular space of brownish mud. It was totally featureless except for small ice-slick puddles.

"Said there was a cellar around the back of a tumbled building or something like that."

"More scalies been here." J.B. pointed to the clear line of boots, etched across a long, narrow bank of snow.

Ryan knelt and peered closely at the tracks. "Recent. Look at the edges. Kind of blurred and rounded. Been this morning. Not last night.''

Both men straightened and looked around uneasily, both conscious of the prickling possibility of sudden, bloody ambush.

''Better find this cellar real quick,'' the Armorer suggested.

The companions looked around the wasteland.

''There,'' Krysty said.

''Behind that broken archway?''

She nodded. ''I can feel it, Ryan. Someone's been there.''

''Still?''

She shook her head slowly. ''No. No, I don't think so.''

''Best look.''

They climbed over heaps of brick, tangled about with iron girders, some rusted to orange ribbons. The sun was bright enough to see clear tracks that said others had been there before them. There was a path between the twin pillars of the arch. Ryan hesitated, looking at the carved figures that had once supported the keystones. More than life-size, they were female, their heads wrapped in stylized shrouds, as though they were frozen in weeping.

''Here,'' he said, seeing immediately that Krysty had been correct. They were too late, probably only by an hour or so.

After ten years, he'd missed the son he'd never seen by a matter of minutes. It was one of the most bitter moments of Ryan Cawdor's life.

Chapter Twenty-Six

The three bodies were so hacked and raggled that it was almost impossible to tell either sex or age. Ryan steeled himself to look more carefully, but J.B. took him by the arm.

"Let me."

Even from where he stood Ryan could see that none of the bodies was that of a ten-year-old boy.

The Armorer straightened, wiping his glasses. "Misted up from somewhere. Can feel heat from... maybe down in the cellar there."

"What about...?"

"No. Two men. Both look late teens. One got a double-stupe face. The other hasn't got much face left. The scalies used cleavers on them all. Pure hacked them to shreds. Third one's an old woman. Bodies are stiffening, but it's cold. Hour or two. That's my guess. Look in the cellar?"

"Sure."

Mildred offered to stand watch outside, her target pistol drawn and ready. The other four climbed down the makeshift steps into the sweltering, noisome darkness.

"Dark night! Like an oven," J.B. said. "And that stink!"

The remains of a great fire still smoldered against the back wall, where there seemed to be a kind of a chimney. The embers glowed with a shimmering scarlet, casting a ferocious heat around the vaulted room. Ryan guessed it was roughly thirty feet long and twenty across, with a flagged floor and a low, arched ceiling.

The worst of the smell came from a shapeless pile in one corner. At first Ryan took it for a heap of butchered corpses, and his heart sank again. Then he moved a little closer and saw that it was bodies all right, but the carcasses were of slaughtered, skinned dogs. Some of them, by the smell, were several days old.

A mound of ragged blankets and coats was thrown against one of the walls, presumably too far gone to interest even the scalies.

"Some dried fish over here," Krysty said. "Rotting meat masks the smell. Seems edible to me."

"Keg of water here," Doc announced, kicking it with one of his boots. "Feels about two-thirds full. Or perhaps it's nearer three-quarters." He kicked it again in a thoughtful way. "Possibly four-fifths, or—"

"We get the picture, Doc," Ryan interrupted, aware of the swell of relief that the boy wasn't lying there with his throat gashed open, cold in a pool of his own blood. That would have been a hard road to walk.

The far end of the underground room held a pile of wood, mostly broken joists and rafters, presumably looted from some of the tens of thousands of buildings that had fallen a century ago.

Ryan walked past the fire, opening his coat and wiping beaded sweat from his forehead. He looked around the cellar, swiping crossly at a slow-flying, buzzing insect.

His sharp eye was caught by something gleaming among the wood, as though it had been tucked there as a hurried hiding place when the scalies came bursting in.

He stooped and picked up the object, angling it to the firelight to see what it was. Aware that the others had all turned to look at him, he waved it. "Knife. Little knife, but the blade's real sharp. Pretty. Hilt carved from what looks like turquoise."

"Small," J.B. said. "And the Navaho use a lot of that green stone, don't they? Remember it from around Towse ville."

"Yeah. Could be."

It was a powerful and disturbing feeling for Ryan, holding something in his hand that might have belonged to his son. It *might* be Dean Cawdor's knife. He found a sheath of soft deerskin, and he slid the blade into it and tucked it into one of his pockets.

Mildred called from outside. "Weather's getting real bad, folks."

"Just what we need." Ryan turned. "Want to get off and try and track them down while the trail's fresh." He punched his right fist into his left palm. "Fireblast! We'll never find him."

Krysty was moving to join Mildred when she paused. "Way Dred talked about them, the scalies control most of this southwest part of the ville. Big base around the docks. They must have taken the boy there. Nowhere else."

"Hey," Mildred said, "there's the biggest mother of a storm I ever saw, and it looks as if it's heading our way!"

Then they all moved to the steps, pushing past a heavy section of wood paneling that had obviously served the hideout as a door.

"Dark night," J.B. breathed. "You're right, Mildred. Seen some big ones down by the Gulf. Acid storms that take the skin off you in a couple of minutes. But this is going to be hard."

"Temperature's up a little," Ryan observed. "Might be rain rather than snow."

"Either way, I think I would rather have a roof over my head. Even if it's this smelly den behind us." Doc hunched his shoulders and sniffed miserably at the prospect.

Ryan desperately wanted to get out after the creatures that had stolen his son. There was no way of knowing whether Dean was still living, but the attempt had to be made.

Would be made.

But not yet. Not with the deep purple and black clouds that were tearing in from the northeast, reaching toward the ville like the clenching fist of an angry giant. Silver lightning crackled and tore at the sky, leaving narrow pink strips through the clouds. The wind was rising, blowing scraps of rubbish across the street opposite.

"No, lover," Krysty said at his elbow.

"What?"

"You were thinking about going after the boy."

"So?"

"Going out into that storm."

"I wasn't."

Then she grabbed him, fingers biting into the flesh below the elbow. "Don't lie to me, you bastard, Ryan!"

"I…didn't really…" he stammered, knowing she was right. He had been about to take an insane chance and go off into the rushing maelstrom.

"You die and what are his chances? You stupe, Ryan! Sit it out and then go. Can't be that difficult to find hundreds of scalies, even in a ville of this size." She let go of him. "And don't lie to me. Don't let this son of yours come between us and the way it's always been."

THERE WAS TIME to throw out the decaying bodies of the dogs, making the cellar a little less oppressive. But moving the carcasses also disturbed nests of maggots and great swollen blowflies, which hummed around them, settling on faces and hands and leaving the shuddering feeling of filth.

One of the insects stung J.B. when he slapped at it, leaving its mark on the side of his face. The Armorer wasn't the kind of man to make a lot of unnecessary fuss, but he stamped and cursed, pressing his hand against the sting.

Mildred offered to look at it for him, but he refused, insisting on helping to dispose of the rotting bodies.

"Should take care," she said.

"Don't fuss. It'll be fine."

THE OLD MAN APPEARED outside just as they were about to batten down against the storm. He came from nowhere, watching them, his rheumy eyes darting toward the heap of dog meat lying in the ice-slick highway. Less than five feet tall, he wore a coat that positively glistened with dirt and ancient grease. His feet were hidden inside boots of different sizes and shapes. The wind was tugging at strands of silvery hair.

Mildred glanced at Ryan. "Can he...?"

"No," he said.

"Why?"

"Because..." His anger flared and he looked at the black woman. "Because he could have any kind of weapon. No point."

The old man had shuffled nearer. "You friends of them they took?" he asked.

"Why?" Ryan dropped his hand to the butt of his blaster, then changed his mind. He struggled to paste a smile on his unshaven face.

It wasn't very successful, as the stranger took several stumbling steps backward, hands up to stop himself from being struck. "Don't, outie. Don't. I was—"

"I won't hurt you. Want shelter against that?" Ryan pointed at the roiling waves of leaden blackness, now almost overhead, blanking out the sunshine.

"In there?" He gestured with a shaking head toward the cellar.

"Sure."

"Don't like being ass-fucked."

Both Ryan and Mildred froze, staring at him.

"What?"

"You heard, mister."

"Well, you have my word I won't ass-fuck you."

"Goes double for me." Mildred grinned.

"Just s'long as it's understood. I heard about you outies and what you do t'each other."

"You can get inside," Ryan said. "First, you said something about the people who were staying here."

"Good they was. Gave me food. Jolt if they had it. I got 'em fish sometimes. Know where t'go. Old docks. Watch for them lizard bastards. Shove their cocks up your ass 'fore you can dodge."

"Thanks for the warning. You got a name?"

"Called Bluff."

"Best get inside, Bluff. Storm's right on top of us."

HIDDEN BENEATH THE PILE of firewood were a number of coils of good rope. J.B. split them up and gave everyone a length to wear wrapped around the waist. "Be useful when we try and get back to the gateway," he told them.

Krysty had been putting more wood on the fire, building it up again from the dull ashes. Doc took a spare hank of rope and used it to fix the makeshift door into place.

Before it was completely shut, Ryan went back out for a last look at the weather. The wind was so strong that he had to steady himself against the fallen wall, his hair lashing all over his face. There was a pelting mixture of rain and hail beginning to fall from the black sky. The lightning still danced, but he couldn't hear any thunder above the screaming of the gale. Visibility had fallen to a dusklike gloom so that he could barely see across the width of the street toward the featureless Chelsea Park.

Once they were battened down, Ryan intended to have a word with Bluff about the group that had been living in the basement. And about the young boy who'd been with them.

His ears sang with the pressure of the wind and he ducked, tears brimming in his good eye. He wiped it with his sleeve, readying himself to return down the steps, when he noticed a flurry of movement low to the ground, near the scattered corpses of the dogs. It looked like a man on his belly, crawling to steal some of the rotten meat. But if it was a man, then he was exceedingly tall.

The curtain of sleet parted momentarily, and Ryan blinked as a great sheet of glowing lightning tore the sky apart.

The sight took his breath away.

Creeping away from the stinking heap of meat were two enormous, pale-skinned alligators as big as anything Ryan had ever seen down in the bayous. In that moment of frozen magnesium whiteness he figured them to be thirty feet long, with gaping jaws and razored teeth.

The lightning frightened the reptiles, and they slithered away, each with its mouth jammed with mangled haunches of dog.

Ryan had once read an old book about people having alligators as pets before sky-dark had come. When the reptiles grew too big, their owners flushed them down the toilets. The book claimed they bred in the sewers and grew to enormous lengths.

But he remembered that the book said the creatures were all a fantastic myth.

Fantastic, yes.

Myth, no.

AT LAST THE CORE OF THE storm came swooping down with a murderous intent on the ville of Newyork.

Ryan clambered inside and lashed the door firmly into place. The barrier trembled under his hands, quivering with the power of the slashing rain. A little water was already leaking around the sides, and he could feel a chill draft knifing into the cellar.

But the fire was now blazing brightly, and he joined Krysty, who was sitting on the stone floor. Bluff squatted opposite them, hands held out toward the lapping flames.

"You knew these people?"

"Sure did. Kind they were, and I gave 'em fish."

Ryan leaned forward. "Tell me about the little boy."

The old man looked puzzled. "Little boy? There weren't no little boy living here."

Chapter Twenty-Seven

"No little boy?" Ryan wasn't even aware he'd moved, but his fingers were locked into the old man's wattled neck. Bluff's seamed face was turning purple, and his yellowed tongue was protruding so far from the mouth that it looked like a dying snake.

"Leave him, lover." Krysty slapped Ryan across the back.

"He said there wasn't any little boy. The lying bastard!"

"There wasn't! No babies at all."

"I didn't say babies. I said a little boy, you deaf stupe!"

Bluff rubbed at his throat, stretching his neck like a trapped turtle. "What do you mean by a little boy? There was a kid there, all right."

"What like?"

"Like about tall as me. Taller. Yes, taller. Not a little boy at all. Be about twelve years old. Hard as... I can't remember his name."

"Try."

"Dean. Real black hair. That was it. Mother was the one with the bad-cut face. Nice, though. Looked after Dean. Like a she-gator with young ones. Dean.

Yeah. But he's not a *little* boy, you murderous bastard. Taller than me, he is.''

Ryan gave a grunting, reluctant laugh. ''Taller than you! Shit.''

BLUFF DIDN'T HAVE too much to tell them about Dean Cawdor.

It rapidly became obvious to Ryan and the others that the old man was a born scrounger, used to attaching himself to groups that might help him to survive, offering any sort of help he could, in any way anyone might want. But he hadn't been close to the previous inhabitants of the cellar.

The old-timer was aware of the boy, though it seemed as if he and the lad hadn't hit it off. He complained that Dean hadn't trusted him and had tried to persuade the others to bar him from the shelter of the cellar.

''But the scalies got him just the same. Dodged the first raid. Clever at that, he was. Got 'em all they did.''

Outside the storm was cataclysmic, seeming to make the whole building shiver. Rain was pouring through the gaps around the door, trickling across the uneven floor, collecting in one corner in a growing pool.

Thunder pealed and crashed, lightning bright around the door's edges. The air was scented with the bitter tang of ozone from the storm, riding over the woodsmoke and the lingering aroma of the dead dogs.

Ryan sat close to Krysty. Conversation was difficult.

"Want to talk about it, lover?" she finally asked.

"I don't know. Yeah, in some ways...course I do. But it isn't real yet. Maybe the woman was wrong or crazy. Or the kid's already dead in some gutter or floating facedown in the river. Maybe he isn't really my...my son. And if he is, then we have to try and find him and rescue him."

"We can do that. A few scalies won't stop the old team."

Ryan smiled and nodded. "I guess so. But that's what's filling my mind, and I can't sort of clear my head to talk about it. Not yet."

THE AFTERNOON DRIFTED BY in a timeless haze of noise and darkness.

J.B. joined Ryan and Krysty. Doc had fallen asleep, and Mildred was also dozing. Bluff had rolled over in a corner, looking like an ugly bundle of rags.

"Getting late to start trying to track the boy," he commented.

"Yeah. Best stay here the night and then move first thing."

"This sting hurts like a bastard. Throbs. Worse than any skitter I ever knew."

Krysty reached over and laid the palm of her hand

on the Armorer's forehead. "Feels hot, J.B. Best take care."

"Too late. Bastard's already bitten me. Be okay in the morning."

THE MASSIVE STORM finally spent itself, the noise and turbulence moving off to the south.

The cellar was warm and snug, the fire whispering to itself, smoke curling up the chimney.

"I'll take a look outside," Ryan told Krysty. "Scalies might be around now the hurricane's gone. Want to see if the smoke's likely to give us away."

"We going to post a guard?" she asked.

"Might."

He untied the ropes, the knots difficult and tight from the wet. The heavy door slid sideways, and he breathed in the cool, fresh air.

It was full dark, with a sliver of watery moon floating uneasily among scudding walls of frayed clouds. The storm was just visible, way off beyond the southern tip of Mattan, the silent lightning still ripping at the blackness.

The temperature was well above freezing, and the street glistened with spilled rain, huge puddles gathering at its edges. The place where they'd thrown the canine corpses was empty, and Ryan glanced around uneasily, wondering if the giant alligators were still crawling in the shadows.

But the ville was quiet, seemingly deserted.

There was a sound behind him, and he turned and saw that Bluff had woken up.

"You moving on?" Ryan asked.

"No. Going for a small walk. Got something I want to hunt on down. Bring it back if I find it."

"Food?"

"Nearly, Captain, nearly. Be a bit of time, then I'll be here again."

"I'M A MITE CONCERNED about John," Mildred said standing at the bottom of the steps.

Three-quarters of an hour had passed since Bluff had vanished, and Ryan was beginning to feel a touch of concern. The hairs at his nape were prickling. It didn't take a giant leap of the imagination to think that the old man had gone to earn himself some sort of reward for betraying them.

"Krysty thought he had a touch of fever. Getting worse?"

"Some."

"Sort of flu? Not like J.B. to go and catch himself a cold."

Mildred joined him, looking out over the silent debris of the city. "God, it's desolate, isn't it? Flu, did you say? Sorry, Ryan, wasn't concentrating. No, not flu. I just wonder about that insect that stung him. The swelling's worse, and he keeps saying it feels like someone's injected him with acid."

"I didn't see what did it."

"Me, neither. And I feel real tired myself. Need something to pick me up."

"Must be plenty of jolt around a ville of this size."

She laughed quietly. "In my day it'd be parties with mirrors and razor blades and a few fine white lines laid out. Wouldn't mind doing a couple of lines right now."

"Addictive?"

"What they called 'psychoaddictive,' Ryan. Means that coke made you feel a new person, and the new person *really* wanted to do some more coke. Sure it was addictive. Most things are."

"Most things are what?" The voice came from the entrance to the cellar.

Ryan didn't even turn around. "Addictive, J.B. Talking about needing something to keep going in the bad times."

The Armorer moved into the open, the moonlight's gleam making him look as pale as death. Beads of perspiration stood out on his forehead and cheeks.

"Nobody needs anything to get through the good times," he said. "I never did. Never will. Times I wonder about what keeps us going. You know, Ryan? What's the point when I'm going to die alone?"

"We all will," Mildred said quietly. "Why not come and keep out of the cold, John?"

"John?" He repeated his own name, running it

around his mouth like someone trying to identify a
fine and rare wine. "Nobody calls me that, Mildred."

"I do. Come on in."

"Fucking cold, Mildred. Body like ice."

Ryan watched as the woman took his friend by the
arm and helped him down into the cellar. The idea
of J.B. being ill was so alien that it was difficult even
to consider.

"Be better in the morning," he called down after
them.

By THE TIME Bluff eventually returned, another hour
had passed. J.B. had slipped into a fitful sleep,
watched over by Mildred. The lump on his face had
grown larger, and she said the glands in his neck and
armpits had also become swollen.

Twice he came to a sort of half-waking and mumbled lines from a song about being up on Cripple
Creek.

"Where he was born," Ryan explained. "It's almost the only thing I know about his background."

"Cripple Creek?"

"Sure."

"Well, I'll be… I took part in a big shooting com-
petition there a couple of years before I got myself
frozen." She shook her head. "Anyway, got to get
back to my patient."

Bluff had returned with a bottle of joltsky that he
grudgingly offered around.

Doc woke up long enough to take a sip, carefully

wiping the neck of the bottle first. He handed it back to the raggedy man with a grimace of disgust. "Thank you, my dear fellow. But no thank you."

Krysty, Mildred and Ryan all refused it. J.B. was sleeping more comfortably by now and wasn't to be disturbed.

Ryan was sitting at the bottom of the steps, keeping a watch outside. The fire was burning well, keeping the cellar cheery and warm. He'd been outside to check on the chimney, but there was virtually no smoke showing. With the Armorer ill, the risk was worth the taking.

"Sure you don't wanna slug of joltsky, huh?" Bluff asked, standing unsteadily in front of him.

"Sure. Man on guard needs to be alert. Not with his head stoned sideways."

The old man giggled. "Nice way with words, outie. Talk good. All of you. All but that old prick. He speaks double-stupe."

"Doc has his own world."

"Stupe. Got to be clever in Mattan. Or you don't pull by."

Bluff was already high, his tongue running away with him. Ryan kept nodding, half listening to his rambling, most of his concentration on watching the street.

"Thought I couldn't remember where I put this little love." He waved the dark green bottle.

"Yeah. Know the feeling."

"Hid it good. Like when you was a kid and you got a reward for bein' good."

"Sure."

"This my reward for bein' good."

Suddenly Ryan focused his complete attention on the small man. "You got that joltsky as a reward, Bluff?"

"Yeah, fucking good." He laid a filthy finger along the side of his nose to indicate his cunning. "Good. Hey, I meant t'ask you if you found somethin' here?"

"What?"

"The kid had a knife. Real pretty. Green handle. Never found it when they came. And they said I could have it. Asked 'em special. Part of my reward." His mouth sagged open in a soft grin at his own cleverness, his eyes rolling, unfocused, blasted by the jolt.

"The scalies gave you the bottle as part of your reward for betraying the people who lived here?" Ryan asked slow and quiet.

"Now I didn't say that."

"You did. I bet you do real well from the scalies, here and there, don't you, Bluff? I truly admire your cleverness."

"You do?"

"Yeah."

In the cellar, beyond the old man, he could see that both Mildred and Krysty were awake and listening, openmouthed, to the conversation.

"Well, that's nice, outie. Got my bottle. Didn't see none of them scalies tonight."

"That's really what I wanted to know. So you didn't tell them about us being here?"

Bluff hiccuped and took another swig of the hallucinogenic liquor. "Course not. Said I didn't see them tonight, didn't I?"

Chapter Twenty-Eight

Ryan pushed Bluff backward with a hard, jabbing blow, the flat of his hand against the man's narrow chest. The little figure stumbled into the cellar, arms waving for balance, the bottle falling and splintering on the cold flagstones.

"Hey…"

The murderous rage totally possessed Ryan, blinding him to everything else. If anyone had come between him and his victim, he would have struck them down without a nanosecond's consideration.

Anyone.

He followed Bluff into the arched warmth and security of the basement, moving instinctively on the balls of his feet, light and ready. His blaster was unholstered, the panga unsheathed.

"Hey, listen, Captain!" The little man was hunched, hands up over his face, seeing a marble-eyed nemesis advancing toward him through the half-light. "Why are…?"

Ryan spoke only once, a single, ice-cold word. "Betrayer."

"You don't—"

One blow was all that it took. Ryan clenched his

fist, leaving the first joints of the index and middle fingers protruding, giving a sharpening thrust to the attack. He drew back his arm a few inches, then jabbed out, exhaling as he did so. He didn't aim at Bluff's head, directing the punch instead at the solar plexus up under the rib cage, tearing into the soft, unprotected area of the old man's stomach. Though Bluff was frail and thin, Ryan's blow buried his fist up to the wrist. He even felt the jar of the vertebrae.

The one-eyed man stepped back quickly, face impassive, watching as the old man commenced dying. He doubled forward, head dropping almost to his waist. Then his knees gave, and he collapsed slowly onto the floor. His mouth dropped open, revealing a half-dozen broken, stained teeth. Breath burst out in a sour explosion, rancid and fouled with bile. The joltsky he'd just drunk sprayed out, splattering noisily on the cold stones.

Bluff's hands folded and clutched his guts, as though he were trying to hold himself together. His eyes protruded from sockets of bruised bone, as if someone were pressing them out from within the skull.

"Jesus," Mildred said quietly.

The nervous damage by the ferocious punch caused vagal inhibition, literally stopping the heart and lungs from functioning. A low, unearthly moaning came from the old man's gaping jaws, loud enough to wake up Doc.

He sat up, seeing Bluff down and done. "What the deuce are...? Are we under attack?"

The keening ceased, and the only sound, apart from the crackling of the wood on the fire, was the scrabbling of Bluff's shoes. Then the lines finally went down and he was still.

Doc was on his feet, staring at Ryan. "I've known you long enough, my friend, to have trust in your actions. But was it necessary to butcher this poor, helpless man?"

"He was a traitor, Doc. Betrayed people to the scalies. Gave them up for drink and his own miserable life. He gave them my son, Doc."

From the corner J.B. spoke, surprising them all. "And the bastard had it coming, Doc. If I felt a little better, I'd have up and chilled him."

Doc nodded. "I see. I did mention that I thought you would have had a cogent reason. And, by the three Kennedys, there can be few reasons more cogent than that."

Ryan stooped over the shrunken corpse, wrinkling his nose at the stench where Bluff had fouled himself in his passing. He locked his fingers into the loose skin at the back of the old man's neck and dragged him across the cellar, up the stairs and out into the open, where he heaved the body into the gutter. "More rotting meat for the gators," he said.

"SHOULD HAVE WOKEN ME UP, Ryan. I could stand my turn."

J.B. was very angry. He was sitting up, with the remains of a gray blanket around his shoulders. He wasn't wearing his glasses, and there were spots of hectic color on his pale cheekbones. His voice was high and strained. The insect bite was very pronounced on the side of his face, pulling at the edge of his mouth.

"Thought you needed a rest. Enough of us to take care of it."

"Not the point, Ryan, you bastard. Cheat me like that again, and you'll wake up with a big red mouth carved across your fucking throat."

"Hey, now you…" Ryan stopped as he caught the warning glare from Mildred.

"Yeah, what, you stupe prick?"

"Leave it lie, J.B. Just leave it."

"Time I can't stand my watch is the time we part company, Cawdor."

Ryan turned away, seeing the concern on the faces of Doc and Krysty.

"Don't show me your back, Cawdor!"

Ryan froze at the unmistakable sound of a hammer clicking back over a loaded chamber. Very, very slowly he looked over his shoulder at the Armorer, who was holding his Steyr AUG in both hands, pointing it toward him.

"I said you wasn't to… What did I say, Mildred? You heard me."

"You said you were tired, John."

"Tired."

"Said you had a headache. Throat felt hot and dry. Sort of sweating and icy all at the same time. You remember?"

He scratched his nose with the barrel of the pistol. His hands were shaking, knuckles white. Ryan had a dreadful, momentary vision of him squeezing the trigger and blowing away his face. But J.B. eventually laid the blaster down on the blanket, sighing.

"That's the way I feel. Why's that? Think I got the mutie flu, Mildred?"

"Could be, John. But it might be some kind of infection introduced by the insect bite. If I had some antibiotic, I'd have you well and up in no time at all."

"Lie down, J.B.," Krysty directed, stooping over him, her cascading torrent of blazing hair seeming to tumble and fold itself around the sick man. She put her hand on his forehead, rubbing gently with the tips of her fingers. "Lie back and sleep. Feel better soon, after a sleep."

The Armorer stretched out his slim body and lay on the floor, tugging the blankets around himself. Doc moved to help him, arranging the covers with careful, solicitous hands.

J.B.'s eyes closed, and he was instantly asleep.

Ryan beckoned to the others to join him near the entrance to the cellar, where J.B. wouldn't be able to overhear them, even if he woke up. "Getting worse fast."

Doc looked at Mildred. "The medical authority in

our little group is entirely vested in you, ma'am. What are your thoughts about our poor ailing companion?''

"Don't know. Not a virus. Something triggered by that damn insect that stung him.''

"How long before he gets better?''

Mildred hesitated before answering Ryan's question. "Not honestly sure.''

"Day? Two days? Longer?''

"I told you, Ryan. I don't know.''

Krysty read the words, unspoken, from the worried black woman. "How bad might it be?''

"Might be as bad as it could be. I *don't* know! But I don't have any drugs at all.''

"Dred said something about a trader somewhere in the ville.'' Ryan closed his eye as he concentrated. "Harry...Stanton. Yeah. King of the Underworld, Retha called him. Said he had everything. Might have drugs.''

"It's serious, Ryan. John's strong. Tougher than any man I ever met. But there's diseases in Deathlands that come at you, and there's no...what's called an immune system to deal with them. If we're lucky, he'll fight it himself and be better in maybe thirty-six hours.''

"If we're not lucky?''

Mildred shook her head. "Can't tell you that.''

Ryan simply didn't believe her. "J.B. seems better this morning. Bitching temper. Doesn't look to me like someone ready for his six feet of dirt.''

Krysty spoke. "I hate to say this, lover, but I sort of feel what Mildred's saying. J.B.'s burning up."

Doc coughed. "Might I suggest that you, friend Cawdor, and I should go out and about these teeming highways? Perhaps to seek this trader and his world of Hades and obtain drugs to help poor John Barrymore? And also cast a net for news of your lad?"

"Makes sense, lover."

Ryan looked up the stairs, breathing in the early-morning smell of wet stone and clean air. "Not too much choice. J.B. can't move like he is. If we leave him, he'll need guarding. More blasters the better. I like the idea, Doc, but I'll go alone."

"Ah… An old man would slow you down and get in the way."

Ryan slapped him on the shoulder. "Don't be the weeper, Doc. Man alone moves quicker, and that cannon of yours is going to do more good protecting J.B. in here."

Doc gave a beaming smile, his double row of perfect teeth gleaming like polished ivory. "Very well. And we will not let you down."

"Antibiotics, Ryan," Mildred said. "You know what to ask for?"

"Penicillin, isn't it?"

She shook her head. "Not just that. John's got a bit of paper in one of his pockets and a stub of pencil. I saw it. I'll write down the names for you."

"Tell me, Mildred. I'll remember them all right. Go on."

She started to recite the list, ticking them off on her fingers. "Tetracyclines. They'd be good ones to get. Cephalexin. Erythromycin. Streptomycin. Colistin. Parom—"

"All right, all right." Ryan held up his hand. "Write them down."

It only took her a couple of minutes, and she gave him the folded piece of paper. "Good luck."

"Yes, the very best," Doc added.

"Come back safe, lover," Krysty chimed in.

"I'll try. I'll aim to be back here before dusk, but if I don't, put up the door and keep watch."

He climbed up the stairs. Krysty was holding the G-12 caseless, watching him. The last thing he heard as he stepped into the ville was a faint echo of J.B.'s voice.

"Keep your back to the sun, Ryan."

Chapter Twenty-Nine

It was an unusual experience for Ryan to be alone. His childhood had been largely a lonely one, often isolated and threatened. Then had come the dark years, when he roamed Deathlands with no friends and very few enemies.

Few enemies?

Alive.

Once he threw in his lot with the Trader, he became part of a team, a highly efficient, superbly trained team.

So many of them now dead. Maybe all dead.

For a moment Ryan had a flash of friends chilled—in mud, in desert, in rain, in fog, in snow, in light, in dark. So much blood. The Trader always tried to make sure corpses were recovered and given as decent a burial as was possible.

"Can't leave a man or a woman to be a rat's supper," he used to say.

You lived, slept, crapped and fought with the whole crew in the war wag. The massive old battle wagons the Trader had discovered in a hidden cache were lumbering brutes. The conditioning was unreliable, and you often baked in the summer and froze in the winter. Though Ryan also recalled a memorable evening up in the Darks with a temperature outside around fifty below. And every vent and ob-slit wide open while the crew sweated in singlets and pants.

Since their first discovery of a redoubt that contained a gateway, Ryan and his companions had been more or less alone, traveling through a largely hostile land, dependent on one another.

Now he was on his own.

He walked on, looking behind him only once. The rubble-strewn street was deserted, except for the stiff body of the old man, which, surprisingly, hadn't been dragged away. At the entrance to the cellar there was the flash of flaming red hair, and he lifted a hand to acknowledge Krysty.

One of the problems of walking alone through territory like the ruined ville was that you had nobody to watch your back. Ryan was so used to having someone in a skirmishing line behind him that his spine crawled at being so exposed.

Though he'd accommodated over the years to only having one eye, it was still an undeniable handicap. It halved his peripheral vision, meaning he had to keep on turning his head from side to side.

The 9 mm SIG-Sauer blaster was in its holster, and his fingers itched for the butt.

He was aware that his biggest danger came from the gangs of scalies that seemed to control much of the region to the south and west of him. But from what they knew so far, he hoped the rigid and noisy regimentation of the mutie patrols would allow him sufficient warning.

The layout of the streets and the ruined buildings made it classic ambush country. It was impossible at any one time to see more than seventy yards in any direction. And generally that came down to about thirty yards.

The air was cool and damp, with the flavor at the back of the throat of burning wood. Somewhere not too far away meat was being roasted and bread being baked.

Ryan proceeded cautiously, trying to keep to the sides of the highways, yet not so close to the piled bricks and stone that someone could jump him. He began to see movement. Now and then, in the distance, figures scuttled over the sidewalks and vanished into the urban labyrinth.

Someone was shouting what sounded like a warning, and Ryan checked his stride, moving into the shelter of a demolished storefront. Broken glass crunched, brittle under his combat boots, and his hand fell to his pistol.

Directly across from him he saw a stout bald man appear and waddle a few steps into the open, moon face turning to the sky. He glimpsed Ryan standing in the shadows and called to him in a glutinous, slow voice. "Better run, outie! The birds is coming."

In Deathlands you didn't live long if you ignored that kind of shout.

Ryan flattened himself against the wall, his good eye scanning the slate sky above him. Others were shouting, and he heard a woman scream a child's name. He remembered a tiny hawk, no bigger than a woman's hand, that had once attacked them with demonic speed and venom. And a condor in the high Sierras with a wingspan that J.B. had sworn was better than fifty feet. The mutated inheritors of the rad-polluted earth had developed in all sorts of bizarre ways.

Now he could see them—white bodies with black-capped heads, wings about six feet across and daggered beaks the color of splintered amber.

Gulls. Four of them.

"Five," he amended as he spotted another bird swooping low over the buildings to the south.

They circled, almost as though they could sense him in the shadows. Then, to Ryan's concern, one of the birds dived toward him, wheeling away at the last moment as he waved his arms at it. In that moment he noticed that the bird didn't have the usual webbed feet of a fishing gull. It had great claws, bigger than those of a bald-headed eagle.

He distinctly heard the hiss of the claws as they razored through the air toward him, missing by less than a foot. The SIG-Sauer was out in his hand, but he realized almost immediately that it wasn't the best weapon to try to hold off a quintet of murderous, fast-moving hunting birds.

For a moment Ryan wished he had Mildred with

him. Her talent with the Czech target pistol was the finest he'd ever seen, and he guessed she could have picked off the circling creatures with five well-placed bullets. He was good, he knew, but he wasn't that good.

The blaster went back into its holster, and he reached for his steel panga.

"Fireblast!"

Two of them attacked him from opposite directions, angling away at the last second, as if they were trying to force him to break and run from the partial shelter of the ruined building.

He was buffeted by the powerful wing tip of the nearer gull, making him blink. A claw snagged at the white silk scarf around his throat, nearly plucking it away from him.

"You bastards are fucking dead," he whispered, though more to boost his own confidence.

He unwrapped the light, thin, strong scarf, holding it in the center, the weighted ends dangling loosely. With that in his right hand and the panga in his left, he balanced himself and waited.

It didn't take long.

Ryan hadn't figured on the birds being fightwise enough to all come at him in a multiple attack, wings flailing, harsh screeches bursting from their throats. His attempt to strike them down with the scarf was a total failure, and he made only a skipping, skating contact with the panga, nicking the smallest of the gulls and drawing a thread of blood.

An old-fashioned phrase of Doc's came to him, describing drawing blood in a fight. "Tapped his claret," he'd say.

One of the murderous birds had certainly tapped his claret.

He'd felt the claws scrape at his scalp as he lowered his head to try to protect his face from the attack. Now he could feel the warmth of his own blood as it trickled down the side of his face on his blind side.

While they gained altitude, squawking angrily, Ryan had a moment to look around to see if there was any better place to be. To run out into the open street would bring the birds down at him from all sides. At least they couldn't get behind him if he stayed with his back to the rough bricks.

This time the gulls chose to come at him one after another, pecking and clawing. But Ryan had recovered from the initial shock of the attack and was ready. He parried the first two, then made his own sudden counter. He swung one weighted end of the narrow white silk, grinning mirthlessly to himself as he felt it tangle and tighten around the bird's body. While the wings fluttered in a beating panic, he used the eighteen-inch blade in a short, slashing blow.

The head, with the blank eyes staring and beak still opening and closing, dropped to the glass-strewn ground. Blood jetted from its neck, and Ryan was conscious of the strong stench of rotting fish.

With a flick of the wrist he released the flapping

body, kicking it away from his feet. "Come on, you bastards," he said through bared teeth.

But the gulls had had enough. In the desolate wasteland of Newyork they could easily find alternative prey that wouldn't strike back with such lethal violence. Still shrieking, they circled once, then flew off toward the west and the river.

As Ryan moved on, the body of the dead bird still moved, in weakening, fluttering movements, the long flight feathers smeared and clotted with its own thick blood.

IT TOOK HIM ALL OF THE morning and the first part of the afternoon to locate the headquarters of the scalies. Ryan was never the sort of man to quickly admit defeat, but he was finally forced to retreat.

There were more scalies than he'd suspected, running into the hundreds, all wearing berets or headbands with the silver lightning flash to identify them as part of a uniquely efficient mutie force.

Every route he tried he found himself barred by the stomping boots of patrol. The main positive result of his extended recce was his learning that relatively few of the creatures seemed to be carrying any kind of blaster. Most had homemade knives and axes, while some hefted spears. Virtually all wore short wooden clubs at their hips.

As with all mutie communities, there were discrepancies in appearance. But this time there was a surprising consistency in the scalies. All were male, mostly between five foot four and five foot nine, though Ryan spotted a few that scraped six feet. All had long jaws and sunken nostrils, as well as the coarse, scaled skin that gave them their name.

They occupied a large part of the Mattan section of the ville. Ryan wasn't sure about street numbering, but it seemed that it ran from roughly West Twenty-third down south about nine or ten blocks, then westward from Ninth Avenue, clear to the ravaged dock area on the North River.

Some freak of blast-and-missile-attack patterns a hundred years ago had left some of the buildings standing, particularly the low warehouses close to the water. Windows and doors were gone, splintered and burned and melted by the nuke-heat, but walls and roofs were often secure.

The other main fact Ryan learned was that the scalies had opened up amazing communication routes through cellars and sewers.

One small group of half a dozen that he was shadowing disappeared into a doorway, and he heard their studded boots clattering down steps.

Moving with slow, infinite care, he closed in on the entrance. But before he'd reached it, the same patrol erupted from an enlarged manhole cover in the center of the highway, a hundred yards away.

They took him by surprise.

"Hey!"

The voice was deep and harsh, like a large saw hacking at a rusting iron.

"Fireblast!" Ryan spun on his heel and sprinted for his life.

At the nearest corner he glanced back over his shoulder, seeing the muties lumbering after him. One had some sort of long gun at his shoulder, and Ryan heard the flat crack as it was fired. But he had no idea where the bullet went.

It was easy to outdistance them, but the whole area was infested with the creatures.

A high, thin whistle sounded, which was answered by others behind him. He heard more to the right... and the left. And ahead.

When you were being hunted, one of the greatest dangers was to run blind. To run blind was to run into the hunters. Ryan flattened himself into the empty doorway of a long-gone store.

The original crosshatched pattern of roads that had intersected the ville was partly vanished. Where there had been great craters and tumbled buildings, alternative routes had been painstakingly cut around the obstacles, sometimes weaving through 180 degrees and making it difficult to maintain any sense of direction.

The whistles and shouts were all around him now. This was the scalies' turf, and there wasn't likely to be any hiding place for blocks around that they didn't know.

Move, Ryan urged himself.

To the right, some way off, he could see the original squad of muties still plodding steadily toward him. To the left, which was the direction he wanted to go, the main highway was clear.

He started off at a fast jog, his pistol in his hand. The whistles were growing louder and nearer, piercing. For a moment Ryan thought he caught the distant sound of a powerful wag's engine. But it vanished, if it had ever been there.

An alley opened on the far side of the street, and he sprinted for it. The walls were three stories high, barely five feet across. The ground was cobbled, uneven, slippery with the damp. A thin layer of phosphorescent green moss gleamed on the stones on both sides of the passage.

Ahead, Ryan could now see brighter light, signaling the end of the cut-through. He slowed down, looking behind him. The noise of pursuing boots was magnified by the alley.

"Stop there!" the voice came from one of several figures that suddenly appeared ahead, blocking the exit.

Ryan spun around.

Scalies waited at that end, as well.

"Oh, shit," he muttered.

Chapter Thirty

"Cacoëthes," Doc boomed.

"What?" Krysty asked.

"Cacoëthes," he repeated.

Mildred stood and stretched. "Yeah, we heard what you said. We don't know what the hell it means."

"Ah, yes, I was just allowing my mind to take a small wander on its own, down into the little rustic lanes of my memory."

"Dangerous paths to walk," Krysty replied. "Never know what you're going to meet, lurking around the next corner."

"Quite so, quite so. Hence, my use of the word. Cacoëthes. An aged poet taught me the word a year or so before the skies darkened. He said it meant an itch that you shouldn't scratch. A kind of bad habit."

"What made you think about that?" Mildred asked. "What bad habit were you remembering?"

The old man smiled in the basement's gloom. "There you have it, my dear. I fear I've completely forgotten what it was I'd remembered. Isn't that the way of the world?"

Behind them, lying bundled in layers of malodorous blankets, J.B. groaned, his head shaking from side to side.

"Had to tie his hands to his belt in the end," Mildred said. "While you and Doc were taking a look around the block, he was trying to tear his face open. The insect bite's driving him stark crazy."

"He worse?" Krysty asked.

Mildred took a long time answering. "I don't think John's going to make it. The coma's deepening, and I don't know what to do. The lump is enormous, and it kind of vibrates when I touch it. Like it's alive."

"Perhaps Ryan will return lathered and spurred, like the man who brought the good antibiotics from Ghent to Aix."

Krysty shook her head. "Truth is, Doc, half the time I just don't know what you're talking about."

J.B. cried out, making them all look toward him. It was close to a scream, sounding as though it had been torn from the depths of his soul. Mildred ran back and knelt down, peering at him. "Oh, sweet Jesus!" she breathed.

THE TRADER HAD BEEN big on logical advice. Even though it might differ from day to day.

"Get in a trap, and your best chance is to go back. Least you know what it's like where you've been."

Then again.

"Find yourself ambushed, and your best chance of

not buying the farm is to go forward like goose shit off a shovel. They won't be expecting that.''

Ryan's fighting brain didn't think about either option for more than a tiny splinter of time. His blaster had fifteen rounds of 9 mm, and one of his pockets held two more loaded mags.

He snapped off three shots, half turned, aiming at his pursuers. He didn't pause to see what happened, knowing that all three rounds must have found flesh and bone. The scalies had packed the end of the alley, making a miss impossible. The SIG-Sauer, with its built-in baffle silencer, only made a rather apologetic coughing sound.

Ryan had already decided he was going to follow the second bit of Trader's battle advice. The ones behind him knew who he was, but those in front of would only have heard shouts and whistles. They knew there was some major alarm, but wouldn't have any idea what to expect.

As he powered himself along the last few yards of the constricting alleyway, he squeezed the trigger five more times, seeing the press of bodies that blocked the light simply evaporate. There were screams and deep-chested roars of agony.

Ryan didn't hesitated or break step, bursting from the mouth of the passage, vaulting a pile of tumbled, bloodied bodies. A squat scalie was swinging a long-handled ax toward him, and he shot him through his gaping jaws.

"Nine," the one-eyed man muttered, keeping score from force of habit.

Now he had a heartbeat to look around and see where he was, weigh up the options and make his move.

The immediate bad news was that there were at least four more scalies, standing with a line of twenty or so chained norms. On the credit side was the open space beyond them, showing a wide stretch of clear street.

At his back was screaming chaos; in front, an unearthly, shocked silence. Once again Ryan thought he heard the distant sound of a wag, but he still couldn't be certain. And he had more pressing matters on his mind.

The scalie guards were absurdly slow to react, stunned by the appearance of the man who'd just blasted down so many of their colleagues. The chained humans were quicker.

"Don't chill us!" one shouted.

"Give in or they'll…" began a skinny man with a narrow, foxy face.

Ryan didn't wait to hear any more. The only chance of freedom lay in their direction.

"Over, under, around or through" had been the Trader's rule, meaning that there was always a way.

The only possibility was "through."

Two more bullets from the blaster took out the scalies guarding the left side of the line. Ryan ran at them, waving the SIG-Sauer, conscious of only having four rounds left in the mag.

The skinny man made a sudden, unexpected dive toward him, pulled up short by the chain around his throat. But Ryan's reflexes were too quick. He snapped off a shot, the bullet only creasing the side of the captive's pallid face as he was jerked backward.

He still went down, screaming, pulling everyone else with him.

Ryan tried to dodge, slipping on the wet, greasy stones, falling to one hand and one knee, barely keeping his balance and avoiding losing hold of the blaster.

"Fireblast!"

The man he'd wounded was thrashing like a gaffed eel, fingers grasping at Ryan's leg. The mark of the bullet stood out, livid, on his skin. The bloody graze, already surrounded by a swelling black bruise, where the kinetic energy of the 9 mm bullet brushing by had been momentarily absorbed by his flesh.

Ryan clubbed him across the temple with the butt of the SIG-Sauer, nearly two pounds of cold metal cracking the skull like a pin hammer.

There was the snap of a small-caliber pistol being fired. A woman with a birthmark across her right cheek cried out as the bullet struck her in the shoulder.

In the shambles it wasn't too difficult for Ryan to regain his feet and spring away, head back, arms pumping, feeling the breath tearing in his chest as he ran, knowing that speed was now his only hope.

Two more guns fired, and he heard one of the bullets hiss past him, only a yard or so wide. He hadn't figured on scalies being able to shoot with that much accuracy, and he began to jink and dodge.

A little dog, with stubby legs and a long, low-slung body, scampered out from a doorway, yapping at the top of its voice. Ryan cursed at it and it backed away, whining.

Now the whistling began again, echoing and bouncing off the miles of ruins around him, shrill blasts that seemed to be warning the whole ville that Ryan Cawdor was loose in the highways and should be hunted down and butchered in the gutter like rabid vermin.

Ryan needed to find his way out in a northerly direction, moving eastward, as well. But this street was blocked at the next intersection to his right, forcing him back toward the west and the river. And the heartland of the scalies.

A long mutie lurched from a covered manhole only fifty yards in front of the running man, trying to heave itself out into the open, struggling to draw a thin-bladed knife as it did.

Ryan swerved away, resisting the temptation to put a bullet through the seamed, reptilian head. Four rounds wouldn't take him far.

He rounded another corner of a devastated block, which offered him the easternly run he wanted.

Ahead of him the street was empty, with a crossroads looming, wide and clear.

Now he could hear the loud rumble of a gas-powered engine.

Scalies didn't drive wags, he thought to himself. Then again, they didn't form themselves into bastard armies with lightning badges on their black berets.

He slowed to a jog, looking behind him and wondering if he had time to change mags on the blaster. But the puff of powder smoke from an old rifle and the ricochet of the bullet near his feet convinced him to keep moving.

In the distance, from a side alley, he saw a dozen scalies appear, most of them armed with blasters.

The net was closing. And fast.

IN THE CELLAR J.B. seemed to have gone into a catatonic trance. His body was stiff and rigid, legs and arms like staves of beechwood, the muscles of his neck taut and quivering. His mouth was pulled back in a rictus of pain, like the grin of a corpse. His eyes were nearly shut, but they showed a narrow strip of white beneath the lids.

Krysty and Doc stood to one side, allowing the light from the fire to fall across their friends, taking care not to get in the way of Mildred as she knelt by J.B.'s side.

Her eyes were fixed on the place where the Armorer had been bitten. Her thin lips were shut tight, and she was breathing through her nose.

"No, Mildred," Krysty said, her voice reflecting the horror she felt.

"Only way."

Doc coughed. "I'll do it."

Mildred looked at him. "Bravest thing you ever said, Doc. I won't forget it. But it's down to me. I've *got* to do it."

ANOTHER SMALLER PATROL of the lizardlike muties had appeared on Ryan's right, shutting him off completely from the direction of safety. The only route still not closed was westerly, where they could herd him through the gray dockside to the edge of the river. And there they would take him.

The sound of the Klaxon was surprisingly loud, booming from the blind side of the next corner. With a screeching of brakes a wag appeared, heading for Ryan. It was less than sixty yards away, cutting him off from the large group of scalies.

At a quick glance it looked to Ryan like an armored recce wag, eight-wheeled. If it held scalies, then the heavy machine gun on the turret would quickly wipe him away.

As the wag came to a shuddering halt twenty paces in front of him, the turret began to swing. Now he saw that the blaster was a Bushmaster automatic cannon.

It stopped, pointing directly at him.

The entry port, just forward of the turret, began to open.

Chapter Thirty-One

Doc had put some thin, dry sticks on the fire, and they now burned with a bright golden flame, filling the basement with warmth and light.

Now they could all see the swelling on the side of J.B.'s face very clearly. Near the angle of the jaw, the lump extended down to his neck.

"They're hatching," the old man said, voice thickened with disgust.

The surface of J.B.'s skin was stretched so tightly that movement could almost be detected—the movement of the wriggling maggots, progeny of the eggs that had been laid in the moment of the mutie fly's sting. There were hundreds upon hundreds of them, coiling and twining as they fed on J.B.'s living flesh.

"Put that can of water in the fire to boil," Mildred directed.

In places the tiny, voracious worms had already begun to eat their way out, perforating the skin of the man's cheek, seething in their warm nest as they hatched.

"Now!"

RYAN BLINKED, unable to believe what he was seeing. Over the years he'd come across a number of books and magazines with all sorts of pix of the times before sky-dark. Any from December showed illustrations of the mythical figure called Santa Claus, sometimes called Father Christmas.

As the entry port opened, a face appeared, rising from the dark depths of the wag. The hair was white and wavy, curling around the ears. A full beard and mustache were also white as snow. The eyes under bushy white brows were bright blue. There wasn't much left to see of the rest of the visage, but the cheeks were rosy, as though the man had been sitting too close to a fire.

To add to the surreal apparition, he was also wearing a bright scarlet sweater with long sleeves.

Behind Ryan a rifle cracked, and the bullet pinged off the front of the wag, leaving a raw scrape of bright silver metal.

"Best be moving, outie."

Ryan didn't hesitate, vaulting up on the front of the black-painted vehicle. The jovial figure vanished, and he was able to slide into the port.

"Close the hatch, outie, or we'll be getting scalies in our laps."

The diesel engine roared, loud in the confines of the steel box. Ryan was aware that there were at least two other men inside, as well as White Beard. One was in the driver's seat, peering out through the ob-slit, wearing goggles. The other could be seen from the thighs down, standing, head and shoulders in the turret.

"Want me to roast 'em, Harry?" the disembodied voice asked.

"Like killing ants with molten silver," came the reply from behind Ryan.

"Back home?" the driver called.

"And don't spare the horsepower." Another bullet rapped smartly on the arma-plate, ringing like a bell.

"Sure you don't want a few rounds up their scalie asses?"

"Haste is waste, Lee. Let's go." He tapped Ryan on the shoulder. "Unless you have anywhere you particularly prefer, Mr....?"

"Cawdor. Ryan Cawdor. You're Harry...?"

"Stanton. People sometimes call me—"

"The King of the Underworld," Ryan completed. "Small ville, isn't it?"

KRYSTY WATCHED, impassive, managing to overcome her revulsion. In the far corner Doc was stooped over, vomiting noisily, unable to control his overwhelming nausea, trying to apologize in between bursts of puking.

Mildred ignored him, ignored everything except the task of trying to save J.B.

Using the point of one of the Armorer's knives, she managed to open up the swelling, lancing it so that the tiny maggots erupted out across his face and neck in a writhing, seething mass. Mildred scraped them away, trying to clear out the suppurating wound. The smell of decay seemed to expand until it filled the entire cellar.

Doc had just started to move toward them when he spun on his heel and retired to his corner again, gagging at the stench.

Krysty had to call on all of her inner power not to go with him.

Mildred continued to breathe fast and shallow through parted lips.

"Can't get them all. I need something like a spoon or a suction pump. Still some buried in the subcutaneous layers."

She straightened, and her eyes met those of Krysty. The redhead was shocked at the look on Mildred's face. "What?" she asked.

"Just realized. There's no compressed-air suction pump here in Deathlands."

"Course not."

"So I have to do it."

"Do what, Mildred? I don't get... Oh, Gaia! No, no, you can't."

"He'll die. Even if I do this, then he'll still probably not make it unless Ryan can come back with some sort of antibiotic."

Doc had straightened and was lifting the dented metal can of water off the fire, using a piece of old blanket. The liquid was bubbling and steaming.

"Ready, Mildred." Seeing what she was about to do, he knelt and placed the can on the floor, with the most painstaking care, before rushing to his corner for a third noisy time.

Mildred bent over, bringing her face closer and closer to the festering sore, with its lacy veil of minute worms.

Closer.

And began to suck it clean with her lips.

RYAN HAD WATCHED through the front passenger's ob-slit as the wag roared at full throttle into the gang of scalies, scattering them. There was the distinctive metallic thud as the wing clipped one of the muties, sending him spinning to the side.

"Nice driving, Sam," Harry praised. "He should be giving his blood at the local blood bank, not on the highway. And this is Broderick Crawford, saying, see you next week." He gave a great roar of laughter. "Bet you never heard of him, did you, Ryan?"

"No."

"Old actor on the vids. Prog called *Highway Patrol.* Had a kind of homily each time. I got a whole run back home. Could show you."

The eight-wheeler skidded sideways on a sharp corner, lifting slightly on one side. Ryan grabbed at a sissy bar in front of him to keep steady.

Harry laughed again. "Take it easy there, Sam. Remember that a clown at the circus is real funny but on the highway he's a killer."

"Where d'you get the diesel for this recce wag?" Ryan shouted.

"Know what it is?"

It was a clever way of avoiding answering the question.

"Think so. Friend of mine would know better. Think it's an LAV. Twenty-five or -six. Got a six-cylinder engine. Close to three hundred horsepower. Does about sixty miles an hour on smooth pavement, and it'll go in water. How's that?"

Once again Stanton replied with a question. "This friend who knows even more than you about weaponry. Name wouldn't be Dix, would it?"

Ryan played him at his own game. "How you hear of J. B. Dix?"

"I know you, Ryan. Remember your face. Remember what a cold-eyed bitching bastard you were. Even as a young kid."

"I don't remember you."

"Only a few weeks after you joined up with the Trader. You were too busy keeping the cheeks of your ass pressed together and walking tough. Me and the Trader went way back. And I knew Marsh Folsom. Him and the Trader found them war wags up in the Apps, you know?"

"I know it."

"Well, it'll take us a while before we're snug in the fortress. Tell me about what you're doing."

"Long story. It'll take time."

Again the merry laughter. "Something we got plenty of."

MILDRED KEPT SPITTING. At first the clumps of frothy saliva contained a number of wriggling maggots. Then, gradually, it became clearer.

Krysty had wiped up most of the newly hatched insects, using a corner of rag, then throwing it into the fire, where it hissed and bubbled among the flames.

"Wound looks clean," Doc said, his face as pale as old parchment.

Mildred straightened. "Get a branch and bring it here. One that's burning brightly."

The old man did as he was told. Mildred also told Krysty to get the can of boiling water ready for use.

"This has to be done. Only way to clean it. Then his system has a chance if Ryan can…" She gave a sudden, gasping breath and swayed, as though she were about to faint.

"Mildred! Are you okay?"

"Fine. I'm fucking well fine, thanks. Look, he'll probably struggle. We got him tied and he's weak. But he'll still struggle. Doc, kneel astride his legs and get ready to hang on. Krysty, you'll have to lie on his chest and then try to hold his arms through the coverings."

"What are you going to do?" Doc looked at the flaming piece of wood in his hand and at the tin can of bubbling water. "Oh, I see."

"It'll leave him with a scar, just on the angle of the jaw. Still, it shouldn't be too easy to see. I hope."

Krysty touched her gently on the arm. "Mildred,

if he lives, I can't see J.B. losing sleep over a small scar. Can you?''

"Guess not. You both ready?"

Doc was sitting astride the unconscious man's legs, pressing down with all his weight. Krysty had braced herself, gripping J.B.'s arms.

Mildred was on the floor, trying to position herself in a way to keep the Armorer's head between her thighs.

Doc suddenly gave a short, cackling laugh. "Sorry. Just thinking that if he wasn't out cold, then our dear friend would probably be taking some pleasure in lying like that, Mildred.''

"Doc," the woman said.

"What?"

"Button that mouth, will you? And give me the burning piece of wood. Krysty, the water as soon as I call for it. Ready?''

Chapter Thirty-Two

Dean had been fast asleep, dreaming of riding on the back of his mother's two-wheeler wag. The big Harley powered over the undulating highway, dust drifting beneath the tires. On either side were a succession of stark red mesas and buttes, sculpted by wind, sun and frost. His mother, Rona, had known the colorful names of them all, telling which was called Owl Mesa and which Mexican Hat Butte.

The boy's sleeping memories carried him on an endless quest, his arms around the woman's waist, face pressed to her back, the scent of sweat and denim mingling in his nostrils with the bitter spice of sagebrush. The roaring of the engine filled his head, the vibration surging through his wiry body.

Now and again he would turn his head to left or right and see the little hogans of the Navaho, hear the hollow sound as they crossed high bridges over silent rapids.

Ever onward.

He never knew how Rona always seemed to manage to find gas for them, but in his dreams they would stop at ramshackle trading posts where smiling men would climb the stairs with his mother. He would sit silently at a corner table until she returned.

And they moved on, the highway unrolling in front of them, the powerful bike hugging the thin white center line.

It was a dream that came back to the ten-year-old again and again. His mother was always smiling and well before the illness settled on her shoulders and began to draw the life from her.

The reality that had reduced her to a trembling skull never intruded.

In the dream the motorcycle seemed to steer itself while Rona sang to him, old songs about shady rivers and brave, roving men. And there was the dark figure of his father, a tall, impossibly handsome and courageous man who wore a black patch over his wounded eye.

One day the boy knew his father would come from around an unexpected corner, and they would live and laugh together forever.

The hand across his mouth jerked him from the sunny, idyllic past into the cold, dark, frightening present.

"Quiet," came a croaking voice close to his ear. The breath in his face stank of rotten fish.

Dean didn't struggle. The mutie holding him felt immensely strong, and he knew from experience how short-fused their tempers could be. He lay quite still and waited.

"Good boy." The hand lifted.

Dean could taste the salt warmth of blood where his lips had been crushed against his sharp front teeth. "What do you want?"

"Quiet! Don't want captain to hear. Poke in black places after me. I be away from him."

Dean sat up, unable to see much in the gloom beyond the broad shoulders of the scalie. The white flash on the beret stood out brightly.

"What do you want?" he asked.

One of the clawed hands touched him on the knee, and the boy's breath froze in his lungs. Rona had warned him about men who would want to do things to him. Awful, hurtful things. And, even at ten, Dean had seen and heard enough to know precisely what his mother had meant.

"You be good to I, and I good to you. Help you in soft work and big food."

The fingers gripped him, making him gasp.

He could just see that food was being served down in the center of the vast, damp concrete cavern and smell the fish-based stew.

"Time to eat," he said, conscious of how small and weak his voice sounded.

"I be saying when time eat. You be good and I be good to you. Know what I say?"

"Yes. I know."

And he didn't even have the slim-bladed dagger with the turquoise hilt. At least he might have opened the scalie's throat and then tried to sneak into another part of the complex.

The scalie let go of him and shuffled upright, looming over the little boy like a reptilian monolith. One hand leaned against the wall while the other fumbled with the cord that laced up the front of its trousers.

"Be careful. Or—"

"I will. I'd like to do it for you, but there's a sort of difficulty."

The hand paused, already reaching inside the gaping slit. "What difficulty?"

The boy managed a tremulous smile, trying to show the right mixture of eagerness and fearful apprehension.

"Can't stop biting." He clacked his teeth sharply together as he spoke.

"Biting?"

"Yeah."

"Biting what?" The long snout quested toward him, breathing suspicion.

Dean was used to lying. Rona had taught him from his earliest memory that you lied to everyone except your closest and most trusted friends. You only lied to them when it suited you.

"Sorry, Captain," he whispered. "Might bite you by mistake and hurt you. I wouldn't want to do that to you."

The scalie finally got the message, straightening up with a long hiss of anger, its fingers fastening its pants again. "I be angry."

"I said I was sorry, Captain."

"I be angry. You bite me?"

Dean shook his head. "No. No, of course not, Captain. That's the point. I don't *want* to bite you, but I might if you made me—"

The scalie swung a cuffing, round-arm blow at the dark, curly head, feeling a satisfying jar as the slap connected. "I be eating, and you not be eating this day," it said as it stalked clumsily off.

Dean was knocked semiconscious by the blow, but he'd seen it coming and had managed to ride the worst of the impact. Going without food was no great hardship. A slip of a lad like him could always duck and dive and creepy-crawl through the shadows and scavenge something to keep belly and backbone apart.

He rubbed his head and lay down again. Sleep returned to him, unbidden. This time it wasn't the sunny dreams of happy times with his mother. Now he was in a ville somewhere among the red and gold trees of the northeast in a spooky house known locally as the old Jackson place. A part of his mind knew he'd responded to the challenge of the local slow-witted, brute-eyed louts and spent a night alone in the creaking frame house. He saw nothing worse than a large, vicious bat.

The dream was different.

Now there were doors in the house and shutters over unbroken windows. Upstairs he heard something walking, walking alone as it had since the dawn of time.

His feet dragged up a wide, candlelit staircase, through quiet dust. Above him the sound had stopped.

Dean lifted his head unwilling to see a man standing at the head of the stairs, reaching out a hand. The face wore a glittering and cold smile, and one eye was covered by a black leather patch.

In the headquarters of the scalie hordes the boy's lips moved, but nobody was close enough to hear him.

"Daddy," he called. "Oh, Daddy."

Chapter Thirty-Three

Doc swallowed hard. He could still taste the bitterness of bile, the result of his earlier vomiting, and the cellar, with the door tugged shut, now reeked of scorched flesh.

Mildred thrust the burning branch against J.B.'s cheek, grinding it deep into the open sore. The Armorer briefly recovered a sort of consciousness. His mouth stretched open in a high, strangled scream of pain, and it took all of their combined strength to hold him still while he kicked and thrashed.

As Mildred took the smoking length of wood away, wiping with her fingers at the smoldering shreds of blackened skin, J.B. fell back into a coma. He didn't stir even slightly as she poured the boiling water into the wound, carefully rubbing with the cleanest bit of rag she could find to remove every possible trace of the insect's eggs.

When Mildred finished, Krysty brought over a large branch, holding it above the unconscious man so that Mildred could examine her work.

The wound looked surprisingly healthy, pink around the edges, brimming with fresh, clean blood at its center. At its widest it was nearly two inches across, roughly circular. It was below the left ear, close to the angle of the jaw.

"He'll have a sizable scar," Doc observed.

Mildred wiped sweat from her forehead, sighing. "Like Krysty told us, Doc. If he does pull through on this, then he's not going to worry much about a bitsy scar, is he?"

"You think he'll make it, Mildred?" Krysty asked. "You got the poison out of him."

"No, I got those creatures out of the hole. It was like a maggot eatery in there. The infection's gone into his blood, deep into his body. Without some sort of drugs he's had it."

RYAN STARTED TO READ the list of drugs from the folded piece of paper, stumbling over the pronunciation of the long chemical names.

"They're all antibiotics. Penicillin, I know about. Tetracyclines, cep...cephalexin, eryth...romycin. Fireblast! Can't read her writing. Strept..."

"Streptomycin," Harry said, reaching out for the list. "Colistin." He nodded. "Which ones do you want?"

Ryan opened his mouth, then closed it again. "Which ones do...? How many you got?"

"All these and plenty more. From what you say about J. B. Dix, I figure the tetracyclines might be best for you. What did the doctor woman say?"

"Yeah. Mildred said they were first choice."

"I'll give this to Labman. He's in charge of that section of stuff."

"How much will it cost?"

Stanton raised a red-sleeved arm, his mouth thinning under the luxuriant beard and mustache. "Not a question I want to hear from someone who rode with Trader. Understand?"

"Sure. And thanks."

"While you're here I'll show you around some more. Probably need some ammo. I got most kinds."

"Could use some .36 rounds for a cap-and-ball pistol."

Stanton slapped his ample thigh and roared with laughter. "Same old Ryan! You think I'll say we don't have any. Well, fuck you, buddy boy. We got a box filled with them. What else? Some more 9 mm for that very nice SIG-Sauer?"

"Yeah. You haven't got any 4.7 mm caseless, do you?"

Stanton rubbed his chin. "Like the guy goes in the restaurant that promises any food on earth. Asks for the foreskin of an elephant on toast. Waiter comes back and tells him he's real sorry, but they've run out of bread." A bellow of laughter made his stomach shake. "You get it, Ryan?"

"I get it. You got the caseless rounds?"

"What the hell kind of blaster's that? Automatic rifle?"

"Heckler & Koch G-12. Lovely piece of hardware, but ammo's not easy in Deathlands."

Harry rubbed his chin. "See what we got. Let's go look around my little place."

THE "LITTLE PLACE" WAS the most amazing complex Ryan had ever seen and contained the most staggering collection of prenuke artifacts he could ever have imagined.

Afterward he tried to remember a fraction of what he'd seen, but found that it all blurred, one room into another.

He wasn't even quite sure precisely where the King of the Underworld actually had his empire. He guessed that it lay beneath one of the nuked areas, perhaps where the tallest of the skyscrapers had been, where miles of underground passages and storerooms linked up. Stanton had cut and tunneled, enlarging his territory, and brought in armed men to cover the many hidden entrances and exits. He attracted those, like Labman, with areas of strange or arcane knowledge.

He admitted to Ryan's questioning that he didn't actually know the limits of his turf.

"But how d'you start to get this much power and trade for all...all this?"

Another laugh. "Garbage bags, my friend."

"You what?"

Stanton reached and topped up his crystal goblet from the decanter of Armagnac at his elbow, offering it to Ryan, who shook his head.

"Black, strong, large bags of plastic, refuse for the disposal of."

"You started by trading those?"

"Not many things, apart from good blasters, worth more in old Newyork. About eight years ago I was digging on the upper east side a couple of blocks in from the big river."

Ryan wiped the remnants of his meal—smoked fish in a cream sauce, with sliced, fried potatoes and canned vegetables—from the decorated plate, using a crust of fresh white bread.

Harry continued. "Broke through into a warehouse. Used the hookups to see what was there. Looked fucking boring, I tell you that, Ryan. Shelf after shelf with pallet after pallet of what looked like paper. Not a lot of use. Got my toothpick out and sliced open the nearest container, and there it was."

"A garbage bag," Ryan said.

"Not just *a* garbage bag. One thousand of the little black beauties."

"Thousand won't go far in this ville."

"Right. What an intellect! The thousand were in one pack. Each pallet held five. Each shelf held five pallets. Each row held 250 shelves. And the whole building had twenty rows."

Ryan had been trying to do his sums on the move, but the quantities eventually defeated him. "That must be—"

"A shit load of bags!" Harry exclaimed triumphantly. "Want to know just how many?"

"Yeah."

"Call it 125 million, give or take a few million torn or missing."

Ryan whistled. "How many you got left now?"

Stanton scratched his chin. "Good question. Have to ask my accountants, but I figure there must still be around half left."

Anywhere in Deathlands, strong, large plastic bags were like a handful of good jolt. You could wear them, shelter in them or under them and carry your life around in them.

"And from that..." He gestured around the room they were eating in, with its strip lighting and thick carpet; the good-quality furniture and the row of video machines and music players; the paintings and the piano in the corner, its perfection marred only by a long gouge across the polished top.

Harry stood, spilling crumbs from his lap. A small dog, looking like a rat in a hairy body wig, scampered from the corner and started licking them up. The man ignored the animal. "Let's go look," he suggested.

And it was the fragments of this tour that Ryan kept struggling to remember.

One thing that struck him early on was that there were no women at all anywhere within the underground empire. The men all seemed to be between eighteen and thirty, with a few of the group leaders closer to forty.

"Women?" the jovial figure replied when Ryan

finally asked him. "Get in the way. *Cherchez la femme* when trouble beckons. Look for the woman, Ryan. No. Not necessary here."

The complex was maintained at a steady sixty-two degrees with air-conditioning ready for the scorching heat of summer. Ryan noticed a large dome of armored glass above one of the linking corridors.

"What's that for?"

"Opens up for some real sunlight. See the flowers all around us?" There were banks of waxen lilies, filling the air with their heavy, funereal scent. "Sun brings out the lilies."

"Sun also brings out the snakes," Ryan replied.

"Best collection of old vids in all Deathlands," the Santalike figure boasted as they strode through a large, high-ceiling room. The walls were lined with shelves, jammed with the cases of thousands of vids.

"How many?"

"Around twenty thou."

"Watched them all?"

Harry Stanton turned to look at Ryan. "Never met anyone with more questions." He paused. "Sure I have. Most are movies, but there's a lot of eighties and nineties teevee. You name it and I got it."

"I once saw part of a vid about a little guy looking for his wife and his brother taking care of him. Never knew what it was called."

Harry looked around the walls. "Could find Vidman and ask him. Got a memory like a triple-comp. Only he's got some sort of flu."

Ryan glanced at his wrist chron. "Look, I ought to be collecting these drugs and getting on back to the others."

"Sure, but just let me show you a little more."

"J.B. needs those drugs."

Harry turned to face him, and the merry little eyes turned into chips of frozen obsidian. "I might not be in the giving vein, Ryan. Just humor me some."

They entered a room that held nothing but dolls, one shelfful with soft, pudgy faces, all of them different, looking to Ryan like the victims of some terrible disease. Another row, at the back, under a failed light, appeared to hold dark green turtle dolls. That idea was so ridiculous that Ryan never even bothered to ask Harry about it.

A long, vaulted chamber held wags, but these were real old, all gleaming chrome and huge, brightly painted bodies. Harry ran his finger along each one, swelling with the pride of ownership. "This is the SS Jaguar and this is a Bugatti. Ferrari and a Corvette. Chevy and a green label Bentley. Pretty, aren't they?"

"You ever drive them?"

"The questions, Ryan. Beginning to get on my nerves some."

There were rooms of clocks and books, jukeboxes and pinball machines; walls with swords and bayonets in serried ranks; pewter mugs and cut-glass vases; trays of gold and silver rings. "Human eye one comes from London originally. Great Frog jewelers. Lovely, isn't it?"

A bookcase ran for fifty feet along a wall and scraped at the ceiling, filled with carefully categorized comics. "Best run of Conan the Barbarian in Deathlands," Harry crowed. And there were necklaces, model ships, embroidered samplers, some with dates back in the 1700s.

One room had its walls covered in black velvet and decorated with whips and handcuffs, and boots with wicked spurs and six-inch spike heels. Mags and some special vids that Harry flicked his hand at. "Porn. Not to my taste. But it's there to be collected."

"Blasters?" Ryan asked.

"Not here. Sec section. Sorry, Ryan. Not even for you."

"Drugs?"

The smile was back. "Sure. In the giving vein again. Should be ready by now. And then you can have a free ride home in the wag."

IT WAS FULL DARK. Krysty was standing at the top of the flight of cold steps. The weather had changed yet again, becoming far colder. The clouds had lifted and been whirled off to the south by a freshening wind, leaving the black dome covered in a myriad sparkling stars.

She held Ryan's G-12 caseless. Her heart told her it wasn't possible that J.B. should be in serious danger of leaving them. Someone like the Armorer had been around so long that the idea of his falling under the scythe seemed to be ridiculous. But her mind and her highly developed mutie sensitivity told her differently.

The stillness that enveloped J.B. in its muffling darkness brought its own story.

She had knelt by his side, reaching for his hand, finding no response at all to her touch. It was like holding warm, dead meat. The vibrant electricity that normally surged through the Armorer was completely lacking.

The ville was quiet. Cooking fires brought smoke ghosting from the north and east of where they were hiding. She felt a few drifting flakes of snow feathering against the skin of her face, holding the promise of more bad weather to come.

Footfalls on the steps made her turn, and she saw the silver-haired figure of Doc climbing wearily toward her. "Good evening, my dear Krysty. Distinctly more chilly, is it not?"

"Hi, Doc. Yeah, getting cold."

"No sign of Ryan?" He shook his head. "Not one of my more intelligent questions. If he'd been back, I suspect you might have informed us. He said he hoped to be back by dusk."

"The key word there is *hoped*, Doc. He's after his boy and also something to save J.B.'s life. Sort of busy day."

"How do you feel about this sudden appearance

of his son? What we used to call 'a bit of a turnup for the book,' back in my day.''

Krysty rested her forearms on the pile of rubble, staring out across the vast wilderness of Newyork. ''I don't know. That's the truth, Doc. I don't know what I feel. I suppose that if a woman had turned up with an armful of children and said she was his wife…might be different. A kid of ten, Doc. You saw the pic of him. Got to be Ryan's son. No, I just don't know. Have to wait and see.''

''Ryan would never do anything that might hurt you, Krysty.''

''I know that, Doc.''

While they'd been talking she'd been idly pricking with her nail at something lodged in the brickwork. It finally came loose, and she peered at it, realizing she was holding a part of a woman's earring. Krysty wondered what had happened to the owner of the slender piece of metal that had been driven into raw stone by the awesome power of the nukings.

''What's that?''

''What, Doc?''

''Thought for a moment that my tired old ears had caught the faintest susurration of mechanized transport far off.''

''A wag?''

''Yes. Can you not…?''

Now she heard the sound, a low rumbling, like a fairly large wag moving in low gear, moving toward them.

"Yes. Could be."

"Shall I tell Mildred?"

"No. Get J.B.'s blaster and come up here, Doc. Might be Ryan. Might not be."

It was Ryan.

Chapter Thirty-Four

There were so many questions after the wag had rumbled away into the freezing night.

The underground monarch hadn't just given Ryan drugs. There was a parcel, neatly wrapped and itemized, of ammunition, including both the rare caseless rounds and the antique .36s for Doc's Le Mat.

A whole rucksack was filled with food, mostly canned meat and vegetables, as well as some dried fish, and a supply of Eau-clenz tablets, which claimed to make any kind of water safely drinkable. A small shrink-wrapped box of self-lights promised to get even the dampest of wood burning brightly.

But it was the drugs that brought Mildred running from the side of the unconscious man. She took the package, which was wrapped tightly in the neatly cut remnants of a black plastic garbage bag, and tore it open, looking down into her cupped hands as though she'd just encountered the Holy Grail.

"Fucking-A!" she whispered.

It was a bubblepack, stamped and coded, of twelve miniature syringes, each containing a measured dose of the antibiotic. Mildred read quickly though the instructions, lips moving, totally ignoring the waiting trio of friends.

Krysty broke the silence. "Well?"

Mildred nodded slowly, her face breaking into a smile. "Pardon the aptness of the expression, but this is just what the doctor ordered."

THE NIGHT PASSED. Ryan took turns on watch with Doc and Krysty, allowing Mildred to spend all her time by the side of her patient. A cold front had come south over the state, slicing down from Canada, dropping the temperature to something like forty below.

The only good thing about the lethal chill was that it kept everything out of sight and under cover. It was only necessary to slide the door open and peer out every once in a while, waving away the frosty plume of your own breath to see what was happening. The streets were utterly deserted. Once the wind blew an old can past, and it rattled and echoed with a strange, sharp intensity.

During the time, Ryan told his companions something about Harry Stanton and the rambling palace of the underworld king.

Mildred was only listening with half her attention. The instructions had said to give the injections every six to eight hours. She'd given J.B. two at once and then a third two hours later. His breathing seemed slower and easier, and his temperature had fallen a little.

But, as she said, there was still a bitterly long row to hoe.

Doc was the most interested in the story of the endless rooms of prenuke memorabilia. But all of his questions passed Ryan by. He wanted to know about certain books or movies or songs.

"Sorry, Doc," Ryan replied, shaking his head. "If you want to go there after this is all down and done and see for yourself, I guess Harry is the sort of guy who'd be delighted to see you."

"You trust him, lover?" Krysty asked.

"You know about me and trust."

"Sure, but as far as it goes? Will he give us up to the scalies?"

Ryan rubbed his hands together, trying to massage some warmth into his fingers. "Don't know, Krysty. I asked him about how he survived, living quite close to the edge of the muties' turf."

"And?"

"Said he believed in living and letting live. Long as they didn't step on his toes, he tried not to step on theirs. But I think the fact that he knew Trader and even knew me years ago gives me an extra card in the game."

"The wag," Krysty said.

"What about it."

"Think he might sort of lend it to us to go after the boy?"

"Stanton's got the biggest collection of wags I ever seen."

"Saw," Krysty corrected.

"I ever saw. But I can't imagine him being so filled with kindness that he'd lend us something like the recce wag I came in."

"Be good against the scalies."

Ryan nodded again. "Yeah. But he did give us a map, showing as much as he knows about the layout of their headquarters. It's right up against the river on the west side. He reckons there could be as many as five hundred of the bastards there."

"Take some doing."

"I know that, lover."

"When do we make our move to rescue Childe Harold from that dark tower?"

"Dean. Not Harold, Doc. The kid's name is Dean."

The old man half smiled. "It was a literary allusion, my dear friend. But let is pass."

"Sure. Depends on J.B.'s health. If he stays the same, I'll go day after tomorrow. If he starts recovering, we could maybe even try tomorrow night. If he…doesn't make it, we'll go as soon as feels right. Can't wait too long. Not with the boy in the hands of the scalies."

"TIME IS IT?" Ryan asked.

"About an hour off dawn," Krysty replied.

"Doc on watch?"

"Yeah. If it gets any colder, he reckons his breath'll freeze right in his mouth."

Ryan laughed quietly. "Might be the only way known in the universe to teach Dr. Theophilus Tanner to keep his mouth shut."

Krysty wriggled under the pile of stinking covers, alongside him. "Mildred says J.B. is holding his own against the infection. She's given him another injection, and she'll try another at first light."

"What a shitting stupid way to go and buy the farm. Bitten by an insect! I reckon J.B. must have had better than a dozen serious blaster and blade wounds. An insect!"

"Not quite as cold under here," she whispered. "You got all your clothes on?"

"Sure."

"Want to try getting out of some of them, lover?"

"Won't be my breath that gets frozen if I do, Krysty."

"Maybe find somewhere hot to put it."

"You gaudy slut."

Krysty giggled, fumbling at the buttons at the front of his trousers. "That's me. Any act, no matter how disgusting, for a handful of jack or a fistful of creds. You name it and I'll do it."

Ryan was kissing her, and he whispered something in her ear, making her laugh out loud. "You filthy bastard perve, Ryan Cawdor."

"You said anything."

"I didn't mean *that* anything. Anyway, we don't have either the honey or the blindfold."

"Or the deaf-mutie with the hand bells."

Krysty was kissing him in tiny, fragile little pecks, all across the side of his face and neck while her fingers reached their destination. He was uncomfortable on his side, trying to find a way into her tighter pants.

"No hand bells?" she said. "Gaia! What a shame. Have to just do it in the boring, old-fashioned way. Never mind."

"Don't mind at all."

Chapter Thirty-Five

The food Harry Stanton had given them made a wonderful change from the strips of dried dog meat and the dubious fish. The four companions sat together around the warm ashes of the fire, huddled against the cold, finishing the meal.

"Any chance of more like this to eat?" Mildred asked.

"Harry told me he'd send his recce wag over to us sometime tomorrow evening. More of the drugs and some more food."

"Why did he not give you a little more of each yesterday and forgo the necessity for a further trip this way?"

"I wondered. Think it's partly the link with Trader. Harry's older than us, and I guess he feels a kind of responsibility toward me."

"Mebbe you're the son he never had," Krysty murmured just loud enough for Ryan to hear. To hear and to understand.

RYAN CONSIDERED GOING on a solo patrol again to try to check out some of the details on the map Harry Stanton had given to him. But he knew now that the network of streets for several blocks around the scalies' base was heavily guarded. From the sketch plan, it looked as if the only way in was from the direction of the river.

The issue that should have been occupying most of his mind was the health of his oldest and closest friend. Yet somehow that wasn't the way it was. It was the faded picture of the solemn-faced little boy with the tight black curls that kept swimming unbidden into the front of his mind.

But the Armorer was already showing encouraging signs of fighting back against the lethal infection. The hectic flush had faded, restoring his complexion to its normal sallow pallor. He seemed to be sleeping quietly, and the gaping wound at the side of his face looked to be healing.

Mildred was delighted. "It's one of the weirdest things about Deathlands," she said.

"What is that, ma'am?" Doc asked.

"Everyone is surprisingly healthy, considering the deadly quality of life. But when someone like John gets an out-of-the-ordinary sickness, there's no resistance to it."

"Forgive me, Mildred, but I think you have already made us fully aware of that."

Slowly, and with an infinite delicacy, Mildred gave him the finger. "I haven't finished, you doddering old cretin."

He bowed to her. "Then I yield the floor to you

for your further elaboration of this most puzzling enigma.''

"It works both ways. Two-edged sword. Just as John went under fast to the bite, so he's responding far faster than usual to the healing power of the antibiotics.''

Ryan stood and stretched. "So you think he's going to make it through?''

Mildred rubbed at her lips, removing a particle of stewed meat. "If I was into gambling, which I'm not, I'd say he was facing a seventy percent chance of recovery. This time yesterday I wouldn't have put it any higher than ten percent.''

By midday she was ready to go up to ninety percent.

The door was pulled three-quarters of the way open, filling the dismal basement with fresh, cold sunshine. Ryan and Doc had gone out an hour earlier on a brief expedition to try to scavenge some more wood for the fire. Twice in only a couple of blocks they heard distant whistles, indicating that the scalies were ranging in their direction. And once Ryan spotted a ragged figure spying on them from an empty second-floor window.

MILDRED CELEBRATED J.B.'s easing back toward health by insisting on cleaning up the cellar. Everything that wasn't nailed down got moved. The piles of rags and blankets were all swept up and kicked to one side, eventually placed in a tumbled mound in the farthest corner of the basement.

"Can't stand housecleaning."

Everyone stopped what they were doing and turned to face the speaker. J.B. was still lying on the floor, but he was propped on one elbow, looking at the subsiding pillar of dust that contained Mildred Wyeth.

"John!" she exclaimed.

"Hi. Been sleeping. My cheek hurts." He raised a hand to touch the cicatrix on his face.

"Don't, John!"

Her shout made everyone jump.

His fingers stopped inches short of the wound. "I remember being bitten and feeling like a scalie had pulled most of my brain out of my skull. What happened next?"

It took some time to bring him up to date with all the happenings of the past few hours.

THERE WAS A FLURRY OF SNOW about three-thirty in the afternoon, which lay in a thin, powdery coverlet over the city's naked ruins.

J.B. sat in a corner of the underground room, propped up by old blankets, sipping at a can of hot stew, courtesy of Harry Stanton. The Armorer had said that he had a vague recollection of meeting him long years ago, but the description of the stout figure with white hair and mustache didn't ring any memory bells.

Krysty was sitting on the top of the flight of steps, only her head sticking out into the open, keeping watch for any danger.

Mildred was helping J.B. to eat, and Doc was fast asleep, lying on his back and gripping his silver-topped cane, like a Crusader on his tomb holding his sword. The old man's mouth sagged open, and he was snoring noisily.

Ryan had decided to fieldstrip his weapons and had just begun with his pistol.

"Company coming," Krysty called.

"Scalies?"

"No."

Luckily the SIG-Sauer wasn't disassembled, and he quickly ran to join her. Behind him J.B. was shouting for his own blaster and Mildred was trying to find her own ZKR 551 target pistol.

Doc was still fast asleep.

Ryan's immediate assessment was that the new arrivals were one of the juvenile street gangs, such as the Hawks, that Dred had run with.

There were about fifteen, wearing nondescript fur-and-skin jackets and pants. All had on fur caps with a bright yellow splash of paint on the side. Most of them carried little homemade zip guns, but two of them had rebuilt carbines. There were three young women in the group.

When they saw Ryan and Krysty, the gang stopped, spreading into a skirmishing semicircle. The leader was tall and skinny, and he had an extremely long blond mustache, the ends dangling beyond his chin.

"You outies?" he shouted.

Ryan didn't reply, glancing behind him at Mildred. "Wake Doc up and tell him to get his ass up here."

"Seen any scalies here?"

Ryan ignored the second question, as well, watching to see how the teenagers at the end of the line were still moving around, trying to enfold them, like the curving horns of a buffalo.

"You stop or you get chilled," he shouted, waving the automatic where they could all see it.

The tall leader hesitated for a moment, then called out an order in a staccato series of yelps that Ryan guessed were some sort of battle code. Everyone stopped where they stood.

"Asked if you'd seen scalies here. They been moving north and east out of their turf, taking our friends for their fucking slaves."

"Seen them near the river," Ryan replied.

"You got many friends there?"

"Enough."

The reply brought general laughter. The boy with the long mustache tried again. "We don't think there's many of you. Maybe only about three or four. And those fine blasters."

"Move on, kid," Ryan shouted.

"We aren't kids, outie! You fucking wrinklies come into our ville and make like you own the place! Well, you got a lesson coming."

"Be a lot of blood spilled," Ryan warned.

The gang was uneasy, shifting feet in the icy snow, breath frosting around them. The nearest was about fifty yards off, and there was plenty of cover for them. Ryan wasn't altogether happy about being held with one narrow entrance to defend. Only two of them could stand there, and if the gang rushed the cellar, then it could be either side who'd win.

"Going down for the caseless," he whispered to Krysty. "Keep 'em talking."

He dived into the basement, allowing Mildred to replace him at the top. J.B. was against the wall, as pale as fresh-fallen snow, gripping his blaster in both hands. Doc was on his feet, looking around for his Le Mat.

"Where in thunderation...? We under attack from hostiles, Ryan?"

"Could be. You haven't lost your blaster, have you?"

"Got to be here someplace, dear boy. Just a matter of laying my hand on... Ah, I have it." He flourished the huge revolver. "Now, damn the torpedoes, I'm ready for them."

"Street gang, did you say?" J.B. said. "Can you hold them?"

"Hope so. About fifteen or so of them. Low-cal blasters. But it's difficult to defend that flight of stairs."

"Want me up there?"

Krysty's voice interrupted the conversation. "Looks like they're going to try it, lover."

"Be there," he called back. Turning to J.B., he said, "Stay here. Best place. Hit any get past us."

"Ryan!" Krysty cried.

"Yeah. Just getting the G-12. Oh, fireblast!"

There was no sign of his precious blaster. The Heckler & Koch G-12 assault rifle had vanished. It had been tucked under the pile of rags he'd been using as a makeshift pillow, before Mildred started...

"Tidying up," he said aloud.

The sound of gunfire prompted him into a whirlwind of controlled violence. The weapon had to be in the cellar. Nothing had been thrown out in the maelstrom of dust and dirt that Mildred had whipped up, so it was underneath the mound of stuff in the corner, beyond J.B.

"Ryan!" Doc yelled in his rich, booming voice.

"Hold them!" The one-eyed man choked and coughed as he delved into the stinking rags, furs and torn lengths of filthy cloth. It was impossible to see, and he worked by feel.

There was more shooting behind him, and he could pick out the distinctive boom of Mildred's .38-caliber revolver and Krysty's lighter 9 mm Heckler & Koch P7A-13. Overlaying them he could hear a barrage of fire from the array of .32s and small handguns outside.

"Got it," the one-eyed man snarled, his fingers

closing on the familiar rectangular shape of the automatic rifle.

He turned, blinked through the haze of roiling dirt and saw that Doc was close to him. Mildred was at the bottom of the stairs, trying to reload on the move. Krysty was also retreating, firing her silvered gun at the attackers. "Got about seven or so, but they don't give a shit," she said. "Just keep coming."

"Out of the way, lover," he shouted at Krysty, pushing Mildred from his path, hearing her curse as he jogged her arm and made her drop the handful of bullets for her blaster.

Krysty dodged him, also reaching for a new mag of ammo. The side of her face was flecked with spots of blood, which caught his eye.

"Just stone splinters off a near miss," she said. "Go on!"

He flicked the main control on the G-12 onto full-auto, pausing a fraction of a second at the bottom of the steps, hearing shouts and screams from outside in the street. He picked his way up until his head was nearly level with the top, then peered out.

The survivors of the gang were obviously gathering themselves for the final assault, conveniently grouping together about twenty paces from where Ryan stood. Behind them he saw at least half a dozen corpses and two wounded boys, one trailing blood from a wound on the side of the head, the other crawling toward cover, dragging a broken leg.

"Ace on the line," Ryan said to himself, squeezing the trigger of the blaster.

With a supply of spare ammo, for once he was able to let the immensely powerful blaster roar out to its full potential. On continuous fire the squat weapon spit out the caseless rounds at more than ten per second. The full magazine was gone in less than five seconds.

And every one of the street gang was down and dying.

At such short range the bullets didn't tumble at all, hitting clean at enormous velocity, leaving untreatable exit wounds. Ryan had fired from the shoulder, absorbing the minimum recoil, countering the slight tendency to drift upward that was a failing with most automatic weapons.

Mildred was first up the steps to join him as he slowly lowered the G-12, conscious of how much lighter it felt with an empty mag.

"Judas's blood!" she said. "You took them all out in one. Even the kid I'd clipped in the leg."

Five or six were still moving, rolling in the light snow, some crying out. In less than a minute there was only stillness and fifteen sprawled bodies.

Ryan turned his back on the bleeding corpses and walked back into the cellar, ready to reload the automatic rifle.

Ready for next time.

Chapter Thirty-Six

The working party had been sent down to the docks to a long shed that had been converted by the scalies from its prenuke usage as a tobacco warehouse. Now it was arranged to gut the quantities of fish that they caught by ranging up and down the Hudson River.

Not that any of them ever called it by that name. To the scalies, and to their captives, it was simply "the river."

Now there was gray ice, lacing on the edges of the steely water, ice on the slabbed counters, ice on the piles of fish of all shapes and sizes.

Twenty of the norms stood along the side of the heavy metal-topped table, each chained to it by the ankle. The table itself was bolted to the slippery stone floor. Iron buckets were positioned at intervals to be used for either the offal or for the gutted fish.

Dean was one of the workers, who were mainly young boys or, in a couple of cases, older women. He held a short-bladed knife in his right hand. Dragging a thick-skinned eel or monkfish from the pile in front of him and holding it still with his left hand—for many of them were still wriggling in their death throes—he plunged the sharp point in behind the skull, drew it along the body and opened it up to reveal the spilling intestines and the mesh of white bone. A turn of the wrist and the guts spilled out in a gray-and-pink clump.

They went into one of the buckets, the boned and cleaned fish into another.

For some of the fish they had also been ordered to hack off the heads. For this they were each given a stump-hafted cleaver.

It was brutal work, bitterly cold and tiring, and they were kept at it from dawn until dusk with only minimal breaks for mugs of hot gruel. When any of the captives wanted to relieve themselves, they had to do it where they stood, or squat, and call for a scalie to hose the mess away from around their bare feet.

At the end of that day the chains were unlocked, and they were marched under guard back to the sleeping quarters. Those who survived. During that single, endless day, one of the women and the youngest of the boys both fell to the ground, semiconscious, and remained there amid the ice and blood. Even a brutal clubbing and kicking failed to rouse either, and they were eventually unchained and dragged out of the doorway. Dean heard the double splash as they were heaved, still living, into the sullen river.

At dusk the gutting tools had to be thrown into a box, under the indifferent supervision of a fat scalie with an M-16. The orders were to shout out as you dropped them in so that he could check that both the cleaver and the gutting knife were returned.

Dean saw, as he shuffled forward, that the scalie wasn't paying attention and merely looked up every now and again as the steel blades chinked against each other.

"Returning two here, boss," called the old woman in front of Dean, and received a casual glance from the guard.

Rona had drilled everything she knew about survival in Deathlands into her young son. "Always take your chances when they come. Don't wait for tomorrow, because tomorrow has a nasty habit of not coming."

The short knife was tucked into the back of his belt. The cleaver in his right hand. "Returning two here, boss," he said, making sure the metal rang against the others in the box.

The scalie didn't even look up.

That night he quietly honed the steel against the concrete floor, relishing the thin whispering sound it made. He felt the brittle edge against the palm of his hand, testing the needle point with the tip of a finger.

It wasn't much, but at least it was better than nothing.

RYAN CONSIDERED going to see Harry Stanton again. The trouble was that everyone wanted to go and see the temple of wonders. Krysty was fascinated by anything that dated from the prenuke period because they had a mythic quality for her. For Doc and Mildred the interest was different. They'd both lived in that strange time of neurosis and betrayal, and to see again the memorabilia that Ryan had described would give their own past an extra layer of reality.

J.B. wanted to go to see the collection of weaponry. Though he was obviously on the mend, the Armorer was still a frail shadow of the man he'd been. Mildred kept giving him injections, at longer intervals, and feeding him from the Stanton food package. He insisted on getting up and exercising, working out in a corner of the cellar near the fire. Outside it was still bitingly cold, the sky overcast and threatening.

In the end Ryan decided that the only safe decision was for everyone to remain close to the basement. With only five of them, and J.B. some way off full health, it would be madness to split their forces— particularly with the scalies active only a few blocks away and with the mangled corpses of some of the street gang still lying in the street.

"Keep where we are. The recce wag should be here sometime after dusk. Before full dark we'll have a council and get our plans together."

DOC FELL ASLEEP during the afternoon, and Ryan and Krysty went up top to snatch a little fresh air. The sky had taken on a strange orange glow, stippled with diagonal slashes of pale clouds. The wind had remained northerly, and the temperature didn't seem quite so bitingly cold.

J.B. was dozing, with Mildred sitting beside him shrouded in blankets like a Kiowa squaw. Her head sagged on her chest and she seemed to be asleep. Ryan and Krysty left her undisturbed.

"How are you feeling, lover?" Krysty asked as they strolled close together through the icy, deserted streets.

"Not bad."

"Not bad?"

"I feel fine, Krysty. Tired. Worried. Old knife wound near the kidneys is playing up with the cold. The blue norther cuts right into the empty socket of my eye and makes it water. That's what I meant by 'not bad.' All right?"

She squeezed his arm. "Sure. I understand."

He turned to face her. "Do you, lover? Does anyone understand anyone?"

"Well as anyone can."

Ryan nodded. "Look, this hasn't been the best of times."

"The worst of times?" she asked.

"No. Not that. But I've known better. To have J.B. go down with that illness and nearly made worm food, then to hear I've got a son I've never seen, a boy who's ten years old."

Krysty looked past him across the lunar landscape of ruined, tumbled buildings. The sun was sinking over the New Jersey swamps, lengthening the shadows. It was a gloomy prospect, filling her heart with melancholy. Suddenly she felt that things were never going to be the same, that they'd somehow crossed a border in the night, not knowing it, and were now doomed to live forever in another country.

"It's going to be all right," she said quietly.

"Think so, lover?"

"Yeah, Ryan, I think so."

"But do you *see* that?"

She turned away from him, taking a few steps along the sidewalk. She kicked at a round pebble in a puddle of gray water, stubbing her toe as she discovered it was iced in solidly. "Shit!"

"I asked if you could see that we'd be fine. All of us."

"You know seeing doesn't work like that. I can't tell you. You know what I've wanted ever since we first met up."

"Some place quiet to take time out of the running and the killing. Somewhere green by running water, where we could live easy and raise children."

There was a long stillness between them, a cold void.

Krysty moved farther away from him. "Think that's still going to be possible?"

"Why not?"

"Dean is why not. Look, don't get me wrong, lover. Gaia! This isn't jealousy about a woman you fucked a couple of times years before we even met. It's not that."

"No?"

She turned and faced him, managing a wry smile. "No. Really."

"So what is it?"

"A kid of ten. If he'd been a baby or if he'd been about fifteen…"

Ryan stepped closer to her. "I don't catch you, lover."

"A baby can be left someplace safe. Older boy can make his own way."

"But Dean, ten years old, is going to come between us."

"Mebbe."

"Mebbe not."

He reached out and folded her into his arms, holding her very tightly, kissing her on the side of the face.

For a moment she resisted, then kissed him back. "Ryan, it might be fine, but I surely know it won't be easy."

"Nobody ever said it would be."

They walked cautiously around the block until Ryan's worry got the better of him and they returned quickly to the cellar.

"If they're all asleep," Ryan said, "they'll be like a bunch of blind kittens. Any swift and evil bastard could come in and take them."

But all was well.

Better than well.

Doc slept like a child, hands folded across his

breast, the gleaming ivory canyon of his open mouth a great tribute to orthodontal expertise.

For a moment, as their eyes grew accustomed to the gloom, Ryan and Krysty couldn't see either Mildred or J.B. Then they noticed movement under blankets at the far side of the fire. A steady, rhythmic movement with low, muffled moans.

"Seems like he's getting better," Ryan observed.

Chapter Thirty-Seven

After J.B. and Mildred had finished their lovemaking, Doc was woken up and they had a brief council of war.

The only problem was whether J.B. had recovered sufficiently to go along on the raid to rescue Dean from the scalies.

"I'll go."

Ryan sat cross-legged across the fire from his oldest friend. "If I'm not certain about you, then I'll be trying to watch your back as well as my own. And that's not a starter."

"Sure. So if I didn't think I was ready, would I want to go?"

Ryan grinned. "Sure you would, J.B. You know that. Miss something like this? Never."

Krysty leaned forward. "Mildred? You're the only one with any professional knowledge. Is he well enough to come?"

"Well, in all my medical days I never saw a man so close to death make such an amazing recovery. Thirty-six hours ago and I'd have been polishing the brass on the coffin handles. Now? Now he's a whole lot better."

"How much better is a whole lot better?" Ryan quizzed.

Doc laughed. "Wasting time, my dear friend. You can never get any professional—doctor, lawyer, whatever—to give you a definite yea or nay. Can't be done. Why, they all suffer from piles—spend all their lives sitting on the fence."

Mildred stood, shaking a fist at the cackling old man. "I'd really like the chance to operate on you for piles, you leering—"

"Come on, come on," Ryan said. "J.B., I guess it stays with you. This is going to be real hard. Might see some farm-buying for us. Long as there's a baseline where you feel you can keep going, then that's fine with me."

The Armorer took off his spectacles and looked at the flames through them, angling to see if they had any smears on the lenses. "Long as I don't have to tackle any full-grown scalies, I'll be all right. Line me up against a platoon of day-old kittens and I'll have a damned good try at kicking the shit out of them. Yeah, Ryan. I'll be there."

"That's good."

Talking through a working plan for the actual attack only took about ten minutes, then all they had to do was wait for the arrival of Harry Stanton's recce wag.

"NINETEEN TWENTY-EIGHT," J.B. said, checking his wrist chron. "Stanton keeps his word."

Outside, the street seemed to be filled with the thunder of the powerful six-cylinder, turbo-charged engine.

Ryan slid the door open, climbing the steps to greet their visitors. To his surprise it was the head of Harry Stanton himself that emerged, beaming, from the turret.

"Greetings and salutations." He was wearing crimson again, maintaining his resemblance to Father Christmas.

"Hi. Didn't think you'd be coming along yourself, Harry."

"Wouldn't miss a chance to have a quick word with J.B. How is he? Those drugs do their stuff for him?"

"Yeah. Not a hundred percent yet, but ninety and rising."

Harry clambered out of the cockpit of the LAV 26, calling, "Sam, stay there. Lee, you come on in with me. Keep the engine running. Looks like there might be some serious snow on the way."

Ryan already figured that. The temperature had risen, and the sky had clouded over just before sunset. Now there were already some stray flakes blowing across the deserted streetscape.

Lee was short and skinny with a hooked nose and thinning hair. He wore a Beretta 92-SB pistol in a fast-draw rig, tied with a leather thong, low on the right thigh.

Harry made a florid entrance to the basement, flapping snow off his hair and shoulders. "By God, but that's a fine ripe smell," he bellowed. "Either you've taken up cheese-making or something's died in here. J. B. Dix, by all the stars in Hollywood!"

He embraced the Armorer, lifting him clear off his feet. J.B. introduced Mildred and Krysty. Doc insisted on introducing himself.

With a low, sweeping bow, hand on heart, he said, "My dear Mr. Stanton, it is a true pleasure."

"Likewise."

"And I hope very much that I shall be able to visit your remarkable palace of memorabilia."

"Good to show someone around who'd appreciate my little place."

Ryan was starting to heave the slab of wood across the entrance again when Stanton turned and stopped him.

"No, leave it. Forgot the damn hamper of goodies! Stupid of me."

Ryan glanced at J.B., seeing the almost imperceptible nod. It wasn't in the plan, but adaptability was always essential.

"I'll go get it, Harry. You warm up. Shall I ask Sam to come in?"

"No, no. Need someone to watch over that baby. Remember that a road accident doesn't determine who's right. Just who's left."

Mildred laughed out loud. "By God! I remember that line. My Uncle Jack used to quote it whenever we went out driving. From some TV program. I know. *Highway Patrol*, wasn't it?"

"Right, lady, right. How come you say you went driving and watched Brod Crawford? You mean you know someone got a collection of vids?"

"No. I mean that—" Suddenly she saw the gaping chasm that yawned in front of her. How to explain to this man that she was a freezie, born on the seventeenth day of December in 1964, that she'd gone into hospital thirteen days after her thirty-sixth birthday for minor abdominal surgery, that it had gone wrong and they'd used her as part of an experimental cryonic program?

"What?" Stanton prompted.

"I mean, it wasn't what you'd call a real collection. Just a couple of parts of bits of one of them. But I saw it a lot."

"Which one was it? Which episode?"

Ryan saw the conversation slipping away from them and interrupted Stanton. "What about this hamper? Want me to go get it?"

"Sure, sure. I'll talk a spell to J.B. here about the old days. Great days. Yesterday was always better than today to us, J.B. and Ryan. Lord, how given we old men are to the vice of lying."

Stanton threw himself onto a pile of torn blankets and furs, wincing at the cloud of dirt that spiraled up from it. "This is where I belong, my friends. Such company I have never met. You know—" his voice dropped and became barely audible "—I have such surroundings for my life, but nobody to truly share it with. What was it that Tennyson's Sir Bedivere said in 'Arthur's Death'?"

It was Doc who answered him. "I know what you mean, Mr. Stanton, for I have often allowed the line to prey upon my own mind. 'And I the last go forth, companionless.' Yes?"

Stanton nodded.

From against the wall Lee cleared his throat and spit into the fire, the saliva hissing in the flames. A look of distaste crossed the red face, half hidden behind the great white whiskers, but Stanton said nothing, lying still and looking around him.

"The hamper?" Ryan reminded.

"Yes, yes. There's some special delicacies from the rearmost shelves of my larder. Quails' eggs and rare fruits in brandy syrup. Some beluga caviar that would have cost a president's ransom. I have smoked salmon and some brandy from the nineteenth century. A good sancerre and a fine claret. Just little gifts to brighten this dark evening and the bitter times in which we few must dwell."

Ryan was conscious of every one of his companions trying to catch his eye, but he ignored them. A plan was a plan.

"I have waited years to meet such a group as you five. With so much wisdom and knowledge, will you not spend some time with me?" Stanton's voice implored them.

"Love to," Doc said, the words exploding from him. "I mean…" His face betrayed his confusion.

His back to Stanton, Ryan silently drew his SIG-Sauer.

"Put your pistol away, Ryan," Harry said gently.

"What's that, chief?" Lee exclaimed, straightening and fumbling for his Beretta. But the flap over the top of the holster defeated his cold fingers.

"Leave it, Lee," Harry ordered. "Had they wanted they could have chilled us as we came in. Since they didn't I wonder why."

Ryan turned around, suspicious of a trap. The Trader had always reminded his men and women to be cautious of people who seemed open, honest and frank. "You have to ask yourself why the bastard's lying to you," he used to say.

Lee stood still, mesmerized by the sight of the blaster. Stanton sighed.

"We talked about taking you out," Ryan said. "Or whoever you sent. Didn't know you were coming yourself."

"And what did you decide in your council of war? Do tell."

Krysty answered. "We agreed we'd try and take them out and hold them. Once we were in the wag they couldn't harm us, so we'd let them go. And you'd get the wag back after we were done with it."

"And now?"

"Same," J.B. said. "You stay here. We go. Then you go."

"Laconic as ever, J.B., aren't you?"

"Yeah."

Harry laughed, shaking his head, the burst of merriment making Ryan tighten his finger on the trigger of the automatic. "Why didn't you just ask me?"

"He gave you the fucking map," Lee snapped.

Ryan ignored the gunner. "If I'd asked you, then you'd have said no."

"Perhaps."

"You didn't get to be the king by being triple-stupe, Harry. Once I'd asked you, then you'd know me and you'd know I'd try to take the wag."

"Correct. Correct in every point. Trader taught you well."

"Yeah. So now you'd better get Sam in and we can demolish this hamper of yours. And then we'll get on with rescuing my son from the scalies."

Stanton stroked his long, silvery mustaches. "Very well. But there is one thing, Ryan, to remember."

"What's that?"

"If we were ever to meet again, I fear I should have to chill you. Hard and slow. You understand. Nothing personal."

Ryan nodded. "I know, Harry. Just business."

Chapter Thirty-Eight

The food and drink were disappointing. After the great buildup Harry Stanton had given his magical hamper, the whole thing turned out to be a letdown. The main problem was the age of most of the contents. Some of the cans showed sell-by dates in the first couple of months of the year 2001. Just after sky-dark.

And not much of it had survived the century untainted by time. The quails' eggs had turned into totally inedible rubber bullets. The fish was undeniably off. The vaunted white wine was like creamy vinegar, and the claret so filled with sediment that it proved impossible to filter. In the end they finished off the dried fish and meat they'd been keeping in the cellar.

Harry leaned back and belched loudly. "Truth is, ladies and gentlemen, that I hardly ever venture to broach any of the rarities from the edible and comestible section of my little home. And now I know why."

"Perhaps I could entertain you with an account of a wonderful eighteen-course banquet that my dear wife, Emily, and I enjoyed once in Paris. The fin de siècle glamour of the city. The women, powdered and elegant. The men of letters and the young bloods, strutting and preening. And the food and the wine. I remember that we commenced with a delicate—"

"Shut it, Doc," Ryan said.

"Yeah," J.B. agreed.

"Don't want to hear about it," Mildred added.

Krysty smiled. "And I go along with everything the last three speakers said, Doc."

Harry coughed. "I'm aware that my position here is a touch precarious. But after that disgusting disaster of a meal, I think it's better if you don't sicken us by telling us about some wonderful meal you had in Paris. In the fin something or other. Whatever that is."

Sensing they were again moving into difficult areas of Doc's time-jumping, Ryan stood. "Time we were leaving."

"How about our blasters, outie?" Lee snarled.

The driver, Sam, punched his right fist hard into his left hand. "Leave us here bare, and we won't make it back to base. Might as well put a bullet through our heads."

"Could still do that," J.B. said, tugging at the brim of his fedora.

Harry heaved himself to his feet. "Yes. Why haven't you done that, Ryan? Or is that still the plan before you go?"

"This won't make an inch of difference, but I don't like taking your wag, Harry."

The blue eyes, hooded by the bushy white brows, stayed as cold as Sierra meltwater. "Talk's cheap, Ryan, isn't it?"

"Sure. You think I relish this, then you're more damn stupe than I figured."

"You go do what you have to and leave us here. You get the wag back to me, that's good. But it won't do anything to change the last page of the book. I'll still take you out if I ever get a chance."

"Doubt we'll meet up again, Harry," J.B. said.

"I can wait."

"Be a long time," Ryan told him, wrapping the scarf around his neck. It had grown cold again, and there was something close to a blizzard raging outside.

"Like I say, I'll wait. Long as the grass grows, Ryan, I'll wait."

"We'll leave your blasters by the wheels of the wag at the last minute. Soon as we're all safe inside. You can come get them then."

Stanton nodded.

It crossed Ryan's mind that he was making a lethal mistake, one the Trader probably wouldn't have made.

"Don't ever," the older man had said, "ever leave an enemy alive. Not if you think there's the smallest chance they might come after you one day. Like placing a cold razor against your own jugular."

But Harry Stanton had saved his life, plucking him

from the claws of the scalies, and he'd been helpful and generous.

"Feel some pangs of guilt, don't you, Cawdor?" Harry stated. "Difference between you and Trader, I guess. Could be I'm lucky like that. Trader would have chilled me. Oh, real courteous and quick. One through the back of the neck. But it don't make much difference at the last how you get it."

"Bullshit!"

Everyone looked at Mildred. She stood, eyes blazing with a ferocious anger, staring at Harry Stanton.

"What?" he said.

"Romantic macho bullshit! Course it makes a difference how you die. My daddy was burned alive by a bunch of cowardly redneck peckerwoods in white sheets. Think that's a good way to go? Just the same as a quick and painless death? You triple-stupe bastard."

The cellar was quiet, with only the sound of the burning wood. Stanton nodded slowly and gave the black woman a half bow. "Sometimes my mouth gets to working before my brain's aware of it. I'm real sorry about that."

There wasn't a whole lot more conversation.

SAM AND LEE REMAINED inside in the warmth. Only Stanton came to see them off. The snow was driving in, great clumps falling and settling everywhere. It softened the harsh lines of the century-old ruins, reducing visibility to less than a hundred paces.

The Light Armored Vehicle was designed to take a crew of only three, and it was a tight squeeze with five of them inside. J.B. took over the driver's controls, and Krysty settled herself behind the automatic cannon. Mildred and Doc niggled ill-temperedly as they squirmed their way into bits of remaining space. Finally Ryan climbed on the outside, ready to take the commander's seat. He held on to the blasters of Stanton and his two men. "So long and thanks."

Stanton blinked up at him, snow gathering on his head and shoulders. The eyes glittered in the golden light of the twin headlights. Ryan had just decided that he wasn't going to get a reply when Stanton finally spoke. "Good luck in finding the boy, Ryan. If you get yourself too big a problem, you could mebbe come see me."

"Thought you were going to have me chilled on sight," Ryan reminded, grinning.

Stanton, straight-faced, nodded at him. "Damn it! You're right. I was, wasn't I? Well, just take care out there and make sure you do it to them before they do it to you."

"That *Highway Patrol*?" Ryan asked, raising his voice over the rumbling of the engine.

"No. *Hill Street Blues*. Good luck."

Ryan lobbed the weapons down into the snow at the feet of Harry Stanton, dropped into his seat and lowered the hatch, sliding the lock across.

Almost immediately he heard the ringing sound of a bullet striking the metal, close by his head.

"That Stanton?" Krysty asked. "Maybe we ought to get moving fast."

J.B.'s voice floated from the dark interior. "No worries. Steel like this'd stop most anything."

"Just his way of saying goodbye to us," Ryan said. "Come on, driver. Let's go."

Nearly nine tons of armored steel lumbered forward as J.B. struggled to master the controls. It was a bit like steering one of the immeasurably vaster war wags. The LAV had top speed of more than sixty miles an hour over good metal, but its effective range on a full tank was a lot less—about five hundred miles if it was coaxed.

In the command seat Ryan had switched on a small overhead light, studying the map that Harry Stanton had so thoughtfully provided for them. It marked all the main avenues and cross streets, indicating which no longer existed because of the nuking, or had been permanently blocked.

The fringes of the scalies' territory was shown in a thin, dotted red line, though Harry had pointed out that this was very approximate. You never quite knew where you might suddenly find yourself among scalies. There were a number of blocks set up to stop any attempt to attack their underground headquarters from above, which left only two alternatives—get down into the sewers and passages with them, or circle out into the river from an entry point farther north, up toward West Forty-sixth Street, then come in slow and careful, feeling your way past the ruins of the old docks.

And this was where Harry's neat map became vague and blurred.

"On your own past here," he'd said, jabbing at the map with a stubby forefinger. "I never got anyone in that deep. Well, I could've got them in, but I sure never would've got 'em out again."

Several times the recce wag slithered sideways in the deepening snow. The brakes protested, and the whole vehicle shuddered.

"Dark night! Like driving a mule up a ladder! Can't see properly through this ob-slit!"

"Take it easy, J.B.," Ryan said. "We get jammed in this and we're in serious shit."

"Can't get the brakes to bite properly. Think they're iced up."

Doc's voice filtered through the black interior. "Might it not possibly be something to do with their extreme age? I have a similar problem myself."

"Yeah." J.B. coughed violently, and the wag skidded around the corner of a block.

"You all right?" Mildred called, unable to hide her anxiety.

"Sure, sure. Just got some dust in my throat. Feel great. Good to be back on the road again."

"Soon have to be making a sort of detour. A right and then left after two blocks. Left again and then another right and left." Ryan angled the piece of paper toward the light. "By then we should be far enough north to head toward the river. Map shows a place where the road slopes in gently.''

The snow continued remorselessly.

There were heaters inside the LAV, but they were overridden by the icy air that lanced in through the open ob-slits. The only good thing was that there wasn't likely to be any kind of ambush. Nobody would be out in a storm of this intensity.

Though a couple of minutes later, Ryan had a strange and unsettling vision. Out of his side window he saw a figure moving alongside them. His instrument repeater showed a speed around fifteen miles an hour. The eight wheels lurched and bounced over rubble and deep potholes, against the background of the roaring engine.

And there, only a few yards away, Ryan could just make out a child. A frail, elfin little girl, looking to be in her early teens. She was dressed in a variety of russet rags, orange, brown and faded yellow, that whirled around her as though she were the epicenter of a fall storm. Her face was pale, the eyes dark and intense.

He didn't say anything to the others.

The creature danced, barefoot he noticed, leaping effortlessly, never slipping or falling, the snow seeming to part in front of her.

"Left here, J.B.," he called. "Better slow down so we can see where we're going."

The engine grated down through the gears as the wag rumbled up to the junction. The nearside wheels slipped for a moment in drifted snow, then found purchase, making the vehicle jerk to the right.

"By the three Kennedys!" Doc called. "Worse than a Frisco cable car."

Ryan peered out, squinting against the cold wind and the wet snow that found its way in through the ob-slit. He glimpsed the child for one last, frozen moment. She had pirouetted on the points of her toes, then she vanished in front of the turning nose of the armored vehicle.

"No," he breathed.

"Dark night!" J.B. exclaimed, stamping on the brakes.

Ryan waited for the thump of the impact of tons of steel against a frail body, but there was nothing. "What's up?" he shouted through the intercom.

"Don't know. Thought I saw someone or something right in front. But it sort of…skipped, yeah, skipped out of the way and vanished."

"Just keep going," Ryan ordered.

"NO GOOD, RYAN," J.B. said.

"Brakes?"

"Partly that. Main thing is I can't see more than about twenty yards. Worst damn blizzard I think I ever saw."

"Mebbe we should stop awhile and wait it out."

"How's the time?" Mildred asked.

"Time we get where we're going it'll be close on midnight," Ryan said.

"I think we should keep going, lover." There was an urgency in Krysty's voice that everyone picked up on.

Ryan responded to it. "Trouble?"

"Feels bad. I think we should keep right on moving."

"Hear that, J.B.? Take it slow but keep going."

"You know where we are?" the Armorer asked.

"Yeah. Course. Well, sort of. I reckon we're about one block south and two blocks east of where we want to drive into the river."

"Forgive a note of doubt from an old man's fevered imagination, but are you certain this tin box is truly amphibious?"

"Sure," Ryan replied.

He knew that this kind of Light Armored Vehicle had been designed to travel with equal facility on land or on water. Ryan pushed to the back of his mind the nagging doubt that the past hundred years might have diminished the recce wag's efficiency.

Krysty's feelings weren't to be ignored. Whatever the risks, they had to keep on.

ANOTHER OF THE SCALIES had tried to put the make on Dean during the evening, only pulling away when an officer shouted at him to get back to his guard post. The squat mutie bent low over the cowering boy.

"Off at the deepest part of night, little one. Be seeing you then. Get ready for what I'll give you."

It patted itself on the crotch and grinned, showing its double row of reptilian teeth.

As it waddled away into the darkness, its boots ringing on the damp stone, Dean relaxed. His right hand let go of the hilt of the gutting knife he'd stolen earlier.

THEY HAD ALL THE OB-SLITS open, and everyone had pressed their faces to the freezing air, trying to see anything that would tell them where they were. But the snow was still cascading down, producing white-out conditions in the streets.

In a narrow compartment in front of his seat, Ryan had found a thick booklet covering driving and maintenance. But the section on amphibious use had been torn away. Something nagged at Ryan about precautions, but it kept sliding away as he concentrated on navigating for J.B.

"See anything, Ryan?" With the ob-slits open it was necessary to use the intercom for any conversation.

"No, but we should—"

The front of the wag dipped suddenly and violently, and the engine raced. Then they fell and crashed. And the armored vehicle began to fill with a gushing flood of icy river water.

Chapter Thirty-Nine

Ryan held on to the metal bar at his side, but the impact was so severe that he bent it away from its fixing point. He lurched forward and took the initial wave of cold, salty water full in the face.

It made him gasp for breath and blinded him.

"Ob-slits!" Doc shouted, surprisingly the quickest in the wag to realize what had happened and where their principal danger lay.

"Close them," J.B. ordered, but the deluge shorted out some of the electrics and his voice disappeared.

It felt like the cumbersome LAV was going clear to the bottom of the Hudson.

Ryan managed to slam the hatch shut, locking it tight, but he was soaking wet and could still hear water pouring in somewhere below him.

"Mildred!" Krysty yelled.

"I'm stuck."

Doc, with a ragged edge of panic riding over his voice, said, "I can't reach past her to shut the port."

The vehicle still hadn't stopped plunging, and Ryan was conscious that they were also being moved slowly sideways by the current. There was another solid jarring thump, and they tipped over farther.

The engine was faltering, coughing and cutting out, barely managing to maintain ignition. Amid the bedlam Ryan was aware of J.B. muttering a calm litany of curses. "Got to close that ob-slot! Can you reach it, Krysty?"

"I'll try. Gaia! The water's twenty below freezing and I'm soaked. I think if… Yeah. Sorry, Doc."

The sound of the torrent suddenly ceased, and Ryan heard locks snapping shut.

Doc's voice, calmer, said, "Don't apologize, my dear young lady, having my mouth filled with the toe of your boot is a small price to pay to render us a mite more waterproof."

Gradually, like a mortally wounded whale, the wag seemed to be stablizing itself, becoming level and rising steadily toward the surface of the river. The engine was still reluctant to fire properly, but at least it was running.

"Intercom's out!" J.B. shouted. "But I got control."

Ryan had fumbled in the chaotic darkness and located a small periscope. He raised it with a hydraulic, hissing sound and looked through the lens. He couldn't see a thing, couldn't even judge whether they were underwater or whether they'd broken the surface.

"Everyone all right?" he called.

"Wonderful," Doc replied.

"Cold, wet and bloody miserable," Mildred called.

"Surviving, lover…"

"We above the water yet, Ryan?" J.B. asked. "I'm stone-blind here."

"I'll risk opening the ob-slit. Rest of you keep 'em shut."

Only a few of the dim lights inside the vehicle were still functioning. Ryan screwed his eye up, shaking wet hair off his face, found the locking handle and eased it up a little. Nothing happened, so he took a chance and threw it clear back, ready to shut it again if the river flooded in.

"We're out," he called. "Still a lot of snow, but I think it's easing some. J.B., can you turn her around and give me a chance to recce?"

"Sure. Reverse port and forward with starboard. And around we go."

The wag began to swing.

Ryan stared out into the night, struggling to catch a glimpse of anything that might give a clue about where the shore lay.

"Can I ask a question?"

"Sure, Mildred," J.B. said.

"Just what happened back there? One minute we're driving along and next moment we're falling into deep water."

Doc's laugh echoed through the wag. "Just like life, isn't it?"

Ryan detected a faint flicker of light, but the LAV

was swinging steadily and he couldn't be certain. He was about to ask J.B. to pull her the other way, but he decided it would be better to let it go around one more time.

"Ran off a dock, Mildred," the Armorer shouted. "Blame our high and mighty nav-man up there."

"What are you complaining about? Fireblast, it's a sure signal you're feeling better, J.B., moaning like this. I said I'd get us into the river. And I did."

"Sure. Want me to stop circling?"

"Not yet. Yeah, there it is. One more time around, but real slow. Ready to check when I say the word. I can see something. Must be the shore. I'll open the hatch and try to get out. Should be able to see from there."

"Make sure we're high enough out of the water," J.B. called. "Open up the big hatch if we're not, and we'll float like a lead balloon."

Ryan eased it open a quarter inch. A little water seeped in, but there was no serious problem. He flung it all the way back, wincing again as the biting gale dashed snow in his face.

Out in the night air it was surprisingly easy to get his bearings. The wind was blowing steadily from the north, and he knew the river ran more or less north-south. So once he stared into the driving blizzard, shielding his eye from the snow, he knew the Newyork shore lay to his right. Over to the other side were the big swamps.

Ryan stuck his head back inside. "You hear me, J.B.? Steer right."

"Sure."

"And open up your hatch, as well. Get a bit wet, but you'll be able to hear me."

"Sure."

They made the turn, heading in a ponderous quarter circle. In the gaps between the snow flurries Ryan thought a couple of times that he saw a distant, flickering light.

Krysty joined him. "Making me feel pig-sick down in there. Rather be wet and cold."

"Don't know where we are. I figure we must've gone in the river a couple of blocks too late. So we need to go south for a quarter mile or so."

"You got the map?"

"Sure. But it's falling apart with the water. I can remember it."

"Think we'll make it?"

She was hanging on to his arm. Though they were so close, the blackness meant they couldn't even see each other's face.

"I know we'll get to where we're going. The rest is..." She felt him shrug.

The flow of the river was another factor in the impossible equation. They didn't know how fast it was flowing, so they didn't know how far south they were being carried. And, since they hadn't known where they were in the first place, there was an awful lot of guesstimates involved.

"Snow's easing some, lover," Krysty said.

The wind was also dropping, but still whipped whitecaps off the tops of the waves all around them. The LAV butted its way through them, its blunt nose making a loud, thwacking noise and kicking up a wall of white spray.

Ryan was steadying himself on the side of the turret, the long barrel of the blaster against the side of his leg. His own G-12 caseless was strapped securely across his shoulders.

"How'm I doing?" J.B. shouted. "Still can't see."

"About as you're going now," Ryan replied.

The map had shown two prongs of fallen rock and stone, like the straight horns of a cow. Stanton said they'd been warehouses once, but now they provided a kind of natural harbor that the scalies sometimes used for their fishing rafts.

Once shore was reached there was a big arched tunnel that gave access, so Stanton believed, to the heart of the muties' empire.

The engine now sounded healthier, and Ryan was grateful for the storm. If the night had been calm, then the scalies would have heard them coming five miles off.

"Can I come up top?" Doc shouted. "I fear the poor remnants of Stanton's feast are about to reappear."

"Careful of the controls," Ryan called.

Three seconds later he was in the blackness of the river, swimming for his life.

One moment he and Krysty had been pressed close, then the turret began to swing around, the barrel of the Bushmaster catching Ryan just below the knees sending him teetering off the slippery, wet metal into the Hudson.

Krysty hung on to the blaster, hearing Doc's voice very faintly.

"Sorry. Caught my foot on some lever. Hope it wasn't important. I said, I hope it's not important."

Ryan heard nothing, just the rushing, bubbling sound of the river beating in his ears. He kicked his way to the surface, hampered by the weight of the rifle. His head above water, he looked around for any sign of either the wag or the shore, but he couldn't see either. He could just catch the distant rumble of the six-cylinder diesel engine.

Then something brushed against the side of his leg.

Chapter Forty

The shock made Ryan open his mouth, and he swallowed a great gulp of freezing water that nearly choked him. He kicked out, feeling his boots jar against something long and solid that floated just below the surface of the river.

As he pushed against it, he felt it move, pressing upward. The panga slipped into his right hand and he reached down, ready for mortal combat—with a long, splintered branch, slimy from its long immersion in the Hudson.

The relief made him yell out loud, fumbling to get the weapon back into the sodden leather sheath at his hip.

But the clinging, smothering cold was already biting at him, making movements clumsy and slow. Ryan had a momentary flash of a tattered book the Trader had once lent to him about the big firefight called the Second War. Convoys of water wags went into the Arctic to supply the Russkies. If a man went in the water when they were attacked, he'd die in less than two minutes if he wasn't rescued.

"Hey! Over here! Hey, Krysty!"

As soon as J.B. realized what had happened, he'd

begun the slow process of turning the wag around, steering it in a big circle, trying as he did so to allow for the effect the current was having on them and what effect it might be having on Ryan.

Krysty, Doc and Mildred were now all on top, grabbing hold of anything they could, scanning the dark surface around them for some sign of Ryan.

"Should be soon!" J.B. yelled.

"Can you cut the engine?" Krysty shouted.

"What?"

"If he's calling, we can't hear him. Can you stop the engine?"

"Daren't. She's hardly firing as it is."

Krysty cautiously slithered to the front, leaning to speak to J.B. through his ob-slit. "If you don't, then we might not find him and he'll die."

"I stop the engine and we all could die. Not the way Ryan'd want it, Krysty. Sorry."

The word of apology was only a token gesture, and they both knew it. Both knew that the Armorer was making the right call.

Krysty wished they had Jak Lauren with them. The albino teenager had poor vision in bright sunlight but excellent sight in darkness. Krysty herself could see better than most, but the intermittent flurries of snow made it very hard. There was no way of telling what was water, sky or land.

By one of those flukes so beloved by the lords of chaos, it was Doc Tanner, with much the worst eyesight, who spotted Ryan.

"There!" he yelled, sliding forward on his belly, grabbing hold of one of the front lights. It was only afterward that it occurred to him that if he'd missed his grip he'd have gone onward and downward, straight under the bow of the wag.

Mildred threw herself after him, grabbing hold of his flailing legs at the second attempt.

J.B. banged the gears into reverse, bringing the lumbering LAV to a gradual halt.

Ryan was hardly moving. The cold numbed his entire body, slowing the blood until the calm of death seemed a pleasant option. He was barely aware of the black mass of the eight-wheeler alongside him. A voice called a familiar name that he recognized through the net of ice that was drawn around his brain, and something poked him sharply in the shoulder.

"Catch hold, Ryan!" Doc pushed the lion-headed swordstick at him. "Damn it, man! Wake up!"

The momentum of the massive wag was carrying it past him, the strong wind pushing it down the river. Ryan was sliding alongside toward the stern. In another thirty seconds or so he'd bob out of reach and vanish once more into the freezing blackness.

Ryan was tired, and the jabbing stick was an irritant. "Fuck off," he mumbled, reaching up to push away the thing that kept hitting him, grabbing hold of its smooth wood.

"Don't let go, lover! Use both hands."

"Krysty," he said, surprised that he knew who it

was. With that realization came a surge of awareness, where he was and what was happening.

He was in the icy Hudson, and he was on the way to dying. "No," he shouted.

J.B. was fighting the controls, struggling to keep the unwieldy monster stationary in the water. Krysty swung herself off the top, feet scrabbling for a purchase on an anchor point on the side, reaching and locking her fingers into the mass of black curly hair, steadying Ryan for a moment.

It was still a ferocious battle to get him up and out of the freezing embrace of the big river. A gust of wind turned the wag broadside, and it lurched, nearly throwing all four of the companions into the Hudson.

Finally they were all huddled on top of the LAV, while J.B. gave it the gun, heading due east toward the Newyork shore.

The snow had finally stopped, and there was a segment of silver moon showing through ragged cloud. Without that pale light it would have been vastly difficult to locate their destination. The entire Lower East Side had been devastated by the nukes, and one pile of rubble looked a lot like another. But they picked their way along until Krysty spotted the two horns of rubble, shown on Stanton's map.

The Armorer throttled back, bringing the engine note down to a muted rumbling, easing the wag in toward the shore, all lights out. Once they were inside the northern spur of rock, they were sheltered from the biting wind.

On top Krysty, Mildred and Doc were clustered around Ryan, trying to keep him from freezing to death. The problem with that was that all of them were soaked and cold.

"Have to get warmed up," Ryan muttered, his teeth chattering. "Or first scalie'll take us all out with one claw tied behind its back."

"Least we're out of the wind," Mildred said. "Lose that chill factor."

"I can see a light. Looks like a fire. Just inside that kind of tunnel opening," J.B. called.

"Could be guards. Best tie up here. Weather like this there's a good chance they won't have spotted us yet."

The Armorer obeyed Ryan's instructions, throttling right back, easing the wag alongside the high wall of concrete and iron.

"Mooring ropes in here," Mildred called, opening a small hatch to the side of the turret.

J.B. cut the engines, and Mildred and Krysty leaped ashore to make the wag secure, fastening it to rusting girders.

There was a gap of three or four feet between the LAV and the makeshift jetty, and it took both Doc and J.B. to help Ryan across. Even then they nearly stumbled and fell into the sucking patch of foaming water.

J.B. was trembling nearly as much as Ryan, and the two old friends clung to each other.

"Can't go on like this," the Armorer said. "Need

a rest. Sickness took too much. Have a rest and I'll be fine.''

"Yeah, me, too," Ryan agreed. "Could do with being drier and warmer."

"That *is* a fire," Krysty said, shading her eyes with her hands. "Can't see anyone near it. Me, Doc and Mildred will go look. You two stay here."

Ryan didn't much like that. J.B. was too bushed to care, sitting down on a slab of concrete, burying his head in his hands.

Krysty led the other two along the dock toward the light. Ryan looked across at J.B. "We're getting too fucking old for this."

IT WAS THE FIRST TIME Krysty could remember leading a scouting team without Ryan, and she knew well enough that there was a better than average chance that the recce could turn into a bloody chilling.

She had her gleaming Heckler & Koch P7A-13 in her right hand. Mildred came second with her target pistol cocked and ready. Doc, at the back, had the Le Mat set on the scattergun barrel. Subtlety wasn't the best way of taking out a scalie.

"Someone there," she said, beckoning her two partners to her.

"Can you see them?"

"No, Doc. But I just know they're there. Muties. More than one."

Ryan had managed to urge caution on her. "Make

much noise and it'll be like sticking your dick in an ant's nest," he'd said.

"Not a problem for me, lover," she'd replied, giving him a quick kiss on the cold cheek before leading Doc and Mildred away.

The jetty, built from old rubble, gradually became lower until it reached a stretch of flatter land. It could be concrete or shingle; the light of the moon wasn't good enough to make sure. The beach was about fifty yards wide, sloping up toward the wide arch where the fire blazed. The other tumbled pier stretched off into the river on the far side.

"Ready?"

"Sure," Mildred replied.

"Apart from a pressing need to relieve a certain tightness of the bladder, caused, I think, by a combination of the bitter cold and the excitement, I'm fine."

"Sure you don't want to piss here and now, Doc?" Krysty asked.

"No, no. But thank you for the kind offer, my dear lady."

"Map shows this as a back entrance to the burrows. Only used in daylight, so Harry Stanton says."

"If anyone's inside, they'll hear us coming across that shingle," Mildred said.

"Only if they're listening," Krysty replied, half smiling. "Let's go and find out."

Chapter Forty-One

Ryan and J.B. hugged each other, shaking like aspens in a hurricane.

"Never been so fucking cold," Ryan stated. "Numb from head to toe."

"Me, too." J.B. was breathing very quickly, his whole body trembling.

"Reckon we should've gone with 'em?"

"I'd never have made it. Be a liability in a firefight."

Ryan nodded. "Yeah. Couldn't draw a blaster. Never find the trigger with frozen fingers. Just wait and listen. Fireblast! That blaze sure looks good."

KRYSTY PADDED across the shingle, leaning a little forward, spreading her weight. Her boots made a faint whispering sound on the tiny pebbles. Doc was about three paces behind her and Mildred another couple of yards at the back.

There was obviously going to be a very unpleasant moment. The fire was so bright that it wasn't possible to see anything in the cavernous shadows behind it. They would have to come around the corner into that dazzling glow, the best of targets to anyone sitting patiently inside the tunnel.

Krysty held up a hand, bringing the others close to her. "No other way," she said. "Triggers tight and in we go. I'll take whoever's on the left. Mildred, pick off the right. Doc, just let rip in the middle. All right?" They both nodded. "Now."

OUT ON THE BREAKWATER Ryan and J.B. heard the sound of shooting, oddly muffled by the distance and the wind. But the three different blasters were all easily distinguished.

"Three from Krysty," the Armorer said, "and two, spaced, from that bitching little pistol of Mildred's. Should mean two dead from her, plus a couple from Krysty."

"And Doc's thunderblaster," Ryan said, managing a grin despite his frozen lips. "Could mean any damn thing."

"Feel up to going to take a look?"

"If we can get near that fire, yeah, let's go for it."

Just seeing the blazing pile of wood made Ryan somehow feel a touch warmer. But as they reached the sloping beach, with the tiny wavelets lapping near their boots, both men were conscious of a sinister silence.

Suddenly the ice in Ryan's body didn't seem so crippling. The SIG-Sauer came out of its holster, smooth as silk. He gestured for J.B. to cover him.

Slowly and cautiously he flattened himself against

the ice-caked concrete of the tunnel wall, sliding his face around the corner to squint, finding the same problem that Krysty had experienced only a few seconds earlier. He was blinded by the golden flames of the big bonfire.

"Come ahead, lover," Krysty called. "Yeah, they were here. Five of them. But they're not any longer. Come get warm. And you, J.B. It's clear."

Five dead scalies were lying where they'd fallen, a tight group, tangled together, their puddled blood soaking into the shingle beneath them.

"They were just on the other side of the fire," Mildred explained, "backs to us, rolling dice."

"You chill them from behind without giving them any warning?" Ryan asked.

"Sure." Krysty looked doubtful.

He smiled at her. "Did good, lover."

Doc was reloading the scattergun chamber of the Le Mat. "Nearly took the head clean off the chap in the middle. Jolly unsporting, don't you know, Ryan. Behavior like that would get us all blackballed from any fox hunt in the English shires."

"If I ever want to go hunt foxes in English—"

"England," Krysty corrected.

"Thanks. If I ever want to hunt foxes…over there, I'll bear your warning in mind, Doc. And now it's time to get warm. You checked out where this tunnel goes?"

Krysty nodded. "About twenty yards back there's a big sec door. That's what those stupes were guarding. Had a quick look behind it. Nothing. Wide passage. Nobody in sight.''

Mildred had finished reloading her ZKR 551. Ryan had already noticed that two of the muties had been chilled by a bullet smack through the center of the skull.

''I'll watch that door while you two get warmed up,'' she said.

Nobody argued with her.

While he sat as close as he dared to the searing flames, Ryan let his thoughts wander past the steel sec door, wondering if the boy was there, safe and alive.

''Think they're going to be replaced?'' J.B. asked, looking down at the slumped bodies of the scalie guards. Already the Armorer was warming up, a faint glow coloring his sallow cheeks.

Ryan was still sitting by the fire, an aura of steam rising around him from his soaked clothing. But like J.B., he was feeling vastly better. Just ten minutes of the blazing heat shook off the horror of the freezing river.

''Bound to have some sort of rota. It's real weird seeing muties with a kind of uniform, like some high-drawer baron with his sec men. Anything's possible, I guess.''

J.B. reached up. Touching the dressing that Mildred had managed to fix over the wound at the side of his jaw. A little blood was weeping from beneath it, discoloring the bandage.

Mildred saw the gesture. "Giving you some trouble, John?"

"Not really. Stings from the saltwater. Not bad. Thanks."

She smiled, her face becoming radiant with pleasure at his acknowledgment of her assistance.

Ryan stood, finding the tongues of fire were so hot that he had beads of perspiration across his forehead. "See if they had some food with them."

"I checked," Krysty said. "Hadn't been touched. Figure that means they weren't due to be relieved for some time."

"What sort of edibles were they, Krysty? I have to confess to a small pang of hunger now and again."

"Thought you might, Doc." She grinned. "You want raw worms and uncooked eel heads? No? Then I guess you have to stay hungered for a while longer."

Ryan walked to the river side of the fire and peered into the darkness. It might have been his imagination, but he thought he saw something moving along the edge of the shingle, something about the same size and shape as a dead tree, but with short legs, a long tail and the whiteness of teeth at the front end.

The gators in the Hudson might be another complication when it came to getting away from the scalies' base.

Assuming they all got in and then out again.

"Everyone ready to move?" he asked, turning back past the fire and walking toward the heavy sec door. Nobody spoke. Ryan smiled at them. "Anybody not ready to move?" Still no word. "Then I guess we go."

The hinges on the doors were rusted from the saltwater, creaking in protest as Ryan leaned his weight against them. He peered around, seeing that the tunnel continued, bending slightly to the right. It was about fifteen feet high and twenty across, with a roof of arched brick. Light blazed from a number of torches stuck into brackets. The smell of the badly refined oil battled over the stink of fish.

"Nobody," Ryan said.

"Think we should split up?" J.B. suggested. "Rendezvous back at the wag in, say, forty minutes. By then we've found the kid or we're all dead."

Ryan hesitated. He'd thought about that option and then rejected it. Now he reconsidered, but reached the same decision. "No."

"Wouldn't we have more chance of finding the boy?" Mildred asked. "Place could be a regular warren."

"Gotta be a shit load of scalies here. Most'll be sleeping, but a few won't. I want to avoid a challenge for as long as we can. The boy—Dean—will likely be sleeping with the other prisoners. Looks like the muties don't have too much firepower, but they have numbers. We don't have numbers, but we've got the firepower. Use what advantage you got. We stick together."

Chapter Forty-Two

Doc leaned a hand against the wall, immediately removing it with an expression of disgust. He looked ahead of them, where the tunnel finally opened up into a huge, sprawling space.

"By the three Kennedys!" he exclaimed. "It's like a glimpse of the bottom circle of Dante's Inferno. Truly this is hell."

In his lifetime in Deathlands Ryan had never seen anything quite like it.

It was impossible to do any more than guess at what the complex of buildings might once have been. In front of them was a great underground cavern. Fires burned at its center, and all around were ranged dozens and dozens of sleeping figures. Many were chained together, and there was the constant chinking of metal as someone moved uneasily. At a slightly higher level Ryan saw a number of the scalie guards, all apparently asleep.

The roof seemed to be high and vaulted, but the lack of light made it difficult to make out. At a rough guess it was a full three hundred feet across. On the far side, toward the ville, there seemed to be the

opening of still more tunnels and passages. The
stained walls glistened with discolored streaks of ice.

Ryan beckoned J.B. to his side. "Must have patrols out on the land side. These are reliefs. Best
move before they start changing shifts."

"Too late."

The one-eyed man led the hasty retreat back into
the darkness of the tunnel, watching from the shadows as squat muties came shuffling in, boots ringing.
They all wore the black berets with the lightning
flash. Most carried self-made blasters or had small-
caliber pistols tucked into broad belts.

They all seemed to know where they were going,
and what they were doing. They woke their replace-
ments with a minimal waste of time, then took their
sleeping blankets. It was all done and over in less
than ten minutes.

"Like to meet the scalie that runs all this," J.B.
whispered. "One day."

One or two of the muties weren't going straight to
sleep. A few gathered near the fire, helping themselves to fish stew from a large blackened iron caldron. There was the sound of rough laughter as one
of them pointed toward a far corner and called out a
harsh, guttural comment.

Eventually that group sat down, huddled around
the fire, and started talking quietly.

"Can't wait any longer," Ryan said. "Won't be
too long before those bodies by the river get found.
Be hard getting away after that. Go around that

way.'' He pointed with the barrel of the G-12 to their right, where the shadows seemed deepest.

It was like picking a way through a breathing nightmare.

The wind outside the scalies' base blew along the nest of passages, brightening the fires, blowing smoke in wreathing clumps all across the great room. Bodies lay everywhere, moving restlessly, as though part of some vast living organism. In among the rags it was virtually impossible to determine the sex or age of the prisoners.

At that moment Ryan felt a wave of despair. There had to be well over a hundred in the muties' slave labor force. How to find a ten-year-old boy, assuming he was still there and still living?

Ryan wound a mazy path through the slumbering crowd, often having to step over sleepers. Once his foot caught in the ragged edge of a torn blanket, snagging it, so that it was tugged away from the figure it had been covering.

''What d'you…?'' a voice mumbled.

Ryan froze.

A trick of the firelight showed him the face. It was a woman, vaguely Oriental with narrowed eyes.

She half smiled up at Ryan. With the smoke billowing around them it was a truly strange, dreamlike moment. All color was draining out and the great cavern was tinted only with a variety of shades of gray, some dark and some lighter.

The woman looked to be in her late teens or her

early twenties. There was a thick chain around her right wrist that had worn a bloody gouge in her flesh, linking her to the sleeper next to her. She also had a fading bruise on her left cheek.

Ryan lifted a finger to his lips, managing a half smile to reassure her.

She blinked, as though she was easing out of a drugged world of half truths. Then she opened her mouth a little farther and screamed at the top of her voice, "Outies! Help, help, outies!"

Chapter Forty-Three

The scream sliced into Dean Cawdor's dozing brain, jerking him fully awake to find the short, muscle-bound scalie looming over him. The creature was holding a short-hafted ax with a curved blade in its left hand, and it had a battered automatic pistol in its belt.

It had been about to throw itself on the ten-year-old, and the front of its pants already gaped open. But the noise checked its lust, and it turned away from Dean. Then it snarled over its shoulder, "Not this time, baby, but I'll be back again."

The boy lay still, fighting the terror that threatened to overwhelm him. He heard thunder from somewhere, then realized it wasn't thunder. It was gunfire, overlaying the yells and screams.

He stood and began to move slowly and cautiously toward the sound of the firefight.

RYAN CAME INFINITELY CLOSE to wasting three bullets by pulping the skull of the screaming woman. His combat training controlled him and his finger relaxed on the trigger. But then she tried to grab at him, clawing for his ankle, the chain rattling. He kicked her once with his other foot, the toe of the heavy boot catching her beneath the chin. Her teeth broke as her jaws snapped shut, and she fell back, unconscious, bleeding copiously from the mouth.

"Fireblast," Ryan breathed.

All the thinking and the planning was shot to hell because of a torn piece of old blanket. Now the only thing to do was carry out as much chilling as possible and head back for the tunnel and the waiting recce wag.

With dozens upon dozens of armed scalies coming awake all around the cavern, it was going to be tough.

The initial danger was the small group by the fire. They were already up, snouts questing toward the source of the noise. One of them, quicker than the others, had his blaster drawn and was leveling it at the invaders.

"Mine," Mildred said calmly as if she were in the butts for pistol practice on a Saturday afternoon.

The revolver fired a big .38 round, and she could hit a mosquito on the wing with it at fifty paces. A scalie's skull at the same distance was like shooting fish in a barrel for her.

The mutie went over backward, landing in the fire, its legs kicking.

"Pick your targets!" Ryan shouted.

Within ten seconds the whole place was a maelstrom of screaming chaos. The prisoners were trying to run every which way, the chains pulling them off their feet and tangling with other groups. The scalies were trying to get at Ryan and the others, but they were hampered by the panic all around them. Some had their clubs drawn and were ruthlessly beating their slaves across heads and faces to get them out of the way.

"Back to the tunnel. I'll cover you with the G-12," Ryan yelled, picking himself a spot against the wall where nobody could get behind him or out-flank him from the escape route.

It wasn't a time for argument.

Doc led the way, his long legs stretching out, knees exploding like firecrackers. Three scalies, one armed with a long pike, lumbered across to try to cut them off. Doc paused for a moment to steady his aim and pulled the trigger on the Le Mat. The .63 shotgun round went off in the faces of the trio of muties, putting all of them down and out. There wasn't time to readjust the hammer on the blaster, so Doc holstered it, drew his rapier swordstick and ran on, brandishing it at any potential enemy.

Krysty was at his heels, picking her shots, going for any of the scalies that seemed to pose a threat.

Mildred was at J.B.'s side, the two of them fighting like a team. He was spraying attackers with the Steyr AUG blaster, while the woman selected her targets with scrupulous care, not missing a single kill.

Ryan stood his ground, watching his friends heading for the safety of the tunnel, trying to judge the best moment to move himself. He kept glancing around at the hysterical mob, looking out for scalies within striking distance.

But he was also looking for something else.

A young boy, solemn-faced, with a shock of black curly hair.

"Dean!" he shouted, the name tasting odd on his lips. "Dean, you there?" But there was too much noise, gunfire echoing off the vaulted roof, mingling with screams and shouts. He could hardly even hear himself calling.

He tried one more time, cutting the cry short as he saw the ultimate bad sight—at least twenty scalies, running in a well-drilled platoon, all hefting carbines. They had appeared from a side tunnel, not far from where Krysty and the others had nearly made it. Ryan guessed they were some sort of mutie elite force.

J.B. saw them first, hesitating and then checking his blaster. "Only got three rounds left in the mag," he shouted.

Doc was effectively blasterless, and Mildred's revolver held only six rounds to begin with. Krysty had fired well over half the thirteen that her P7A-13 held.

The Armorer gave Ryan the hand signal that meant they were nearly out of ammo.

Putting the smooth butt of the G-12 to his shoulder, Ryan got ready to do business. If he failed to get all aces on the line, then life was just a few heartbeats long.

The triple-fire rate of the Heckler & Koch caseless

was so fast that a burst sounded like a man snapping his fingers. With fifty rounds in the mag Ryan had only sixteen chances.

If anyone who was totally deaf had been watching the squad of muties, they'd have seen an odd sight. It was as if they were all possessed of some demonic dancing sickness. One by one they went spinning sideways and backward, grabbing at one another as they staggered. A few tried to return the fire, but Ryan was death, the destroyer of worlds, cold and ruthless, picking the scalies off one by one.

It was over in less than fifteen seconds.

Twenty scalies were lying, dying, in a welter of gushing blood and shards of splintered bone, some still crying out in their harsh, croaking voices. Immediately a few of the quicker-witted prisoners moved in to grab the carbines from the clawed hands.

Other muties were trying to shoot at the outies, but the human slaves were milling around, causing such a shambles that it was impossible.

Someone tipped the huge bowl of fish stew into one of the fires. There was a hissing sound as a great cloud of noxious steam filled that part of the scalies' base. Another fire was extinguished by bodies falling into it, and the light was fading fast.

"Go!" Ryan yelled, waving the empty rifle above his head, gesturing to J.B. to lead Doc and the two women back toward the river.

The Armorer paused, dropping an empty clip from his blaster and reaching in his coat pocket for a fresh mag. Ryan shouted to him again, urging him to get moving out. J.B. shrugged his shoulders and turned on his heel, leading the other three in a sprint along the tunnel.

The massacre of the top squad of scalies had redoubled the panic and bedlam behind Ryan.

He glanced around once, his good eye piercing the gloom and smoke. He somehow still hoped that he might see a small figure running toward him, arms wide, calling out his name, yet knowing the absurdity of the idea.

The attack had failed miserably. Now the scalies would be that much more careful and vengeful. It wouldn't be surprising if they carried out reprisals against their own prisoners. Any future rescue attempt would be unimaginably more difficult and would probably take weeks to organize and execute.

Faced with the terrifying firepower of the Heckler & Koch automatic rifle, the scalies weren't interested in coming at him again, contenting themselves with making their own escape across the bodies of their victims.

Just one of their big central fires was now burning, and the scattered wall torches threw only small pools of distorted light. Apart from the general impression of twisting bodies and ear-bursting screams, it was impossible to pick out any individual.

Ryan remembered the old maxim of the Trader—"he who fought and ran away saved his ass."

"Time to go," he said to himself.

As he began to back off along the slippery wall, a spear came hurtling out of the gloom and smashed into the stone less than a yard away from him, its point bending from the force of the impact.

Ryan ducked, combat boots slipping in the wet, bringing him to his hands and knees. Then he straightened, and faced a heavily built scalie, standing less than fifteen feet away from him. The creature held an ax, short-hafted, with a polished, curved blade, in its left hand. In its right was a rusting Smith & Wesson 459-M, pointing straight at Ryan's chest.

"I be blasting you into blood and bits," the creature said in a croaking voice.

The long, lizardlike skull was thrusting toward Ryan, a twisted grin of triumph on its peeled lips. The hooded eyes stared unblinkingly at him, and the clawed fingers tightened convulsively on the butt of the automatic. It grinned. "You be chilled, outie."

Beyond the mutie Ryan thought he caught a flicker of movement in the shadows, but it vanished. The empty G-12 hung in his hands, useless. At that range there wasn't even a chance of throwing the rifle at the scalie. The SIG-Sauer P-226 was fully loaded in its holster, equally useless.

"Do it, then, you mutie piece of shit!" Ryan snarled.

The one-eyed warrior's last conscious thought contained a mixture of killing rage and regret at the futility of dying in a stinking hole under a ruined

ville. And he felt a deep pain at not seeing Krysty
again.

Behind the straddle-legged scalie there was another movement in the blackness, a tiny flame of
light off steel.

DEAN HAD FOLLOWED the menacing guard as it ran
toward the scene of the gunfire. He gripped the little
knife as he chased it, not knowing why he was pursuing the scalie. All his life Rona had drummed into
him to keep out of trouble and remain inconspicuous.
Now, for the first time, he was going directly against
those instructions.

The whole place was in mind-blowing confusion.

His heart pounded at the thought that someone had
actually dared to come into the home base of the
scalies and start chilling them. There was a burst of
gunfire like he never heard before, and he glimpsed
a whole squad of twenty or so of the killer elite muties go down in a twisting, lurching massacre.

But the light was dimming and he couldn't see
properly, just enough to track the scalie with the ax
as it moved toward the big tunnel to the river. Then,
with breath-stopping finality, he saw the tableau,
only just ahead of him. The broad back of the guard
masked the man that it was holding at blaster point.

Dean padded silently closer, half crouched, the
knife held point up, the way his mother had taught
him.

Readying itself to shoot, the guard shifted a little

to one side, legs wide, braced to kill. And Dean, for the first time, saw the man who was about to die— the lean face, the matted black hair and the patch over the left eye.

And he *knew*.

RYAN WAS REACHING for his blaster, knowing that it was an utterly pointless gesture, when he saw the strangest thing.

The scalie rose onto its toes, dropping the blaster, dropping the ax, which rang like a bell on the concrete. Its mouth gaped open and a strangled, bubbling cry came from its throat.

Dean used every fiber of his strength as he struck at the creature, aiming his blow between the scalie's thighs. He thrust the point up and into the soft genitals, twisting as he drove it home. He felt the roughness of cloth against the back of his hand and then a convulsive, shuddering contraction of muscle. A warm wetness streamed over the boy's wrist as he withdrew the knife.

Ryan didn't waste time wondering about the apparent miracle. He drew the blaster and put a single round through the scalie's throat, the bullet angling upward and exiting through the top of its skull, bringing a fist-size chunk of bone and a splatter of brains with it.

As the creature fell, Ryan saw behind it the person who had saved his life, still holding a short-bladed skinning knife in his right hand, the steel smoking a little in the cold, damp air.

It was a boy, lightly built, wearing a collection of patched rags. His face was partly in shadow as he looked down at the thrashing corpse. Then he looked up, and Ryan saw the curly black hair and the deep-set, serious eyes. The boy appeared to be around eleven or twelve years old, maybe a little younger.

And Ryan *knew*.

He holstered his blaster and held out a hand to the silent boy. "Hello, Dean. Hello, son. It's time to go."

Take
2 explosive books
plus a
mystery bonus
FREE

Mail to: Gold Eagle Reader Service
3010 Walden Ave.
P.O. Box 1394
Buffalo, NY 14240-1394

YEAH! Rush me 2 FREE Gold Eagle novels and my FREE mystery bonus.
Then send me 4 brand-new novels every other month as they come off
the presses. Bill me at the low price of just $16.80* for each shipment.
There is NO extra charge for postage and handling! There is no minimum
number of books I must buy. I can always cancel at any time simply by returning a shipment at your cost or by returning any shipping statement marked
"cancel." Even if I never buy another book from Gold Eagle, the 2 free books
and mystery bonus are mine to keep forever.   164 AEN CH7R

_____
Name   (PLEASE PRINT)

_____
Address   Apt. No.

_____
City   State   Zip

_____
Signature (if under 18, parent or guardian must sign)

* Terms and prices subject to change without notice. Sales tax applicable in
  N.Y. This offer is limited to one order per household and not valid to
  present subscribers. Offer not available in Canada.

Shadow THE EXECUTIONER®
as he battles evil for 352 pages of heart-stopping action!

SuperBolan®

#61452	DAY OF THE VULTURE	$5.50 U.S.	☐
		$6.50 CAN.	☐
#61453	FLAMES OF WRATH	$5.50 U.S.	☐
		$6.50 CAN.	☐
#61454	HIGH AGGRESSION	$5.50 U.S.	☐
		$6.50 CAN.	☐
#61455	CODE OF BUSHIDO	$5.50 U.S.	☐
		$6.50 CAN.	☐
#61456	TERROR SPIN	$5.50 U.S.	☐
		$6.50 CAN.	☐

(limited quantities available on certain titles)

TOTAL AMOUNT	$
POSTAGE & HANDLING	$
($1.00 for one book, 50¢ for each additional)	
APPLICABLE TAXES*	$ _____
TOTAL PAYABLE	$ _____
(check or money order—please do not send cash)	

To order, complete this form and send it, along with a check or money order for the total above, payable to Gold Eagle Books, to: **In the U.S.:** 3010 Walden Avenue, P.O. Box 9077, Buffalo, NY 14269-9077; **In Canada:** P.O. Box 636, Fort Erie, Ontario, L2A 5X3.

Name: _____

Address: _____ City: _____

State/Prov.: _____ Zip/Postal Code: _____

*New York residents remit applicable sales taxes.
Canadian residents remit applicable GST and provincial taxes.

GSBBACK1

Desperate times call for desperate measures. Don't miss out on the action in these titles!

#61910	FLASHBACK	$5.50 U.S.	☐
		$6.50 CAN.	☐
#61911	ASIAN STORM	$5.50 U.S.	☐
		$6.50 CAN.	☐
#61912	BLOOD STAR	$5.50 U.S.	☐
		$6.50 CAN.	☐
#61913	EYE OF THE RUBY	$5.50 U.S.	☐
		$6.50 CAN.	☐
#61914	VIRTUAL PERIL	$5.50 U.S.	☐
		$6.50 CAN.	☐

(limited quantities available on certain titles)

TOTAL AMOUNT	$
POSTAGE & HANDLING	$
($1.00 for one book, 50¢ for each additional)	
APPLICABLE TAXES*	$ _____
TOTAL PAYABLE	$ _____
(check or money order—please do not send cash)	

To order, complete this form and send it, along with a check or money order for the total above, payable to Gold Eagle Books, to: **In the U.S.:** 3010 Walden Avenue, P.O. Box 9077, Buffalo, NY 14269-9077; **In Canada:** P.O. Box 636, Fort Erie, Ontario, L2A 5X3.

Name: _____

Address: _____ City: _____

State/Prov.: _____ Zip/Postal Code: _____

*New York residents remit applicable sales taxes.
 Canadian residents remit applicable GST and provincial taxes.

GOLD EAGLE®

GSMBACK1

Follow Remo and Chiun on more of their extraordinary adventures....

#63220	SCORCHED EARTH	$5.50 U.S. ☐
		$6.50 CAN. ☐
#63221	WHITE WATER	$5.50 U.S. ☐
		$6.50 CAN. ☐
#63222	FEAST OR FAMINE	$5.50 U.S. ☐
		$6.50 CAN. ☐
#63223	BAMBOO DRAGON	$5.50 U.S. ☐
		$6.50 CAN. ☐
#63224	AMERICAN OBSESSION	$5.50 U.S. ☐
		$6.50 CAN. ☐

(limited quantities available on certain titles)

TOTAL AMOUNT	$
POSTAGE & HANDLING	$
($1.00 for one book, 50¢ for each additional)	
APPLICABLE TAXES*	$ _____
TOTAL PAYABLE	$ _____
(check or money order—please do not send cash)	

To order, complete this form and send it, along with a check or money order for the total above, payable to Gold Eagle Books, to: **In the U.S.:** 3010 Walden Avenue, P.O. Box 9077, Buffalo, NY 14269-9077; **In Canada:** P.O. Box 636, Fort Erie, Ontario, L2A 5X3.

Name: _____

Address: _____ City: _____

State/Prov.: _____ Zip/Postal Code: _____

*New York residents remit applicable sales taxes.
 Canadian residents remit applicable GST and provincial taxes.

GDEBACK1